THE
TRUTH
ABOUT
GOODBYE

A Novel

Russell Ricard

ISBN: 978-1-63489-787-7
eISBN: 978-1-63489-378-7

Library of Congress Catalog Number: 2017935005

Printed in the United States of America
First Printing: 2017

21 20 19 18 17   5 4 3 2 1

Cover design by Emily Mahon
Interior Design by Kim Morehead

Published by Wise Ink Creative Publishing.

Wise Ink Creative Publishing
837 Glenwood Ave.
Minneapolis, MN 55405
www.wiseinkpub.com

For my husband, Scott

"To me every hour of the light and dark is a miracle."

—Walt Whitman

Chapter

ONE

Sebastian taps his wedding band against the underside of the table. *Does goodbye really mean forever?* The *click, click, click* sound, paired with the cavernous restaurant's chorus of voices, makes him shiver. He looks toward the wood-beamed ceiling. This isn't how he planned to step into forty, without Frank.

"You with me, birthday boy?" Chloe says, snapping her fingers.

"Yeah, right." He scans the room. The squat-bodied waiters— old men in white shirts, black pants, and ties to match—glide effortlessly through the cramped space. With him as their choreographer, they'd be adorable doing the famous waiters' number from *Hello, Dolly!*

Chloe whistles. "Like I was saying before you ghosted me . . ."

"Sorry." Sebastian grips a lock of his black hair.

"I'm really digging this Gerald dude." She picks at her fruit salad.

"Yes, Auntie Mame. Especially after he whisked you off to Brazil." Sebastian's mouth turns upward at a thought: if Frank were here, he'd probably reach over and steal a bite of his husband's chocolate cheesecake.

"*Namaste*, my little love." Chloe offers prayer hands, which Sebastian notices are a shade darker than her natural olive tone, closer to his own caramel complexion. "Brazil was all business."

"Right. Living on the beach for six days is business as usual."

"Guilty, Your Honor. Gerald's a sweetie. And it's supercool learning something new." Chloe's dark brown, shoulder-length curls bounce as she swivels her head. "I'm going to rock this publicity thing."

"Nothing stops you," says Sebastian. "A man drops you, and you move on to the next. The Rockettes don't offer you another contract after a zillion years, and you pick yourself up, dance your way into a new career. I'm jealous."

"Really?"

"A bit." Sebastian nods.

"You hear that, Ma?" Chloe says toward the ceiling as she rewraps the purple Hermès scarf around her neck. "Get that, Daddy?" she says to the floor, straightening her Gucci blouse. "I'm putting my degree to good use. And you, darling one," she says to her best friend, "are an artist."

Sebastian shakes his head. "I'm just a forty-year-old Broadway chorus boy who wants to be a choreographer." He dabs at the remnants of cheesecake on his plate, savors the chocolaty taste, and licks his finger dry.

Chloe retouches her lipstick. "Just saying: until you're given the chance, my little love, you never know what other talents you have." She blots her kisser with the white dinner napkin and folds it into a triangle.

"So you think you're in love with this Gerald guy?" Sebastian sips his chamomile tea.

"Please, you know full well that marriage is not my gig."

Sebastian pouts. "But something lasting. A special vow with just one person is—"

"Unrealistic, from where I stand. Sometimes I wonder why

you even fight for all this legal marriage crap. For me it's about freedom, not a piece of paper and all the other blah, blah, blah. Ultimately everyone exits stage right. Or stage left."

Maybe she's right. After all, not one of Sebastian's dead loved ones had bothered to give him a proper goodbye. He looks toward the ceiling. *Happy fucking birthday, Seb.*

"Ooh, don't look now."

"What?" Sebastian glances toward the bar area. He's startled by the clinking sound his teacup makes as it hits the saucer.

"Incredible guy staring at you," Chloe says in a singsong voice.

Sebastian rolls his eyes. "Incredible? What are you talking about?"

"I'm talking about *him.*" She waves toward the bar. "Yummy goodness, Robert Redford circa *The Way We Were*, sitting at the bar. He's been staring at you since we came in."

"Stop it." Sebastian cups his brow. He sinks lower into his chair until Chloe's body hides his view of the bar.

"Don't be silly." Chloe taps his chest until he sits upright. Her touch induces a giggle from Sebastian. "See," Chloe continues. "You're intrigued, right?"

"Absolutely not." Sebastian looks toward the bar. A smile comes as he notices the man perched on the stool. *Handsome.* Sebastian catches his breath; he checks the ceiling. Is it possible Frank sees all this? Absolutely yes, his husband's on guard. Sebastian closes his eyes and sighs, intertwining his fingers under the table.

"Confession." Chloe takes his hand. "I invited him."

"Excuse me?"

"You know my style. Speaking of . . ." She tucks the feathery sides of Sebastian's hair behind his ears. "Time for a trim, George Michael the *Wham!* years."

Sebastian finger-combs his wavy hair. "I know. I know."

"Anyway, I met him in the laundry room of my co-op. I've never seen him in my building before, not even in Hell's Kitchen. So I got to talking while we both folded."

"Of course you did."

"I told him you live just two blocks away."

"And your point?"

"You can guess the point."

Sebastian grips his wedding band. "I can't believe you."

"Hello, gorgeous. Just look at him! He said he's some swirl of German, Scotch, and Irish."

"Did you do a credit check? Get blood work?"

"Ha-ha. That can be arranged, you know."

"No." Sebastian tucks his hands under his knees.

"Ooh. I've got the perfect nickname! Let's call him Schatz."

"Huh?" Sebastian glances toward the bar, just enough for a snapshot; Is that reddish-gold hair? It's hard to be certain—the restaurant's low lighting bounces off the wood-paneled walls and tangerine carpet, giving everything an equally orange glow. Still, the man's the polar opposite of Frank.

"Yes!" Chloe snaps her fingers. "Schatz it is. It's German for 'treasure.'"

Sebastian releases a breath. "Thanks a bunch, Sesame Street."

"Actually, today's lesson is brought to you by the letter *P*, as in my problematic parents. See, Daddy dearest," she says to the floor, "that German poetry class at Queen's College wasn't a waste."

"That's for sure," Sebastian says.

"Okay. First of all, Schatz has some really cute underwear. Not boxers, not briefs . . . what do they call them?"

Sebastian bites his lower lip. "Boxer-briefs?"

"Exactly. Very sexy, even when folding said boxer-briefs."

"You're such a perv." His focus shifts toward the dark ceiling. Sebastian swears he hears Frank's baritone voice nudging him to do his own laundry.

"Second, he's definitely the commitment type, which I know you love. And he's spawn from the same pool: two parents, still happily married for at least a zillion years. If memory serves, there's one brother and two sisters. He's not an only child like you."

Sebastian covers his face again. "Geez, you really did yak his brain away. Did you make sure to tell him I'm adopted, too?"

"And third," Chloe continues, ignoring him, "he bought his apartment with someone else, but that's over—he'll fill you in. Apparently it was long term."

Long term. Is another long term even possible? Sebastian wonders. He angles his torso to face the bar. Schatz licks beer foam from his lips. He tips his glass toward Sebastian and mouths, "Cheers."

Sebastian's throat locks. No, he hasn't seen this guy around the neighborhood; he would've remembered. *Okay, fine: he's Technicolor hot!*

Schatz stands to adjust his bar stool. He sits back down, his taut ass anchored over the edge. But why is Sebastian staring at a stranger's ass? *Ass:* why is he even thinking the word? He can't help himself; his eyes widen to take in the whole package.

Schatz is probably around six foot two, definitely taller than Frank, and looks as if he stepped straight out of an outdoor menswear catalogue. He wears blue jeans and brown work boots, and the sleeves of his tan chamois shirt are rolled up. From a distance, his forearms appear muscled, like a man who works with his hands all day. *He didn't overdress, even though he knew we'd be meeting for the first time,* Sebastian thinks. *That's refreshing.*

And on closer inspection Sebastian can tell his spiky hair is, in fact, reddish gold. Chloe's nickname was on target: *Schatz.*

Sebastian can't help but steal more snapshots. There's a muted glow to the stranger's skin under the halogen bulbs above the bar. His eyes seem to be aqua blue, although it's hard to tell exactly from a distance. His build, however, is noticeably rugged—broad shoulders and chest. Sebastian furrows his brow. *Okay, he's handsome. Movie-musical handsome. Still, he's not Frank.*

"Ooh, honey," says Chloe. "Your dark skin against his vanilla would look hot."

"Don't be crude."

"And don't you be such a prude. All I meant is that you'd be beautiful together."

Sebastian shrugs. Who cares if this Schatz is nice to look at? Nothing could be more beautiful than Sebastian plus Frank.

"And all the time you interrogated him you didn't get his real name?"

"Maybe I did, maybe I didn't. I guess you'll just have to call him over here and find out his real name yourself. Or invite him to your tap class."

"What?"

"When I told him I was a Rockette, he said he was a tap-dance kid. You could use another student."

Sebastian huffs. "I should go."

"Come on, Seb. I told him all about you. And Frank, and—"

"Are you insane?" Sebastian chokes out a cough, his eyes wide.

Chloe offers Schatz another wave before turning back to Sebastian. "Just meet the guy. It won't kill you."

Sebastian downs some water to cool the flush radiating across his face. Chloe hasn't the slightest clue what could or couldn't kill him. He slams thirty dollars on the wooden table and rises to his feet.

Facing the bar, Sebastian notices Schatz's contorted brow, an expression that looks eerily like a big question mark. *Questions are good, but not tonight.* "Sorry," Sebastian mouths to Schatz.

"Aw, honey. You can't afford it—it's my treat. Your birthday."

"Enough! You shouldn't have assumed anything." Sebastian wads the cash into her palm.

"I just wanted you to feel good on your fortieth."

"Is my birthday the only significant event on this particular day?"

"Of course not. I know it isn't, but—"

"I'm not like you. I can't go from one man to the next." Sebastian heads toward the door, careful not to trample any of the penguin waiters. Chloe follows him out of the restaurant and up the basement stairs that lead to Thirteenth Street.

The spring night breeze sends a shiver through Sebastian's body; he tugs at his black blazer. "Look, what Frank and I had can never be replaced. Never!"

"I didn't say anything of the sort." Chloe drapes the Hermès scarf around her neck.

A gust of wind rushes against Sebastian's face. Is Frank here? *No.*

"You don't understand, Chloe."

"Why not? Because you're the only person on the planet who knows what it means to lose someone?"

"That's not what I meant."

"Then get off your ass. Stop feeling sorry for yourself."

"I am. I am." Sebastian buries his face in his hands. "I'm working on it."

Chloe rubs his back. "Be open. Meet someone else."

"I told you, I cannot and will not do that." Sebastian pats his tight chest. "Besides, no one else who lost a spouse would be expected to meet someone else in only a year."

"I know, sweetie," she says, wrapping her arms around him.

Sebastian catches his breath. "It sucks that we had to run off to Massachusetts to get a license, that New York and the federal government still wouldn't recognize our marriage." He wipes the tears with the back of his hand. "Damn them. It's 2008, and still no full marriage equality."

"I'm with you, not against you." Chloe dabs away his tears. "I get it."

Sebastian twists his wedding band around his finger. "This July would've been seven years for us." He rests his head on her shoulder.

"Seven years?" Chloe channels a Valley girl: "Oh my God, that's like, twelve in my book."

They laugh and hug again. Then, more tenderly in his ear, she says: "I miss him, too."

"You do?"

"Of course. Sebastian and Frank. Frank and Sebastian. Fuck New York, and fuck the Feds. And if the next president isn't for equal marriage rights, McCain or that other new dude running, Obama, well then, fuck 'em!" She clears her throat. "Actually, in or out of the White House, I'd tap that Barack dude."

Sebastian sucks his teeth. "Really, right now?"

"Kidding." She shrugs. "Well, maybe not kidding. Seriously though, you and Frank, you were the real deal."

Sebastian wipes away the sniffle with his blazer sleeve. "That's the first time I've heard you talk about us like that."

"You know me," she says, anchoring her hands on his shoulders. "I get that you loved Frank more than anything, and that

8

you're the kind of guy who believes in all that Technicolor, blah, blah, blah, happily-ever-after, drama-queen shit." She covers her mouth. "I mean, all that musical theater, lovey-dovey stuff is definitely your specialty."

"What's wrong with wanting a forever with one special person?"

"Nothing. But honey, you don't have to exchange vows or anything with anyone else, just have a date. Maybe there's another Prince Charming out there."

Sebastian exhales. "Not possible."

Chloe throws up her hands. "I better get back in there and apologize to Schatz. Sure you won't join me to find out his real name?"

"Still not possible. But can you tell him again that I'm sorry?"

"All righty." Chloe pecks his forehead. "I'll give you a buzz tomorrow."

Sebastian nods, closes his eyes. He turns away and notices the red DON'T WALK hand signal on the corner stoplight. His heart races; he tells himself to exhale. When he turns back to Chloe, she's already dashed back inside—back into the restaurant filled with penguins and Schatz, their "treasure," or whatever he is.

Chapter
TWO

The end credits from the black-and-white movie *Swing Time* roll on the TV screen; the song "Pick Yourself Up" has just ended. The screen blackens—three thirty a.m. Sebastian sighs. After dinner with Chloe, the copycat has grappled all night with Fred and Ginger's steps from the video: *Flap shuffle hop, flap shuffle hop, flap shuffle hop . . . toe hop step* still rings in his head. *Ugh!* Only two months left to finish the recital number.

Sebastian gasps as Arthur, his twenty-pound tuxedo, jumps in front of the TV. In silhouette, his eyes shine like underwater coins against the screen. Two sandpaper licks on the spot where Sebastian wears his wedding band, on his right hand, then Arthur's off. He burrows into the sofa bed's mound of comforters.

"Sweet dreams, baby boy," Sebastian offers as he turns off the DVD. When the monitor switches to TV mode, the twenty-four-hour news channel, New York One, fills the screen. G. W. Bush's face, an extreme close-up, invades his senses, file footage of the outgoing president. He spouts gibberish, something or other about "turrists." A chuckle fills Sebastian's head—Frank's signature laugh, a *ha-ha* like the sound in *hat*.

Arthur scales the mound of comforters and rumpled sheets and bullies his way onto Sebastian's chest. He stands briefly, makes a half turn; he wraps his black tail around his rear, which nearly touches Sebastian's chin. Arthur coos like a mourning dove.

Sebastian whispers: "Thank you for trusting me. For loving me." Arthur rolls onto his back, his white belly exposed, his purr now a soothing rumble. It's sometimes hard for Sebastian to believe that his fur baby was once the feral rescue that he and Frank adopted. *Or was it Arthur who rescued them?*

Sebastian blows air from his mouth. In the most nasal twang he can produce, he mimics the president's voice: "Turrists." Be it turrists or terrorists, doesn't he have enough to worry about? The seventh anniversary of 9/11—with all the mourning and memories of death and destruction—is still six months away. And with his skin color (a homeless dude, just outside his apartment building, actually once called Sebastian a dirty Muslim terrorist), it's not something he needs to be reminded of today, moving further into forty.

TV off, ear buds in, he presses play on the CD Walkman and reclines on the sofa bed. He taps out the bouncy rhythm on his stomach, tickled as usual by Fred Astaire's jovial singing voice. After a while, he shuts off the Walkman. He shakes the sudden chill away, then smiles at the thought: Frank loved this song almost as much as Sebastian's parents had.

It's been exactly a year, and Sebastian still feels cheated out of life. Worse is the guilt—it was, after all, Sebastian who started the argument that night over Greg. *That night!*

To add insult to injury, the apartment is a disaster area; Frank must be mortified. The side table next to the sofa bed holds a brushed-metal frame, which is home to a picture of the couple. They both wear black suits. Frank sits on the sofa with a stoic yet loving half smile, the perfect expression for the psychiatrist he would've been today. *If I hadn't stopped him from finishing his residency.* He wears a burgundy tie with yellow teardrops. With his curly, light brown hair and olive skin, he has the look of a Michelangelo statue, such a contrast to the caramel complexion and black hair of Sebastian, who wears a toothy, boyish smile and a striped, multicolored tie. He sits perched behind Frank on a bar stool, his arms draped over his husband's chest.

A red bejeweled lamp from Pier 1 and faux-walnut alarm clock sit on the bedside table. A bottle of pills, glass of water, and box of tissues also hog the surface. Nearly everything Sebastian has read, or is attempting to read, is scattered. Books on movie musicals, choreography, dance terminology, all seem to end up on the floor—Fred Astaire's *Steps in Time: An Autobiography, RKO Movie Musicals, Broadway Musicals: The 101 Greatest Shows of All Time, Hollywood Hoofers.* And Sebastian dares not remove the hefty volumes on anatomy, personality, physiology, and Jungian psychology that live inside Frank's cherrywood bookshelf. Nor can he get rid of the green scrubs that still hang from a blue plastic hanger on the closet door.

Crammed in the corner of the small room, a desk holds everything else Sebastian can't seem to reasonably organize. Dozens of movement sketches and notes monopolize the surface, while CDs and DVDs fill any space that remains on top.

His tap shoes roost on a nest of clothes in the center of the room. The silver taps underneath are scraped away, and the toes are smudged blue-black from two decades of dance steps: riffs, wings, toe stands, and the like. Dark-colored clothing—blue jeans, black khakis, T-shirts, and a few pairs of navy shorts that he hasn't worn since last September—is also strewn about the floor, all peppered with stray white hairs from Arthur's tux.

An orange wingback resides against the wall opposite the sofa bed—Frank's favorite chair, to Sebastian's ongoing shame, has become yet another clothes hamper, currently housing several pairs of socks and dry cleaner–ripe button-downs. In short, it's a clusterfuck apartment.

Dizziness floods Sebastian's body. The mess clouds his mind, which is why he must recreate dance numbers from movies like *Swing Time*. Night after night it's the same, no progress on creating original choreography, just the blur of Fred and Ginger's steps comforting his senses toward sleep.

The alarm's high-pitched tone, coupled with its *one . . . and two . . . and . . .* syncopated beeping pattern always reminds Sebastian of a dump truck backing up. He rubs sleep from his eyes and catches a glimpse of Arthur's ears as they rotate backward at the piercing sound.

Sebastian bats several times but misses the clock's silencer. After a few more tries he bolts upright and presses firmly. "Off," he grunts, obliterating the piercing sound.

Six? Great! Awake most of the night, and now all he craves is sleep in the nest. He turns on the bedside lamp. Nothing. Damn: he forgot the bulb died last night, yet another thing to replace.

He downs the two white-and-mint "depression" capsules with a long swig of water, wishing they really tasted like peppermint, like anything other than required-for-breathing pills. He never takes them one at a time; better to get it done in one hard swallow. His wellness counselor, Andrew—whom Sebastian prefers to call his guru—promises he'll speak to the consulting psychiatrist, unfortunately more Sigmund Freud than Carl Jung, about a dosage reduction.

He slowly twists his white-gold wedding band and rubs his fingers against the tiny scratch lines and pocks along its surface. He looks up; these days, Frank generally seems to reside near the ceiling.

Arthur leaps on top of the cluttered desk. His yowls sound like the drawn-out baritone of a country tomcat on the prowl—memories from Sebastian's childhood in Margaretville, New York.

"What's up, buddy?" Sebastian asks as he smooches the top of Arthur's head. "Shit! Do we have mice again? Is that what's bothering you?"

He cracks the blinds. There's sunshine, but the temperature's crisp. Spring has sprung, and starting the day is unavoidable. He shuts the window, turns on the overhead light.

Arthur kneads the pile of Sebastian's sketches, then knocks over the stack of CDs and DVDs. Sebastian gasps—there go the copies of *Swing Time*, *Easter Parade*, and *Silk Stockings* that Chloe burned for him when they aired on the Turner Classics Movie channel.

"Great. Now you're on my case about all the mess, too?" He wonders if his fur baby's teamed up with Chloe, and the thought of his friend makes him angry again. How dare Chloe think he's ready to move on? Especially with some stranger she met in the laundry room. He fumbles with then ultimately gathers the sketches and shoves them into the file cabinet. A guttural meow follows.

"Wow. I get the picture." Sebastian strokes the white part of Arthur's distended belly. "I'll make a deal: you go on Weight Watchers, and I'll clean up this joint one of these days. Got it?"

Arthur cocks his head. His black ears rotate backwards before he bolts for the sofa bed.

"Whatever." Sebastian fingers the picture frame. His eyes—*Frankie's eyes*—are just as beautiful as they were in life. It seems as if they could reach into his heart. Sebastian rolls his eyes. Such fantastical delusions. "Musical theater" plotting is exactly what led to Frank's death, isn't it? He nods toward the ceiling. Frank's probably laughing right now and saying, "Always the drama queen."

Sebastian lurches forward, startled by the alarm's musical reprise: that *one . . . and two . . . and . . .* syncopated beeping pattern. The smack of the frame as it strikes the hardwood floor incites a hiss from Arthur.

"Sorry, boy." Then, "Damn it!" The glass has cracked into four jagged pieces, which awakens a tableau in Sebastian: he and Frank, hands intertwined, staring out a window. The image vanishes as quickly as it arrived, shattered by the insistent alarm clock. Sebastian turns it off with a grunt, and then places the frame back in its rightful station. He plops down on the bed and stares at the ceiling a moment, *only a moment*, because he must keep going.

. . . . .

Sebastian takes in his nude reflection in the bathroom door's mirror. He'd swear his sideburns have gotten whiter since the dinner with Chloe the night before. It's only been a year, but Frank might not even recognize him. He runs the brush through his wavy mane; it still holds strands of Frank's brown intertwined with his own black hair. Deep exhale; when he checks it tomorrow morning, there will probably be even whiter hairs added to the mix. He puts the brush back on the counter and forces a smile at his reflection to evaluate the progress of his crows-feet—yes, day by day, they're becoming more pronounced.

He scans his body again: the caramel color of his skin is more yellowish from the winter months. He sucks in his gut; to think that he had a twenty-eight-inch waist when he moved to New

York at eighteen. Now, at forty, his waist is thirty-three inches. He pinches the bits of meat around the midsection—not too much fat, but still, he never thought he'd edge toward a spare tire, especially with no one to rotate it. He cranes his neck to stare at his ass, where faint stretch marks have decided to plant themselves. It's all quite *Invasion of the Body Snatchers*. "Hmm," he says to himself in the mirror as he tugs at his ass. Although it isn't as taut as it once was, at least gravity hasn't completely taken hold.

The shower steam creates a fog. Turned upside down with two capfuls left, Frank's favorite container of bodywash still lives next to their razors in the chrome rack beneath the spigot. Back home, after a thirty-six-hour hospital shift, Frank would sometimes use it as a bubble bath and soak for nearly an hour.

Would the bodywash smell as cucumber fresh on someone else? Sebastian wonders. And what would another man possibly smell like, anyway? He shakes away the thought, forces an inhale of steam, and sits on the closed toilet lid, elbows on his naked thighs and one set of knuckles propped under his chin like Rodin's *The Thinker*. He wonders how Chloe, night after night, can share her body with a different man.

If only Frank were physically here now, also naked. *If only.* In many ways, however, Frank's evergreen, definitely around, Sebastian tells himself. When you're with someone for so long, you know his habits: the way he tastes and smells, his morning breath (pretty or not), the good-night kiss after he's brushed his teeth, the sweet yet sour smell after hours away from home, the salty taste on every trace of him as you make love, the post-sex cucumber smell that gloves his body in the shower. You grow accustomed to every mole, blemish, scar, and patch of hair, every vein. Sebastian knew Frank inside and out. Therefore, he reasons, Frank must still really be here.

Sebastian steps underneath the shower spray. As usual, he chuckles whenever he twists the single-handled faucet, reminded of their routine. While Frank would always set the temperature to lukewarm, the very center of the gauge's blue section, Sebastian would set it directly in the center of the red section—hot.

"Shit!" Sebastian yells as he shuffles backward. The gauge is set at the farthest end of the red section. He must've really been out of it moments before. Why on earth did he set the temperature to scalding? he wonders.

The apartment door buzzer sounds like a handbell choir. "Hold on," Sebastian yells as he opens the medicine cabinet. He rubs on deodorant, sneaks a whiff of each underarm—the baby powder and chamomile scent comforts him.

Arthur, who stops for a quick yawn and a long meow, meets him near the center of the living room. "Good boy," Sebastian says, giving him a quick peck on the nose.

"Cheers!" the raspy alto voice streams through the peephole. Sebastian opens the front door to find Chloe, who bursts into the room and offers kisses on either cheek. "Lordy, lordy, you're officially forty," she continues, hanging her metallic-brown handbag on the wingback chair and draping her matching coat and scarf on top of it. He's always imagined Chloe as a gazelle, and that's what she looks like today with her lean yet muscled body in the mocha gown.

Sebastian finger-combs his wet hair. "What are you doing here this early?"

"The question is, what are you doing?" She points to his crotch.

"Ha-ha." Sebastian folds his arms. "Getting ready for work, sassy pants."

"Oh really." Chloe's dark eyebrows dance up and down. "Sure you don't have some hot guy stashed away in the other room?"

She flicks his nipple.

Sebastian jumps. "Don't be gross!" he says, covering his chest and trying not to smile.

"I'm just asking. Maybe our newfound treasure from last night?"

"You know I left early." He tightens the towel around his waist.

"Gotcha." Chloe falls into the wingback. She flicks her nose and says with a British accent, "Chop, chop! Your fur clients await their morning jaunt."

"Exactly." Sebastian heads to the bathroom. He slips into a pair of camouflage-green undies. Every time he wears army colors he reminds himself that his days are often like a war, and combat doesn't get easier with age. If only life were like a musical: press a button and you live happily ever after.

"Hell no, to all this," Chloe says as Sebastian comes back into the living room. She pulls the bedsheets taut and flattens the mounds of comforters and blankets. "Aren't you tired of the Howard Hughes act? I told you I can loan you money for a cleaning lady." She winks. "Or a hot houseboy."

"No thanks," Sebastian says. "I'm fine. Besides, with no more Christmas show, you must be strapped yourself."

Chloe bevels her showgirl legs. Her dark, curly locks bounce as she cranes her long neck forward. "Damn straight I wasn't a Rockette for the money."

"I know. But you can't live off your inheritance forever."

"Oh really? Mommy?" she says toward the ceiling, then: "Daddy?" she continues with a sneer, her eyes aimed at the nest of clothes on the floor. She bats her eyes at Sebastian. "Darling. I know what I'm doing. I'm a big girl." She curtsies.

"For your information, maybe I'm also a big girl," Sebastian says, batting his eyes in return.

"Ooh!" Chloe fans her face, laughing. "Touché! But you're just going to walk dogs, temp at a troglodyte universe, and waste your talent on wannabe tap dancers?"

"I love my students. They work very hard. It's not their fault that I can't successfully choreograph a routine."

Chloe purses her mouth. "Cut it out, you're a genius talent."

Sebastian closes his eyes. *Tell that to my three a.m. brain trying to put together steps.*

"So again, why the early drop-in?" Sebastian sniffs a black T-shirt: not too dirty; there still is a hint of lavender detergent. He sets it on the dresser.

Arthur gallops toward Chloe and jumps onto the bed. She gives his white belly a quick stroke, then picks up the picture of Sebastian and Frank. "Today being what it is concerns me." She squints, then does a double take. "It's cracked."

"I'll replace it." Sebastian resituates the frame on the side table. "Cross my heart, I'm fine. Except for the big forty thing."

"Queen, please. Mind your elders. You didn't see me go underground six months ago when I danced into forty, did you?"

Sebastian sticks out his tongue. "Tell that to the Rockettes."

"Fuck the Rockettes." Chloe shuts her eyes and heaves a sigh. "I don't give a queef."

"Eww." Sebastian pauses, then continues more gently: "Seriously, it doesn't bother you at all that they refused to give you another contract?" Until this past season, Chloe had done the Radio City Christmas Spectacular for ten consecutive years, a gig that has always been the envy of every New York dancer—and singer, for that matter—good, steady money to get a gypsy through the year ahead.

Chloe shrugs. "I told you I don't care."

"Really?"

Through gritted teeth Chloe says, "Have I ever lied to you?"

"No . . . you never lie," Sebastian says with a knowing look.

"That's right," Chloe says. "I'm all about honesty." The way she tiptoes her narrow fingers along Arthur's spine, her nails colored to match her metallic-bronze lipstick, reminds Sebastian of Cyd Charisse's solo in *Silk Stockings*. A final step along the now-hypnotized cat's back, she then gives him a gentle tap on the head. He meows and starts grooming.

"Anyway." Chloe grabs a few tissues from the box on the side table and blots the fur from her hands. "I'm pleased as shit to be working with that publisher." She slam-dunks a wad of tissue into the trash can near the desk and puts on an even more highbrow British accent. "Mummy" (a kiss toward the ceiling) "and Daddy" (a sneer at the floor), "they'd be so proud my BA in English is being used for a worthy cause."

Sebastian perches on the arm of the wingback. "At least you have a college degree."

"It's not too late for you to go back, if that's what you want. *Is* that what you want?"

Sebastian shrugs. "I have no idea."

"Hmm. I think you do."

"What's that supposed to mean?"

"Nada." Chloe waves the air as she heads toward the bathroom. "Anyway," she continues over the sound of running water, "I was in the neighborhood. Just finished with a hot, hot item. Cuban." She glides back into the living room. "Yummy." She pats her face with her still-wet hands. "A tad darker than you, just shy of the color of this dress, actually."

Sebastian folds his arms. "Good for you, an equal opportunity gal."

Chloe offers the peace sign. "You know that's right."

But they're countless: the mornings, evenings, and afternoons Chloe stops at Sebastian's door, having been in the neighborhood on a date with one "yummy" guy or another. Isn't it scary getting older and not having someone to share her life with? And what about HIV? Sebastian sometimes wonders if Chloe's one of those straight people who assumes they're immune. God only knows, as his father might say, what kinds of men she's hooking up; some of them might have the same Russian roulette philosophy she does.

Sebastian slips into the black sweatpants and T-shirt he unearthed moments before. Chloe gives him the once-over.

"What?" Sebastian checks his body, sniffs his underarms again.

"Bon anniversaire, mon ami." Chloe reaches into a pocket of her overcoat and hands Sebastian a plastic bag. "Found it in the village last night, after our din-din."

Sebastian rolls his eyes. "And pre–Cuban rendezvous?"

Chloe clucks her tongue. "Exactly. It's belated, but it looks like you could use something to start the morning after forty."

"Oh." Heat spreads across Sebastian's face. He opens the bag to reveal a black T-shirt; CREATE, in gray block letters, is displayed across the chest. "Is this a hint?"

"Maybe. You like?"

"Yes, Auntie Mame," Sebastian says with a smile. "It's actually cute." He takes off the old and slips into the new T-shirt.

"Fabulous. I'm glad you think so. And you better wear it in good health," she says. "Anyhoo, I knew you'd be up so I figured . . ." She takes a bottle of lotion out of her handbag and starts to rub some into her hands. The strong scent tickles Sebastian's nose. It reminds him of gardenias, of Margaretville.

"Seriously, though," Chloe continues, "we're still on tonight, right?" She shakes her hands in the air as if to dry them and

21

tosses the lotion bottle into her handbag.

"Tonight? Going out? No." Who knows what surprise Chloe would spring on him? It could be some other so-called date item, or maybe even Schatz himself, back for another try. Sebastian rifles through the pile of clothes on the floor and eventually unearths his black Pumas. He notices Chloe appraising their condition. Of course he's embarrassed about the scuffed toes and worn soles, but he'd rather save his money for bills.

"Come on, Seb. Frank would definitely want you to celebrate all birthday month long."

Sebastian glances at the ceiling. "I'll just stay in tonight. I'm going to have a long day with the dogs, the office, and tap class. I still have to get them to learn that Fred and Ginger number."

"And 'therapy,'" Chloe says, putting the word in air quotes. "With Heir Wellness Counselor?"

"Don't make fun. He's my guru."

"I thought he didn't like it when you call him that."

"He's a guru to me."

"Hey, it's not my call." Chloe flicks her hands. "Guru, therapist, wellness counselor . . . whatever works."

"Truth." Sebastian bites his bottom lip. Chloe's therapy is mixing pills with alcohol and seeing what happens, to Sebastian's ongoing annoyance. "Anyway, I won't see him until the end of the week."

"Good. That'll work," Chloe says with wide eyes.

"What?"

"Not to add to your day, but I ran into Greg last night."

"I don't want to talk about Greg."

"This isn't about him, trust me. Only he told me, being the little Nelly Big Mouth he is, that there's a private call for a new show. Broadway. Production contract." She rubs her fingertips together. "*Dinero, dinero,* anyone?"

Sebastian's throat locks. "I can't crash a private call. Besides, I'm rusty. My last audition was two months ago." He coughs, swallows hard. "And that was a singer's call."

"Go anyway!" Chloe grabs him by the shoulders and shakes him. "You know they might consider you for a singer in a show, even at a dancer's call. You've got the pipes, and you've been cast as a singer before. Whatever will get you in there and make some money." She throws both fists in the air in a V.

"Listen, *Evita*, performing isn't supposed to be about the money."

"Tell that to half the fuckers on Broadway right now. Look, you don't have to crash anything. My other date item, Gerald, the publisher, knows the casting director."

"Like I can keep all your date items straight."

Chloe smooches the air. "As long as *I* keep 'em straight, we're fine."

Sebastian groans. "Chloe, be honest: are you playing safe with these guys?"

"Sebastian Hart, do I look like an idiot?"

He raises an eyebrow. "There was that one guy."

"Ages ago. Only time I slipped up, I swear. Anyway," she says, switching to a high-pitched voice, "they're seeing people at two."

"The office won't let me off for an audition."

"Bull. It's only temp work and—"

"And I need it to pay my bills." Sebastian points to a half dozen sealed envelopes that help clutter the desk.

Chloe pulls gently on his ear. "Sweetie pie, if you get the show, you'll get back on your feet." She strokes his cheek. "And maybe out of this dump."

"It's not a dump." For almost seven years it's been—*still*

is—Frank and Sebastian's home. It doesn't matter if it hasn't been cleaned since Frank left. Every bit of mess was a piece of what they accumulated as a couple.

Chloe sighs, then murmurs, "Sorry. You know what I mean. Not that it's a dump. It's just not like it used to be around here."

"Wake up!" Sebastian clenches his fists. "I told you last night, nothing's the same anymore." He looks toward the ceiling and closes his eyes.

She wraps her arms around him. "Aww, sweetie, I know." Her hair smells of lemon with a hint of tobacco, maybe the Cuban guy? The mingled scents remind Sebastian of his parents.

"You're right," he says through a sniffle. "I'm such a fuckup." He wipes away his tears, then pulls away to cram the stack of bills into his backpack. "Frank is probably so upset with me for letting things get this way."

"Stop it." Chloe blots the wetness around his eyes with a tissue. She takes his hands in hers. "You'll get through this. I promise. And I'm always going to be here for you." She checks her watch. "Oh shit, except right now. I've gotta dash. Gerald needs me to clock in early to go over client blogs and some royalty stuff." She scoops up her things and heads toward the door. "By the by, I heard Tom Streeter got several grand a week in royalties for choreographing the London revival of *Me and My Girl*."

"No surprise. He's brilliant."

"And you wouldn't be?" Chloe grabs his chin, making Sebastian laugh. "You can only do so many community center tap recitals before you're officially wasting your talent. Get your odds up, Seb."

"I don't know. I'm starting to think I'm not much of a gambler." A cramp invades his core. He folds his arms across his stomach.

"Crappers." Chloe jostles his shoulders. "You get that show, do the dance captain thing for the last friggin' time, and make your move into choreography. That's how you win the game." Chloe anchors her hands on either side of her waist and walks pigeon-toed. "Become the next Bob Fosse. Become a serious choreographer."

"Who said anything about becoming a serious choreographer?"

"Jeepers, you're such a closet case!"

"Says the smartass."

Chloe winks. "Right back at you."

Exhale. Sebastian reminds himself to "facilitate his breath," as Andrew would instruct. He inhales deeply, exhales with an even tempo, and rubs his brow as he traces his best friend's footsteps. *Easy for her to say. The Rockettes cut her at the audition and don't re-up her contract (for being too old, or so they both believe), and she just moves on to the next thing.*

"Why do you do all this?" Sebastian opens the front door.

"All what?"

"The jobs, the pampering," he says, helping her into her coat. "The looking out for me."

"It's cold out there."

"It sure is."

"Exactly." Chloe rubs his back. "And perhaps I'm just your fairy godmother who helps keep you warm." She bats her eyes and raises her arms toward the ceiling.

"Yeah?" Sebastian falls into a low curtsy. "Or maybe I'm *your* fairy godmother."

Chloe harrumphs. "Not likely." She pecks his cheeks. "Now, *please* go to the audition this afternoon. Do it for Frank."

Frank. Sebastian's screamed his husband's name, aloud and to himself, every day since last year: to the ceiling, to the scrubs that hang on the closet door, to the shelf full of medical books, to that damn hairbrush. But today, in Chloe's low alto, it sounds so much louder.

Sebastian watches Chloe slink down the dingy hallway until she descends the staircase. Inside again, he leans against the apartment door and rubs the heat that has gathered in his chest. He arches his upper back; he flattens it firmly against the rectangular, steel portal to the outside world—a stretch he's often seen Arthur perform. He wonders if cats actively engage in breathing exercises, meditation; their moves certainly are yoga-like. Sebastian closes his eyes. If he squeezes them tightly enough, maybe the pain will simply disappear.

Chapter
THREE

Fifth Avenue, Seventy-Second Street. The dogs await Sebastian's arrival. As they begin to walk, a Great Dane pushes to the front, forcing the entire pack into a triangular formation. There's a gray-coated schnauzer, a chocolate cocker spaniel, a duet of pigeon-toed pugs (one fawn, the other black), and a golden retriever. Sebastian trails behind, a rainbow of leashes wrapped tightly around his wrist.

Aside from the gray CREATE on his chest, Sebastian's fully dressed in black: the T-shirt, the sweatpants, baseball cap, and fleece jacket. His stuffed backpack, which carries a gaggle of clients' keys, also holds a change of clothes for the office.

Sebastian flinches as Olga marches toward him, her feet turned out in first position, like a duck. She wears a pink-and-white Oscar de la Renta suit, typical attire for an Upper East Side grande dame. Her own dog, a brilliant-white standard poodle, pulls her along the avenue. Edgar (the Great Dane) drags Sebastian and the rest of the pack toward Boss Lady.

"Shit!" Sebastian yanks the gathered leashes. "Sorry, Olga!" he calls as she and her pooch beat a hurried retreat in the opposite direction. Big mistake. That wasn't the right pair to chase off the sidewalk. The pack barks and strains at the leashes, forcing him into unplanned choreography: *hop step, hop step, hop step.* His wrist flexes from their pull. "Ow!" He loses his grip for a split second and they're off, barreling down Fifth Avenue.

"Edgar, Biscuit, Oscar!" Sebastian calls out as he dashes past, nearly tripping over several people on the sidewalk. Despite himself, he chuckles—with a little fine-tuning, this chase would make a great production number. Thankfully, he finally halts the stampeding pack. As he gathers the leashes, he sighs. *Olga's never going to let me hear the end of this.*

. . . . .

Next stop: Park Avenue South near Grand Central. Although it challenges him the most, because he hates corporate settings, the software development company pays the least of all his gigs— even less than his tap class at the community center. Sebastian's convinced that the office regulars—with their bug eyes trained on him, all probably hopped up on their third cup of Starbucks— call him Copy Boy behind his back.

The hospital-green walls are appropriate for the fast-paced environment; tons of dead and walking wounded in this ER, though no one would actually admit it. The ceiling is depressingly lower than that of the other floor they occupied when Sebastian first started work here six months earlier. That location had to be vacated because of budget cuts.

Gray work cubicles run along the center of the space like an endless chain of railroad cars. If only Sebastian could take the train out of this place. But he needs the cash. Along the outer walls of the cubicles are glassed-in offices, some with windows that look onto Park Avenue South.

No caps, sweats, fleece jackets, or CREATE T-shirts allowed

here, not even on Friday. Sebastian changes out of his all-black dog-walker outfit and into his all-black office uniform: slacks, button-down, tie, and dress shoes. On some level, he knows all the dark clothing, while slimming, is awful on him. But every morning, when he rifles through the piles of shit in the middle of his apartment, the color that wins is black. It's a sharp contrast to the stacks of white folders Sebastian hauls from cubicle to cubicle, office to office.

Sebastian's a glorified copy boy. He Xeroxes and distributes things. It's busy yet uncomplicated choreography, which is good because his office skills are limited—*What the fuck are PowerPoint and Excel, anyway?* he wonders; lucky he's lasted six months.

He checks his watch: only four hours until the audition. He exhales, catches his breath at the thought of the impending battle. Suddenly it's a dreadful proposition, having to be on display as the now forty-year-old chorus boy.

. . . . .

Sebastian closes the dance studio door. As he heads down the hallway, Frank's former "date item," as Chloe would say, startles him.

Greg's twenty-seven now, and not necessarily the spring chicken he pretends to be; still, the troll's in twink territory, Sebastian reasons. He'd just turned twenty when he seduced Frank. They met at a benefit performance for Broadway Cares/Equity Fights AIDS. Greg was in the opening production number, while Frank had volunteered his services as a drop-in mental health counselor for several months before the benefit. According to Daddy Frank's version, Twink Greg had cornered him at the postshow reception. *But that was before us*, Sebastian reminds himself. It was a mismatched liaison that had lasted only two months, much to Sebastian's delight then and now.

Although Sebastian hates to admit it, Greg's stunning. His dark hair and green eyes make matters worse. He's chiseled where it counts: pecs, arms, butt, and face—a typical chorus boy any casting director would want, so long as he keeps his mouth shut.

"Sebastian! Haven't seen you in at least a month!" Greg squeals through pursed lips.

Yep, Sebastian tells himself. *Still looks like Superman and sounds like Lois Lane.* Aloud he says, "Nice to see you too, Greg."

Greg rests his chin on a knuckled hand. "And how'd you get in on this call?"

"Chloe has a friend." Sebastian hugs his notebook to his chest.

"Hmm." Greg licks his lips, his green-eyed stare locked on Sebastian. "Still got connections, the old hoofer."

Old. The word rings in Sebastian's head. When did it become such a dirty word to him? The *New York Times* review of his last Broadway show is archived in his brain: "As for the chorus members of this monster musical, erroneously titled *There Shall I Go*, one wonders if Geritol should be passed out at half-hour, curtain, intermission, and before the eleven o'clock number."

Sebastian clenches his jaw. It's true: He's forty years of skin crammed into black slacks and a matching button-down. But compared to his competition, Sebastian's earned his hide over the years, avoided slaughter. Most of these boys huddled along the wall in their tightly fitted spandex, some as young as eighteen, probably couldn't even moo through a song, much less carry a tune.

No! Sebastian's earned his place here. He lived through the aptly named cattle calls of the late eighties, got herded into countless sweaty dance studios with only a number safety pinned to his chest for identification. He's a veteran compared to these boys.

Sebastian sizes up the wall of hopefuls. So much for Chloe's assurance that this would be a "selective" chorus call. Other than Greg, no familiar mugs in sight. Either way, chances are it's flooded with twinks from the casting director's "I wish I could screw him" files. Some are probably even friends of the director-choreographer.

"Believe it or not, Greg," Sebastian says with a sigh, "maturity does have its privileges."

Greg rolls his eyes. "Note taken."

Sebastian clenches his jaw. Even though he knows it would hurt his hand, he wants to sock the troll square in his chiseled jaw. The thought that Frank ever dated him is repulsive.

"Did they have you read after you sang?"

"No," Sebastian mutters, stepping away from the doorway.

"Did they ask you to dance?" Greg persists.

"No. They didn't."

"So they asked you to stay to dance?"

"Hello? I said no." Sebastian pictures himself whacking Greg upside his block head. "Anyway, I don't think they're having people stay to dance today."

Greg purses his lips and snaps his fingers in the air. "They asked me to stay."

Sebastian's heartbeat revs to an allegro pace. "Good for you." This is exactly what he hates about the whole audition game. There's always a prick eager to compete with him. This one is just better at raising his blood pressure than others.

"Yeah, getting older sucks, doesn't it?" Greg scratches the tip of his nose, seemingly too bored to wait for an answer.

"*Excuse* me?" Whenever this troll stands before him, Sebastian can't help but remember that night, the last time he saw Frank. It was obvious *that night*, wasn't it? Greg wanted Frank back. *That night.* It wasn't just the hospital paging his husband that made Sebastian angry. Greg's a huge part of the reason they fought the night Frank died.

Greg's eyes widen. "Wake up, Sebastian! It's not like you can be a chorus boy forever."

The urge to play Rock 'Em, Sock 'Em Robots with Greg's face grows stronger. "I really have to go," Sebastian says through gritted teeth. "Another job."

"That's right." Greg shakes his block head. "I heard you're still teaching at that community center."

The groan that rises from Sebastian's belly rumbles inside his head. Chloe probably blabbed his business during some drunken club outing.

"Yeah," Greg continues, "I guess you're strapped since Frankie's gone."

"Frank!" Sebastian barks. He allows the exhalation four counts before he scoops up his backpack.

"Sorry, darling. But he didn't mind me calling him Frankie."

Sebastian shoulders his backpack. "To you, it's Frank."

"Whatever." Greg narrows his green eyes. "Here's to a second callback," he says, licking his lips. "Because I know I'll definitely get one."

"Yes, I'm sure you'll use your charms to get under the director, as usual."

"Aww," Greg says, patting Sebastian's back. "How nice of you to say." His mouth corkscrewed, nostrils flared, he shrugs his broad shoulders. "And good luck to you with . . . whatever." He pivots in the opposite direction and saunters away.

Sebastian grunts as he raises both middle fingers at Greg's back. "Whatever," he says in as mocking a tone as he can muster before bolting out the studio door.

Chapter

FOUR

The tap class holds steady in the center of the room. Mrs. Woo, as tall as the black upright piano, bangs out Gershwin's "My One and Only" with the fullness of a fifty-piece orchestra. With his arms draped over the back of the console, Sebastian feels the piano's vibration running through his body.

"That sounds fantastic." Sebastian knocks out the beat on top of the piano. "The more bass you can get into it, the better," he says. "It helps us keep tempo."

Mrs. Woo bites her lower lip, salutes him. "Sure thing. I'll kick it up a notch." She hammers out a heavy-handed bass line. Sebastian snaps his fingers as he tries a set of steps (which he picked up from Gene Kelly when watching the DVD of *An American in Paris*): *Step scuff heel back flap back flap shuffle heel cross step.*

Sebastian continues the sequence of steps on his right then left side and then repeats them again, his eyes trained on Mrs. Woo, whose neck swivels in sync with her honky-tonk creation, her hair fixed in place like orange cotton candy. With black glasses that take up half her face, she's a stuffed toy owl.

Sebastian stops dancing. The class applauds. "I didn't know you had that in you," he adds with a wink to Mrs. Woo, hands on his hips to allow for full breath cycles.

Mrs. Woo beams and sits up taller. "There's more where that came from." She cranks out a syncopated ragtime beat without a thought. Sebastian could swear the old woman channels Scott Joplin. She bounces up and down, bobs her head, twists and swivels on the bench to the tune of her one-woman orchestra. Both Sebastian and his troop snap fingers and clap as they move to the music.

After a few bars, Sebastian waves his arms in the air. "Okay, okay." He taps Mrs. Woo's ample arm. She hoots and cackles as if another spirit has entered her body, craning her head backward as if to say, *Don't stop me now.*

Sebastian anchors his hands on Mrs. Woo's shoulders. "Thank you, my dear." The students applaud and Mrs. Woo curtsies.

Sebastian shakes his head in awe, reminded of meeting Mr. Woo a few months before his death. Like his wife, the old guy was reminiscent of a bird, a towering Japanese gentleman who was at least six feet tall. He was a giant compared to his five-one, pudgy Irish wife, Mrs. Woo.

"Okay, everybody." Sebastian whistles. "Try it again, a bit faster now. Let's see if we can do all the sequences in succession."

"Succession?" Hank asks. Slender, with a head of white hair, he reminds Sebastian of Fred Astaire, the later years, especially in his gray slacks, white button-down, and pink ascot.

"Without stopping!" Millie says with a finger wag toward her husband, herself an older Ginger Rogers with her signature champagne-colored coif and gauzy canary-yellow gown.

"Precisely," Sebastian offers, even though he knows they'll never master, let alone get through every step.

"But it's confusing," says Kathleen, her pudgy arms folded across her chest. Her dark eyes are reminiscent of a middle-aged

Shirley Temple—that is, Shirley Temple Black.

"Exactly," Beau, who could be the love child of Ricky Ricardo and Donald O'Connor, chimes in. "I don't remember which section is which, Sebastian."

"I guess we get a little confused by thinking of the steps out of order," Hank adds, his eyes focused on the wooden floor.

"They're not out of order, silly," says Millie, her dress rippling as she shakes her head. "That's why they're called sequences."

But Hank is on point. The routine's disjointed, if not beyond repair. Sebastian could never learn from a choreographer such as himself, the way he's teaching the pattern of steps, jumping from one set to the other. What bullshit: *sequences.*

"I hear you, Hank," Sebastian says. "But just try to think of sequence A as the riff section, sequence B as the cramp roll section, and sequence C as the time step section with all the turns."

Hank nods, but Sebastian figures the old fellow probably doesn't buy it, and neither do the rest of them.

"Let's hit it, you guys," Sebastian says. Although he wonders: Does Hank really have an inner Fred, and does Millie truly aspire to be Ginger? Or is it his imagination, some trick of his inner View-Master lens that makes Kathleen look like an older Shirley Temple and imbues Beau with Ricky Ricardo's looks and Donald O'Connor's spirit?

Sebastian points to Mrs. Woo and claps his hands on each count. "And a five, six, seven, eight."

His back to the students, Sebastian faces the mirror and joins the routine. After a few measures he notices, in the mirror's reflection, the studio door swing open. He squints: a man stands in the doorway. He squints again. Is the mirror playing tricks on him? His heart accelerates to allegretto, much faster than Mrs. Woo's current tempo. No tricks. Sebastian's eyes widen, and he gasps.

It's him, Schatz, from the restaurant! The pair of white tap shoes, laces tied and draped over Schatz's shoulders, remind Sebastian of the ones Fred Astaire wears during the "Begin the Beguine" number with Eleanor Powell in *Broadway Melody of 1940*.

As the routine continues, Schatz waves with a smile. Just as Sebastian had guessed the night before, his is a square jaw. He sports a trio of dimples, one on either cheek and one on his chin. Chloe, no doubt, is responsible for this surprise visit.

Okay, okay, he's gorgeous. Sebastian catches himself, diverts the thought. Frank was—Frank *is* gorgeous. A widower is supposed to think of his husband, not another man. *Still,* Sebastian tells himself, *I shouldn't be rude.* Returning a smile and nod in the mirror's reflection is harmless, right?

"Faster," Sebastian shouts to Mrs. Woo. "Allegretto!"

The floor-to-ceiling windows of the studio allow for the usual ray of sunshine on days like this, which causes Sebastian to squint further as the light bounces off the mirrors. And he knows what magic to expect next. Here it comes: Mrs. Woo's garnet ring reacts to the light from the window as she continues to play, casting a rainbow onto the mirrors. The first time this light show occurred one day last spring, Mrs. Woo said that it was a telegram from Mr. Woo. *She's probably right,* he muses. Why couldn't it be possible for a dead husband to send a love note to his beloved? Sebastian gives her two thumbs up.

The students stop dancing; their captain knows full well that they're unable to continue at the vigorous pace he's set. *How sadistic,* Sebastian scolds himself, but he can't help but keep the metal taps under his feet striking the wooden floor, his legs radiating heat with their constant movement. His troops, apparently too tired and lost in the routine to keep going, clap and cheer to the music as he continues. He tries his best not to glance too often at the square-jawed hunk's reflection—no matter how convinced he is that Schatz watches his every move.

Guilty? Sure. But when necessary, Sebastian can be quite the show-off. And the smile inside keeps his feet going. Schatz holds the rhythm of the music as well; he snaps his fingers along with Sebastian's dance steps.

Then a cramp filters through Sebastian's belly: *the white tap shoes*. Schatz intends to join his crew?

Sebastian refocuses, stares at his own reflection and shakes his head. Instead of himself, he sees Frank: his face, smile, and his body in the mirror, all of him.

"Frank?" Sebastian calls. A chill followed by intense heat floods his body. His vision narrows. Three Franks now stare back at him. He feels dizzy; his legs are heavy yet unsteady . . .

Sebastian hears the gasp for air he takes. His eyes flutter open. Flat on his back, he watches the whirl of the ceiling fan. Mrs. Woo and the other students stand over him. He wonders how long he's been out.

"Frankie?" Sebastian shakes his head. He tries to open his blurry eyes even wider. All colors; it's as though he's stepped into a 3-D film version of *An American in Paris*. Everything's Technicolor: Mrs. Woo's orange hair, her black owl glasses; Millie's canary yellow gown, and Hank's pink ascot; Beau's white teeth and Kathleen's large, onyx eyes.

"Frank," Sebastian mutters again.

"Who?" Schatz asks.

"I guess I channeled a bit too much of Scott Joplin's spirit," Mrs. Woo says as she presses lightly on Sebastian's temples. Her fingertips, still warm from her ragtime, are as soft as his mother's were whenever she offered the same comfort to his childhood self.

Sebastian squeezes her doughy hand. "Thank you, Mrs. Woo."

"All right. Let's give him some air, everybody," Schatz's baritone voice booms.

Mrs. Woo shoos Kathleen, Beau, Hank, and Millie.

Hoarding the opportunity, Sebastian stares into Schatz's eyes. *Are they really that color, aqua blue? Maybe. But no one's that perfect,* he quietly reminds himself.

"You okay?" Schatz asks.

The weight of the hand that now rests on his chest gives Sebastian the hypnotic sensation of lying under a comforter on a blustery night. "I'm swell," he says. He clears his throat and uses an exhalation to help himself sit upright. "Just fine. Really." Yet the lie makes him feel even weaker. He flinches as Schatz reaches for his right hand; he doesn't want to call attention to his wedding band that still lives there. He pulls his hand away and tries to stand.

"Not so fast." Schatz pats his back. "Take it easy."

Sebastian offers his left, bandless hand. Schatz's grip is firm but not too stiff. It's a hand that knows work but not moisturizer.

On his feet again, Sebastian rubs his eyes. "I'm okay, really. I thought I saw . . . oh, God."

"You saw God?" Schatz asks. His chin dimple and the tiny half-moons that line his cheeks rise as his reddish-gold eyebrows knit together.

"Not God. Not exactly." Sebastian smiles, albeit on the inside. *Wowsie!* There's a hint of some garden herb. The guy smells as if he's just taken a bath or maybe gargled with peppermint. Sebastian pinches his brow: *Frank is the real treasure, not Schatz!*

Mrs. Woo hands Sebastian a bottle of water. "There you go, sweetie." She purses her mouth. The lipstick is a deep purple today. Everything in the room still screams in vibrant, oversaturated hues. "You always warn the crew here," she continues.

"Remind them to get enough water before, during, and after the dancing. And here you are probably dehydrated yourself."

"You're right. Thanks, Mrs. Woo." Sebastian downs half the water bottle in one gulp.

.....

Moments later, Sebastian and Schatz stand in front of the community center building on Fourteenth Street and Second Avenue.

"I can't believe Chloe did this."

"Don't be angry," Schatz says. "I sort of forced her to tell me where I'd find you."

"Forced her?" *By flashing that smile, those cute dimples, the aqua blues?*

"You know what I mean. Not forced."

Sebastian gives his wedding band two twists around his finger. "And why did you need to find me?"

"Let's just say I miss some parts of my childhood. Like my happy feet." Schatz tugs at the tap shoes draped over his neck.

Sebastian folds his arms across his chest. "I see."

"Yes, sir. Believe it or not, back in the day, I could twirl for days. In fact, you're looking at the official whirling dervish of Miss Sheila Jean's School of Dance." Schatz clinks the metal taps of his shoes against each other.

"Whirling dervish, huh?" Sebastian grips both straps of his backpack. "How sweet that you have those memories."

"Mmm-hmm." Schatz's face reddens. He looks down at his brown work boots.

Sebastian pictures it: a shy, twirling boy with reddish-gold locks who does a triple pirouette, chaîné turn, inside turn, outside turn, and then, like a perfect little gentleman, takes a final bow. All this executed in miniature white tap shoes to the song "Stepping Out with My Baby."

Schatz adjusts the shoestrings around his neck. "It's true. I loved every minute of that recital stuff when I was a kid. The costumes too, tacky as they were. Didn't you?"

"No, sir. No recitals for me. I mean . . . I danced when I was a kid, but it was just with the TV, at home." Sebastian stares at his black sneakers, grips the straps of his backpack tighter. "I'd watch movie musicals with my parents and sort of futz around, and with Broadway records in my room, you know, and . . ." *Exhale, Sebastian.* "But I didn't take my first official dance class until I was here in New York, at eighteen."

Schatz nods. "Well, well, well," he says, his eyebrows raised. "Very impressive."

Sebastian smiles. The final verdict is in—Schatz's eyes truly are a real-life aqua blue.

"Anyway." Schatz tucks his hands in his back pockets. "I came today because I thought we should meet under better circumstances."

"You call my fainting in the middle of class a better circumstance?"

"Well, I did surprise you."

And Frank surprised me too. Sebastian closes his eyes and feels the same vertigo he had just before he fainted. "I know it's crazy, but thought I saw . . ."

"What?"

"Nothing." Sebastian intertwines his fingers at his chest. "No one. It's not important."

"Do you faint often?"

"I'm just overworked right now."

"Afraid I was going to have to give you CPR."

Heat spreads across Sebastian's cheeks. It's been over a year since Frank left, and since he's felt another man's mouth pressed against his own. He swallows hard, licks his lips. "Oh . . . well . . . I have to run," he mutters. "Thanks for your help in there." He juts his hand forward. "By the way, I'm Sebastian." *Finally. Dummy.*

Schatz's chin dimple lifts as he smiles. "I've never known a Sebastian. Except, of course, jolly old Sebastian Cabot from *Miracle on 34th Street.*"

Does he think I'm jolly as in fat? Old as in geriatric? Sebastian forces a return smile.

"I adore that film," Schatz adds.

"Really?" Sebastian looks toward the cloudy sky. Frank called it a silly propaganda flick.

"And for the record, even at forty-five years old, I believe in Santa Claus."

Sebastian covers his mouth as he laughs. "Me too."

"It's Reid."

Reid. Sebastian exhales. A bold name that fits his profile: the reddish-gold hair, straight nose, square jaw, and the dimples.

Sebastian initiates the shake. "I'm—"

"Nice to meet you, Seb."

"No!" Sebastian's face radiates heat. "I'm sorry. I prefer Sebastian."

"Of course." Reid sucks in air through clenched teeth. "Apologies. I guess it just stuck in my head when Chloe referred to you as Seb. Maybe we could grab a bite sometime."

His business card is white with cobalt-blue lettering. Sebastian reads it aloud: "Dr. Garden?" *Not again.* "Chloe didn't tell me you were a doctor."

Reid winks. "She didn't get everything out of me."

"Oh." Sebastian feels a twitch in his scalp and runs his fingers through his hair. "Like I said, I have to go." He puts the business card in his front pocket. "See you." A quick nod and wave, then he heads across Fourteenth Street toward Third Avenue.

"Wait up." Reid grabs Sebastian's arm. "I'm Dr. Garden, as in my firm."

"Your firm?"

"Rooftops, parks, sometimes homes on Long Island. I'm a landscape designer."

"Oh . . . cool." Sebastian nods. "Hence the footwear."

Reid shuffles his booted foot on the pavement. "You pegged me."

Sebastian smiles. "I love gardens. When I was a kid I planted a Japanese maple."

"Beautiful. Maybe someday I'll kidnap you, take you on one of my jobs. Dr. Garden"—he gestures in quotation marks—"that's just my persona, you know, an alias. Although I am a kind of surgeon—good with my hands, with growing things."

Sebastian runs his hand through his hair, takes another snapshot: turns out Reid's hands are as large and calloused as they felt in the handshake. And although Sebastian hadn't noticed it earlier, Reid's nails have dirt underneath.

"Anyway," Reid continues, "my real name is Reid Becker. At least when I'm not playing doctor."

"Great." *Playing doctor?* Sebastian closes his eyes. Frank probably sees this right now, and no doubt he's jealous. While there have been some very attractive men who've flirted with him in the past year, Reid is the first one that makes Sebastian feel a spark of who knows what.

"All right, then. I'll see you in class, Seb." Reid sucks his teeth. "Sorry. I mean, Sebastian."

"You bet." Sebastian stops at the curb like one of his obedient dog-walking clients, eyes closed. The way this man says his name feels like a lullaby. He opens his eyes. "Here's to tap class," he adds, miming a toast and immediately feeling like a dork. "I'll see you then."

.....

Sebastian wrestles under piles of blankets and comforters. Arthur, with his twenty-pound body, bundled in black-and-white fur, lies sprawled on his back, taking up most of the bed. Sebastian bolts upright with his husband's pillow hugged against his core. He couldn't have seen Frank in tap class. And there's no way Mrs. Woo ever actually sees her beloved Mr. Woo, because he's gone. Just like Frank, he's dead!

Arthur rolls onto his stomach and arches his back. He jumps off the bed and leaps on top of the desk. He uses his full body weight, as if he's at a disco doing the Bump with someone, and knocks the books and papers to the floor.

"Arthur!" Sebastian punches Frank's pillow, then clutches it tighter. "What's going on?" he begs of his cat, whose meows are incessant as he walks a figure eight around the books and papers that are now on the floor. Sebastian should take notes—Arthur's creating decent choreography, a tribal dance that would be great set to bongos and flutes. The cat siren continues and crescendos toward a more aggressive tone; with that squawk he sounds part chicken. Sebastian can't decide whether to laugh or cry.

"What do you want?" Sebastian calls again. He slams Frank's pillow onto the bed. His internal thermometer dances back and forth: hot, cold, chill, heat. He can't quite decide what temperature it is inside his body or, for that matter, the room itself.

Arthur slips on a sheaf of papers as he makes a running jump on top of Sebastian. He springs off the bed in a mock grand jeté, a leap with his front and back legs stretched outward. He runs back to the pile of books and papers. The dance seems to have turned into a game of tag. His ears cock back as he kneads at the mess.

"Please, Arthur!" Sebastian wonders if the cat's antics are a sign unwanted guests have checked into the apartment. *But it's too warm for mice, right?* Besides, every nook and cranny has been filled with steel wool and patched since last winter's visitors were caught and paraded around the apartment by Prince Arthur, the new dance star who finally seems ready to take his last bow of the evening.

Sebastian exhales. He lies on the floor now, his face pressed into Arthur's fur at that too-fat place between his front and hind legs. He strokes Arthur's back, the top of his head, massages the tiny space between his shoulder blades. "I don't understand what you want." He rests his chin on one hand and kisses the top of his fur baby's head.

Arthur snakes sideways, away from Sebastian. He uses his paws to weed through the pile of papers. The meows stop after he has cleared away the documents that were sitting on top of a massive hardcover book. Now, finally, it seems as if the number is complete, the game over. He settles onto the floor and tucks his paws under his chin. No more squawking chicken; instead, his standard buzz-saw purr has commenced. His nose scrunched up and his eyebrows raised, he darts his greenish-gold eyes from side to side for a moment, then closes them.

"Breathe," Sebastian commands himself. Should he dial Chloe? Call his guru, Andrew? Would they be able to answer the question that's plaguing him: *Is Frank here?* He looks more closely at the hardcover book Arthur unearthed: *RKO Movie Musicals.* Sebastian suddenly feels as if he's falling in slow motion from a great height. He looks around the room and finally at the ceiling. "Frank?"

Chapter

FIVE

H is last round of dogs, then Sebastian transitions to client. Or is it patient? No, client. He never dreamed he'd still depend on therapy or antidepressants all these years after his parents died. At eighteen, he wasn't sure whether to believe his father, who claimed to have visions of his dead mother. At the time, however, there was no question of Sebastian's anger over the fact that the man's secondhand smoke led to her lung cancer and the subsequent loss of them both. But those goodbyes aren't something he dwells on every day, except maybe during these sessions.

Sebastian changed therapists after Frank died because he didn't want one as traditional as the previous five had been. He needed to breathe. He craved homework assignments, not just talk. He wanted a push, a guru. Enter Andrew Cooper, a combination of Buddha and Jung who, much to Sebastian's irritation, prefers to call himself a wellness counselor.

The Wellness Box—a dwelling of wonder and work—is covered in linen wallpaper. An antique brass floor lamp capped with a linen shade is the primary interrogation light; it stands beside the cherry desk, on which sits a lucky bamboo plant (apparently, it's supposed to bring good things to your life) and a box of tissues. There's also a mocha-brown lounge Sebastian loves to run his fingers along every time he passes it. But as hypnotic as this place is, it's still a workout room. Proof positive? Early in their sessions, when Sebastian protested the abundance of questions about his childhood, Andrew teased that when he applied for the job as wellness client, the fine print stated that he not be afraid to work with a shovel. Consequently, their relationship has lasted just shy of a year.

Eyes closed, facing Andrew, Sebastian sits on a blue yoga mat. He wears his signature black-on-black attire, his naked feet tucked in a cross-legged position. His hips, tight as usual, took several Downward-Facing Dogs to relax. The only noise during the past twenty minutes has been Andrew's voice, along with the breath as teacher and student inhale and exhale in unison.

Sebastian takes in the ocean sound of their synchronized inhale through his nose and the subsequent exhale through his mouth for another five counts. It's so much easier to ingest the environment when his guru is along for the ride. But allowance for the inhalation is still difficult when Sebastian's alone. Who knew that something as easy as breathing could feel as hard as the most difficult piece of choreography?

"And now, Sebastian. Slowly . . . open your eyes."

He does as the guru directs.

"Back to your revelation," Andrew continues, "what you said about the cat."

"Arthur."

"Excuse me. Arthur." Andrew adjusts his square, black-rimmed glasses. "You really believe Frank's spirit was being channeled through Arthur?"

"No. Yes, he was—well, not really. But then again, there was the book . . ."

"I'm with you. Take your time," Andrew says. His smile, showcased by his salt-and-pepper beard, brings comfort to Sebastian. Still, it's hard to maintain the good breath technique from moments before.

Sebastian places his right palm, the hand that holds his wedding band, on his breastbone, and exhales with sound: "Ahh . . ." As he fills his chest with air, he imagines his body in flight, hovering inches above the yoga mat.

"And exhale," Andrew's baritone voice intones. "Continue the cycle. Your thoughts."

Sebastian grunts but tries to do as his guru demands. Still, there doesn't seem to be enough room in his chest cavity for an inhalation. "What I was trying to say is that the *RKO Movie Musicals* book, which I swear Arthur practically handed me, is the one I use to research dance numbers."

"I see." Andrew readjusts to a cross-legged position, his khaki pants rolled up to the ankles. "And the first time you thought you saw Frank, in the mirror at the dance studio, was in conjunction with this new guy, Reid?"

"I don't know what you mean by 'new' guy." Sebastian exhales. "But yes. First I saw Reid, then, soon after, Frank appeared in the mirror."

"I hear you." Andrew clears his throat. "And how quickly after this Reid entered the studio did you see Frank?"

Sebastian closes his eyes and shakes his head.

"Open, Sebastian. Be careful not to use closed eyes as an escape," Andrew says. "Now's the time to be present, not merely inside yourself."

"Sorry." Sebastian blinks his eyes open. He rests his palms on his belly, covets its expansion and release. "I just don't think any of this has to do with him."

"Remember what we've discussed: within the grief process, delusions are possible."

"I'm not crazy!"

"I didn't say you're crazy. Is that what you heard?"

"Maybe," Sebastian says while chewing his bottom lip. He's afraid that Andrew will suggest another visit to the psychiatrist, who'll want to up his dosage of antidepressants.

"The thing is, Sebastian, it's been exactly a year now. Guilt over Frank's death—"

"I don't feel any guilt."

"Let me finish," Andrew says, his baritone voice dipping toward a bass. "What I'm saying is that these visions might be asserting themselves from a need to blame yourself for what happened. Like symbols, signs."

Sebastian can't help but roll his eyes. *Blah, blah, blah.* "Frank chose to leave me that night. He's the one who just had to answer his work page." Although part of him still wonders if his husband was really headed to the hospital *that night.* "I can't go into this."

Andrew clears his throat. "Sebastian, you're not a child. And even if you were, I'm not here to make you do anything you don't want to. I'm just trying to encourage an awareness of the moment, not just what's inside your head. And, of course, a sense of how everything from the past affects how present you are today, moment to moment."

More blah, blah, blah, Sebastian thinks. *Besides, what's so horrible about living inside my head?* Doesn't every man, woman, and child have an active inner world? Isn't that what meditation is, a pathway to the inner self? Even Andrew must sometimes swirl around in his own thoughts to make sense of himself and others. Sebastian huffs. Besides, wouldn't Andrew's own guru, the late-great Carl Jung, say that an inner imagination filled with symbolism is healthy?

Sebastian closes his eyes, gives his wedding band two turns around his finger.

"Let's transition," Andrew murmurs. He places his hands in prayer position, and Sebastian follows suit. "Okay," Andrew continues, "I notice you touching your ring a lot."

"My wedding band?"

Andrew nods. "Yes, your band."

Sebastian's hands curl into fists in his lap. "Why shouldn't I?"

Andrew smiles. "Prayer position."

Sebastian groans. He presses his palms together as he's told.

Andrew adjusts his glasses. "Perhaps we might consider what we discussed about the ring . . . sorry . . . wedding band." His eyes are hazel, but until now, in the year Sebastian's been coming here, he hadn't noticed just how long Andrew's lashes are—*beautiful.*

"My wedding band." Sebastian's fingers, locked in the prayer pose, begin to stiffen. "I just can't."

"Relaxed shoulders, please. And breathe. Don't cheat your inhale. Wide eyes, my friend."

Sebastian rolls his shoulders back and down. He exhales; his chest still locks as he attempts to allow air inside.

"You don't have to throw away your wedding band." Andrew's inhale through his nose makes him sound as if he's sucking air through a straw. "But it might be helpful to put it away, in a safe place."

"Like I said, that's not something I can do right now." Sebastian wonders if Andrew would ask a straight man to do the same if his wife had only died a year before. And would a woman be expected to just forget her husband, *put* him somewhere else so soon after his death?

"Okay. That's enough of that for now," Andrew offers more

tenderly. "Let's move on." He returns to a steady, deep breath cycle.

When Sebastian mirrors Andrew's breath, pushing air from his core out through his mouth, he fully realizes the exhale; the tightness in his chest evaporates. As air fills his lungs, he feels his heart ingest oxygen and the space between his eyes expand. Even so, Sebastian's glad to forge onward, his brain exhausted from too many confusing thoughts about Frank.

Andrew places his hands, palms upward, on his knees. He looks pointedly at Sebastian.

"Fine," Sebastian says as he does the same, placing his hands on his knees. The issue of his wedding band, his bond with Frank, has once again been safely put aside . . . for now.

. . . . .

Midnight. Sebastian tries, once again, to work on the steps from *Swing Time*. He plays a short section of "Pick Yourself Up." He presses pause, freezing a shot of Fred and Ginger. A tiny clear section of the otherwise cluttered living room floor serves as his dance space; he's run into a barricade of clothes several times during the past three hours.

Two sources of light: the lamp on the unruly desk (bombarded still by piles of papers and the open *RKO Movie Musicals* book) and the iridescent glow of the computer screen. He slams the book shut.

As a couple, they were never this messy; even before Frank, Sebastian wasn't a slob. Of course, his parents weren't as kempt as they might've been, especially near the end of their lives. Still, Sebastian should know better. He shakes away the thought of Frank's disappointment.

In a notebook, he writes the steps he's extracted from the zillionth private screening of Fred and Ginger's dance number. He clutches a lock of his hair; the process shouldn't take this long. Another breath, then he transcribes the stolen goods onto the computer: *flap shuffle hop, flap shuffle hop, flap shuffle hop toe hop step.*

He retrieves an expanded folder from the cabinet below the desk, which contains typewritten pages of text and movement sketches. Leafed among these are so-called dance sequences and half-finished routines. He takes the five-inch stack of notes—his original, if not entirely complete, ideas—out of the folder. He grips the unbound text and flips through the pages. His words, his drawings, his ideas, the handwritten numbers on the upper right-hand corner rush by in a kaleidoscope, like a film strip. The last page, which is 225, initiates a showdown. He's manifested 225 pages of what? It's just not complete.

He blows air from his mouth as he envisions his new CREATE T-shirt. As much as there appears here—225 pages of his creative spirit—it isn't enough.

He tidies the stack of notes and places them back in their rightful home inside the file cabinet. He enables the computer's caps lock and types CREATE over and over. The click of plastic against plastic is hypnotic, induces an easy breath cycle.

His eyes dart between the screen and his hands as his fingers tap dance along the keyboard. The monitor's glow evokes the sensation of a patch of sun blanketing his face; it's not bright enough to make him squint, but he knows, at times such as this, what it feels like when his dark eyes dilate and provide room for more light. And each keystroke forces him to see the wedding band he still wears on his right hand.

By the time he finishes, he's filled ten pages with the word

CREATE, and the clock on the computer reads 12:15 a.m. He rubs his eyelids with the heels of his hands, pinches his brow. He needs to finish some dance numbers, not just hazy sketches and notes on possible choreography. He rests his head on the desk, using the *RKO Movie Musicals* book as a pillow. As soon as he does, he thinks he hears the clicking of the keyboard.

He bolts upright. "What?"

The clicking stops.

He commands himself to exhale. "Arthur, you scared me." But the breath is hard to catch. The damn inhale always trips him up. He slowly pushes his chair away from the desk.

"There's nobody here, right?" He pecks the top of Arthur's head, scoops him up, and stands alongside the desk. Kitty lets out a squawk; the force of his leap from his captor's hold makes Sebastian lurch.

Arthur jumps on top of the desk, rubs his hindquarters against the edge of the computer monitor. He morphs his black tail into what looks like an exclamation point as he glides past the glowing screen. Finally, defying his girth, he springs off the desk in what can only be described as a split leap, one that would rival any that Baryshnikov might've done in his prime.

Arthur's greenish-gold eyes are trained on the computer screen. Sebastian hoists him up again and slowly backs away from the desk. With furry bundle in tow, he heads for the bathroom. But the low-toned meow (an insistent, guttural sound) conveys, "Let me go, you nervous bitch." Or something to that effect, judging by the force Arthur uses as he springboards off Sebastian's belly and sprints out of the bathroom.

But why isn't Arthur freaked out by all this?

Sebastian shuts the bathroom door, steps in front of the medicine cabinet, and rubs his eyes. He reaches for the tap. "Ouch!"

He pulls his hand away from the flow of hot water, adjusts the temperature. He tests it again; the lukewarm splash of water against his face is a welcome coolant.

"Everything's fine," Sebastian tells his reflection. He opens the bathroom door and peeks around the corner. "Right, Arthur?" he yells toward the kitchen. "Everything's great." Back to the sink, he splashes more comfort on his face. *Frank's gone. He's not really here.* He shuts off the water, leans forward, and presses his hip-bones against the white porcelain basin, appreciative of the physical support that allows his body to rest.

Present? Sebastian grunts. *Who the hell cares what Andrew says about actually being present?* If he closes his eyes, the crazy thoughts will go away, and his easy breath cycle will return.

After forcing several rounds of air in through his nose and easily pushing it from his mouth, Sebastian uses his arms to push himself upright. He towels his face dry. One more exhale, his eyes closed. Everything feels realigned, and his heart rate settles back into a midtempo pace. He checks the mirror. Nothing.

Sebastian closes his eyes. Despite himself, he imagines Reid's smile, that damn half-moon chin dimple, the aqua blues . . .

Suddenly, Sebastian could swear he feels someone twist his wedding band.

He gasps. "No!" He rushes out of the bathroom and into the living room. In bed, he covers his face with a pillow. If he squeezes hard enough he can smother himself and be done with all this. He punches the pillow. Maybe there's guilt because, wrong as it may be, he can't help but think of Reid.

Eyes closed. Eyes opened. Sebastian cradles his head on the pillow, turns on his side, and tucks his knees toward his chest. The other one, Frank's pillow, fits cozily between his knees. Eyes closed. Eyes opened. He doesn't see anything. He bolts upright, clutches his husband's pillow to his gut.

The phone rings, making him jump. *Maybe it's Chloe?* The ring stops just as he reaches for it.

He looks toward the ceiling. "Frankie?"

Chapter

SIX

———————

Psychopathology. It's absurd for Sebastian to reduce himself to such a clinical word. But how else could he explain the surreal communication with his dead husband? *Psychopathology.* A few days after eighteen-year-old Sebastian buried his father, the psychiatrist gave the poor old man that label. After all, six months before his own demise, the elder Hart claimed to have seen and heard his dead wife, Sebastian's mother.

He dials Chloe. Ten minutes later, as if by magic, she stands in his doorway. Dazed and blurry, Sebastian sees her in double vision.

"I hightailed it. What's the—"

"Okay."

"What is it, honey?"

Sebastian blows away the wisps of hair that cover his eyes, tucks his locks behind his ears. "I still can't believe it." He stands with locked knees. His eyes widened, he tries to adjust them to form a single image of his best friend.

"Please come in?" Chloe waves her hands in front of his face. "Have you been hitting the peace pipe or something?"

"You know I don't do that. I focus on my breathing."

"Mary Jane could help you find all the breath you need."

"Not funny." Sebastian blinks until finally there's one Chloe. He pulls her inside and shuts the door.

"I'm not laughing," she says.

"Don't call me crazy or anything." He pushes her to sit on the sofa bed where Arthur sleeps.

"You use that word way too much, Seb."

Sebastian chews his nail. "What word?"

"*Crazy.*" Chloe makes a circular motion with both fingers pointed toward her temples.

"No, I don't." Sebastian winces, covers his mouth with flexed fingers. "Do I really?"

"Yes, ma'am."

Sebastian closes his eyes. "I'm just afraid you won't understand."

"Ooh." Chloe jostles his shoulder. "Did something happen with Reid?"

"Yes—no! It's not Reid."

"Anything to do with what you told me, about how you haven't slept since the night of your birthday?"

Sebastian catches his breath. "That's just it. I first saw him, and now he keeps . . ." He takes her hands. "Frank."

"Frank?"

Sebastian bites his lower lip. "I believe he's . . ."

"He's what, darling?" Chloe pats the top of his hands, nods as if she were a mother talking to her six-month-old. "We need a drink."

"No." Sebastian grabs her wrist. "I really don't want a drink. Please." He guides her to sit on the bed.

"I was just going to fix you a little pick-me-up."

Sebastian sits beside her. "He's here," he says, his vocal chords pinched.

"Who?" Chloe strokes Sebastian's hair.

"Frankie. I saw him. I think." He tucks his hands between his thighs. "I know. I really saw him. I *feel* him."

Chloe lowers her head, which forces her thin neck to crepe. Her mouth purses like one of those shrunken apple-head dolls, and her eyebrows arch. Sebastian nearly trips over himself when she abruptly pulls him by the wrist, leading him toward the kitchen. "You sit." She points to her target. "I'll tend."

First Andrew, and now Chloe's the choreographer? But Sebastian does as she directs. He pushes aside a pile of bills that clutter the kitchen table. "I'm serious. He was here."

"Keep on. I'm with you." Chloe takes short glasses out of the cherrywood cabinet. "Peach stuff?"

"Next one over."

Chloe manhandles the bottle of schnapps. She slams the cabinet shut, then unearths the vodka and ice tray from the freezer. "Deux?" she asks Sebastian with a smile, her fingers in a peace sign.

Sebastian huffs. "Fine." He shrugs with an eye roll. The clinking the two ice cubes make as she drops them into his glass summons a memory, reminds him of when his parents used to throw their keys in a glass bowl just off their foyer.

Chloe drapes her slender frame over the counter. She places her pointer and middle fingers against the glass, fills it with vodka up to the level of her pointer finger. As she works she whistles an unrecognizable tune and does a cha-cha step toward the refrigerator. She adds a splash of orange juice and another dollop of cranberry and peach schnapps to her lava creation. She holds the glass further away from her body and gyrates her wrist in a careful motion until the drink turns the color of pink grapefruit. It's like watching a prize-winning chemist in her laboratory. Sebastian chuckles. Her father, the dastardly pharmacist, would be so proud.

"Your favorite," Chloe says. "Sex on the Beach." She does a mambo step and hands him the drink.

Sebastian smiles and cups his hands around the frosty glass. "You think I live in a fantasy world, don't you? That I see everything through a candy-colored lens."

"Don't be silly," says Chloe. Still, she flashes her signature "you do know you're nuts" look again: the wide eyes, the creped neck. She nods and pours more vodka into his glass.

"That's too much for me."

"It'll help you sleep, my little love."

Sebastian takes a sip and coughs at the burn. He imagines this is what it would feel like to take a swig of Shoe Stretch, the pungent solution dancers use to break in new shoes. He sets the drink on the gray Formica table, slides it an arm's length away. The sound of the glass as it moves against the surface floods him with more memories of Frank: long nights seated across from each other at this very table, Sebastian helping his husband study for one med school exam after another; the heavy textbooks and piles of flashcards; the heated discussions about Doctor "There Are No Accidents" Freud versus Doctor "Everything Is Symbolism" Jung; the glasses of Dr. Pepper that accompanied each TV dinner; the plates of apple pie married to cups of English breakfast tea.

"I can't handle this," Sebastian finally adds. Then to Arthur, who has slinked into the kitchen to quietly chow down kibble, "Please tell Auntie Mame I can't drink this."

Chloe still roots in the cabinet. "Have you mentioned this Frank stuff to your therapist?"

"Technically, he's not a therapist. He's a wellness counselor. A yogi."

"Well, pardonne-moi," Chloe says before clearing her throat.

"Your wellness counselor, your guru, or whatever the hell he is." She takes another glass from the cabinet. "Have you told him about Frank's recent visits?"

"I've told Andrew," he replies evenly. His eyes follow her as she prepares her own brew. No fruity blend for Miss Chloe, just "deux" ice cubes, four fingers of vodka, and three wrist gyrations.

Chloe runs her finger along the inside rim of the glass. "Yum, yum." She licks her finger. "And what did this guru of yours, Herr Cooper, say about your seeing Frank?"

"How did you know his last name?"

"I've chatted him up a bit after yoga class." She licks her lips. "So what did Andrew say about Frankie?"

Sebastian huffs. "Would you stop interrogating me and just listen?" He knows he sounds like a five-year-old, feels the tension in his brow as he scrunches up his face.

Chloe holds up the same two fingers she used to mix her potion. "Scout's honor, I absolutely, positively am listening to you." She gulps most of her drink and slides Sebastian's toward him.

"You may be listening, but you're not hearing me." Sebastian slams the drink on the table. "Sorry, boy," he calls after Arthur who, obviously startled by the sound, waddles out of the kitchen.

Chloe rubs his upper back. "I am listening, sweetie."

"Trust me, I'm not just seeing things, Chloe." *Or am I?* Sebastian bites his lower lip. "I'm not going crazy. I'm not like my father."

"There you go again with the crazy talk. I didn't say you were crazy."

Sebastian rubs the tension from his chest. He keeps his hand on his breastbone, as if ready to recite the Pledge of Allegiance. "He was—Frank definitely is here."

Chloe downs the rest of her drink. "Look," she says, "you've got to chill the fuck out." She leads him toward the sofa bed. "Come on, I'll tuck you in," she continues as she sprints back into the kitchen and returns with Sebastian's drink.

The vodka hasn't done its magic yet, at least not that Sebastian can tell. He's physically tired, yet his wide-awake brain tap dances to its own syncopated beat. He sips more of Chloe's brew. No burning sensation or coughs this time. He gulps down half the glass, savors the sweetness.

"See, my dear, you can work that much vodka." Chloe clucks her tongue and blows him a kiss. "As they say, you never know what you can handle until you try it."

"I'm not sure 'they' know what I'm up against." *And neither do you,* a voice inside adds. After all, Chloe's never lost anyone. Her parents have passed, but from what she's reported all these years, their death didn't seem to bother her in the least.

Sebastian falls back onto the bed. He squints; to his surprise, the ceiling isn't very high, not as much as he once imagined, anyway. The mound of covers and pillows underneath his body force him into an arched position. As his neck cranes backward, blood rushes to the top of his head. He giggles.

"What's so funny?"

"Nothing," Sebastian says with another chortle. Either he's drunk or, once again, being a drama queen. The latter is perhaps the more appropriate diagnosis. He twists from side to side, reaches around to pull the covers from underneath his back. He cradles his head on Frank's pillow and rolls on his side to face Chloe. Arthur folds his limbs under his torso and nestles between the two humans.

"Well, well, well," says Chloe. "Aren't you boys just too cozy for words." She reaches into her black Coach bag and shakes a bottle; its loud rattle makes Sebastian cringe.

"Voilà." Chloe hands him an oblong pink pill. "To help you sleep."

Sebastian rolls his eyes. "What is it?"

"The lowest dose of Xanax." Chloe flicks her hand. "Just take it."

Sebastian groans as he sits upright. Arthur lifts his head briefly, then recups his paws, covers his brow.

"Come, come." Chloe hands him his glass. "Have it with your Barbie-pink beverage."

"With the alcohol and the Prozac?"

"Trust me. With all the shit I've mixed, I know this won't kill you."

Put me out of my misery. Sebastian sighs. He's tired of the voice inside that needs to remind him to exhale, to not be ashamed of breath. It shouldn't be this hard. No, it can't be this hard. The pill slips down his throat with ease, aided by the remainder of his drink.

"I'll stay the night." The bed rocks gently as Chloe stretches her lean body toward, then away from Sebastian as she places his potion on the side table. Chloe turns to stroke Arthur's belly. "We'll have a slumber party."

"I'll be fine. You don't need to hang out here." Sebastian joins in with scratches on top of Arthur's head. His black-and-white face offers a welcome smile and a motorboat purr.

"I will not leave you on your own tonight."

"I'm not alone. Right, Arthur?" Sebastian says. "Don't worry, Auntie Mame." He rubs her arm as his hand grows heavy. It's increasingly difficult to keep his eyes open.

"You rest," Chloe says, tucking him in.

Sebastian revs up for a good breathing cycle: a short, forced inhalation, like a yawn that's abruptly stifled from social embarrassment, then an easy exhalation. He reaches for the air.

Chloe taps his forehead, settles him deeper into the mattress. She begins to morph before Sebastian's eyes: two, three, four images of her blur together as if trapped in a slow-motion slideshow.

Sebastian's heartbeat slowly descends from allegro to legato. For once, the slower pace feels natural as his entire body falls into the relaxed state Andrew would call Shavasana—Corpse Pose.

Chapter

SEVEN

Sebastian brushes away the nose tickle. He feels his mouth turn upward in a smile. Arthur's purr vibrates in Sebastian's head as he continues licking his guardian's nose, the weight of his twenty-pound body mounted on Sebastian's chest. A striation of light peeks through the blinds. An unexpected and effortless exhale comes to Sebastian in the form of a full-throttled yawn. He feels rested, as if he's finally had a good night's sleep. He massages Arthur's neck and turns away from his wet kisses.

A piece of paper, rougher than the kitty's tongue, crinkles against Sebastian's cheek. He reads the note:

My Dearest BFF Drama Queen,

You can keep your lumpy-ass mattress. Next time, the slumber party's at my place. Arthur's not invited, though, because he's a bed hog. (Did you know he actually snores?) Regrets I had to dash early, but didn't want to wake you. Call me this afternoon from your friggin' "landline." By the by, why the hell won't you get a cell phone already? (Just bustin' your balls. Someone's got to, right? Hardy-har-har.)

Love you,
The Big C

Sebastian folds the note in half. He wonders if Chloe scribbles as much correspondence for her date items when she dashes out after their interludes.

He sets the note on the side table and holds Arthur tight against his body. The hug lasts a mere five counts before Arthur shimmies out of Sebastian's grip and quicksteps (well, he does wear a tuxedo coat) toward the kitchen.

"Shit!" Sebastian swings his legs over the side of the bed and presses the top of his clock to display the alarm mode. "Twelve thirty?" He gives himself a pat down and realizes he's still in last night's outfit. "What the hell?" He rakes the pile of clothes on the floor and finds his sneakers, rifles deeper, and finds the black baseball cap and windbreaker. Should he alert Madam Olga? No, no time. He rushes toward the door.

When he makes it outside, he's struck by the pleasant weather. *Warm, not hot; definitely feels like spring today.* The sky appears content to be dressed in powder blue—or is it really aqua? Then, serendipity—the moment Sebastian steps toward the loading zone at the corner of Forty-Ninth and Tenth Avenue, the bus arrives. He chuckles; sometimes luck throws him a moment he can actually embrace.

He grabs the M50 across town to Lexington Avenue, then hops onto the faster 6 train to the Sixty-Eighth Street/Hunter College stop. He despises the fact that his tardiness has become chronic. If he were choreographer of a huge production number, and a dancer was consistently late on the same vital count of music, he would be more than frustrated. Of course! He charges up and out of the bowels of the subway station and bolts across Sixty-Eighth.

Out of breath, he lurches forward uptown on Fifth Avenue. He stops abruptly; the traffic flows in the opposite direction. In the twenty-two years he's lived here, he's never noticed the upper

Manhattan portion of Fifth Avenue is a one-way.

But now he's trapped behind the L. L. Beans. Mr. Bean is rail thin and tall. His stringy brown hair settles over his brow like a well-bred sheepdog. He wears khaki shorts, a white button-down with sleeves rolled up, and black loafers. As family tradition most likely dictates, a white canvas tote with nautical trim completes the outfit. If Sebastian were closer, he'd get a good whiff of the Polo cologne Mr. Bean most certainly sports.

Mrs. Bean is also thin but only stands as tall as the middle of her husband's chest. Yellow embroidered bees dot her navy-blue shorts. She has shoulder-length, platinum-blonde hair and holds a small, white Louis Vuitton bag in the crook of her arm, an odd complement for the preppy ensemble. Maybe the status bag was gifted to her by another man? Or perhaps she wears open secrets and Mr. Bean doesn't even realize?

In Mrs. Bean's other hand is a green leash, the umbilical cord to a terrier. Junior Bean, who appears to still be a puppy, darts from side to side, poking his nose at pieces of refuse along the sidewalk: a candy wrapper, a soda can. He pounces on what seems to be a glossy postcard for a fashion boutique. Incredible— isn't the renowned Fifth Avenue supposed to be cleaner than this? But Mrs. Bean forges ahead, her hand attached to Junior Bean's lifeline.

Sebastian laughs; it's almost absurd, this family's lack of self-awareness, the impact their improvised choreography has on him as he tries to maneuver around them but can't. *Ugh!* Nothing gets in the way of the Bean family, this pas de trois that blocks the entire sidewalk.

Still, Sebastian needs to pass, *now!* By the time he gets to his own pack of the day, Madam Olga will probably be ready to unleash him. He ups his speed; maybe he can snake around them as Junior Bean steers Mrs. Bean to the left? Nope, that doesn't work either. He countermoves right. Nah . . . still no break in the trio's hold over the wide sidewalk. Damn, they won't surrender the downstage position. Don't they sense someone wants to share the playing space? Truth be told, however, Sebastian digs the challenge. It's as if he's the choreographer now and needs to take charge and restage them.

On just the right count, he tells himself as he prepares to initiate the moves, *the back line will pass the front line. Not yet, not yet. No . . .* Junior Bean moves left again toward a set of scaffolding. *Yes!* Sebastian finally chases one foot under the other, a bastardized chassé forward, and claims the downstage position.

He's exhausted by the time he finally steps into the sixties high-rise on Fifth Avenue and Seventy-Second Street, the Madam's place. *Madam* seems appropriate since that's the way Olga makes Sebastian feel, as if he's a prostitute. Inside, a doorman sits behind a wooden podium. The tip of his blue hat peeks over the top of the *New York Post.*

Sebastian waves. "Hey, Miguel."

Miguel tilts the paper forward. His face is nearly as brown as Sebastian's, yet round and owl-like as Mrs. Woo's. "Tardy again, my friend?"

Sebastian scrunches his face. "I know."

Miguel's short whistle is like an afterthought, but the message to Sebastian isn't hard to translate: "*Pobrecito*—poor thing" is what his dark eyes say before he nods and goes back to his paper.

I wonder what Olga has in store today? Sebastian thinks as he plants himself on the red suede bench. Chills rush through him at the sight of gold veins that streak the mirror on the opposite wall and disfigure his reflection. The visual of himself entwined in the veins creates the sensation of being bound from head to toe. He giggles; Chloe would tease him if he revealed such imagery, and probably whip up something sexual—an S&M joke, no doubt—with Reid added to the formula. Sebastian slaps his wrist to chase the thought out of his head.

He writes the word *trapped* over and over until a half page of his notebook is crammed. He notices the front-page headline on Miguel's paper—*9/11: Another Anniversary on the Way*. He closes his eyes at the thought. Hard to believe it's the seventh anniversary of 9/11 that's *on the way*. But there are enough anniversaries to think of at the moment, he reasons. Besides, who knows where he'll be or how he'll feel on that day next September, which is still six months away.

He documents more *trapped* on the page, then skips a few lines down to write, *If I were to choreograph a tap number to convey a trapped man, what would it look like?* He claps the notebook shut, follows suit with his eyes. Something bold, aggressive; a Stravinsky symphony would work for the music—dissonant sounds. A plethora of fast chaînés and pirouettes, zillions of scuffs and riffs would highlight *The Dance of the Trapped Man*. Steps that make the feet go crazy and force the dancer to really dig into the floor, from the ball of the foot to the heel at unexpected intervals, would also signify the character's struggle. And his dream ballet might well include a stop-time section, a sequence of steps that initiate themselves for several counts, are suddenly silenced (forced to concede as several more counts pass), and whose pattern finally starts again, over and over.

But to what end? How would the routine and the dancer called to play the part of Trapped Man find closure? Sebastian tucks the notebook between his thighs and massages his tight jaw. These rants are just more ideas to add to the unfinished stack of routines at home. Eyes open: "Be present, Sebastian," he says to his warbled reflection in the vein-streaked mirror.

Then, as he puts pencil back to paper, an off-white envelope is placed on his open notebook. This intrusion makes his hand veer sideways and scrawl a long, unruly streak. The pale, wrinkled hand attached to the envelope, knotted like a piece of gingerroot, is streaked with blue veins, its claws lacquered a bubblegum pink.

Sebastian narrows his eyes on the all-too-familiar rings: one is gold with a coin on top that depicts a scene with a Trojan warrior, his cape flowing as he straddles a charging horse. The other ring is crowned with an ice-blue crystal that juts outward by at least an inch. *Must be costume jewelry*, he thinks.

"This is for last week and the first part of this week," says the ring bearer. Yes, it's the one and only Madam Olga. And surprise, surprise, she's dressed in yet another Chanel suit, this one cobalt blue with white trim. Or is it a knockoff?

Sebastian's eyes wander toward the raised lines that track from the center of Olga's earlobes to the bottom of her jaw. Doesn't she know there are scars? Isn't she ashamed of those reminders of her past? If so, she hides it well. With her face pulled back as it is, she'd be allowed office space with the other amphibians at the Actor's Equity lounge. Actually, Olga might still hold her union card; after all, she's a retired Broadway gypsy who, according to Chloe, was an amazing performer in her day. In addition to being in zillions of shows, she was Gwen Verdon's understudy in Fosse's *Redhead*. All the same, Sebastian would never want to share the stage with her.

"I'm very sorry, Olga," he says through a forced smile.

"Whatever," Olga responds in her signature wannabe Bacall baritone. She pushes the envelope toward Sebastian.

"For this morning," he adds. "I'm sorry."

"Sorry, Sorry, Sorry," Olga drones, bobbing her head.

"Well, I am—let's say regretful."

"Regretful?" Olga shakes her gnarled fist. "No. *Let's say* I've heard that quite a bit from you lately."

"I know. I'm sorry." Sebastian covers his mouth: *Stay away from the S word*. It suddenly occurs to him that Olga's bitchy enough to have spawned a certain chorus boy. Maybe the old hag was Greg's long-lost grandmother.

"You do know that I nearly twisted my poor ankle the other morning when you lost control of the dogs. And little Maxine was so traumatized."

Like hell. Sebastian sighs. The poodle probably was thrilled to finally have some fun.

"I couldn't get her to take a walk for two days. Not even a real dump," Olga continues. "Poor thing is still resting upstairs from the ordeal." She looks around, then whispers, "We've been reduced to Wee-Wee Pads, for God's sake."

Translation: Sebastian obviously isn't the only drama queen in Manhattan. Madam's just pissed that she can't always control her purebred, and doggie's depressed that she's always being controlled by Madam.

"I feel terrible, Olga. I swear." And he really does feel bad that any animal has to live with this biatch, including Doctor Frankenstein, her plastic surgeon husband.

"I can't even tell you how cross this has made me." She juts her neck forward, her dark eyes bulging. The scar lines on the sides of her face move backward as if she's dislocating her jaw.

"I can just imagine how terrible it makes you feel that Maxine's so upset. I love my cat to death."

"Don't even try it." Olga scrunches her face. "Cats are not dogs."

Sebastian stops himself from hissing at her and clenches his jaw. He doesn't trust people who don't like cats. People like Olga are just scared of their inability to control kitties: independent, intelligent, and mysterious (although very loving) creatures.

"Again, Olga, I'm deeply sorry."

"Ah, ah, ah." The scars on her jaw redden as she speaks. "You'll have to give it up. Now I must admit you're fairly good with animals. Although, truth be told, you used to be better at it. You know that, yes?"

Sebastian nods.

"My clients depend on me." Olga wags her calcified fist. "What's my motto?"

Sebastian exhales, then says, "Although they drool, the clients rule."

"Exactly," Olga adds with another finger wag, that obnoxious Trojan warrior charging toward his face. "Several of the clients have been unhappy with your mess-ups."

A cramp locks in the center of Sebastian's belly. He closes his eyes. "I know I messed up, but—"

"No but!" Olga says. It sounds like tree branches cracking as she snaps her fingers. "Keep your 'but' to yourself. I'll do the honors this last time."

"What?"

"The sorry routine," Olga says, her dark eyes wide. "Sorry." The S sound swims slowly toward, then finally sinks into Sebastian's head.

"You're sorry?"

"Yes, I am. I really am sorry." Olga pats her coif. "Because I've given you a bunch of shots, and Doggie Duties has a reputation to uphold. My business must maintain its stature. *Finito!*" She claps her hands for emphasis.

"*Finito?* That's it?" Sebastian groans. "Come on, Olga, don't do this." He's tempted to add "pretty please," but it probably wouldn't suffice.

"The keys, Mr. Hart!"

Sebastian's heart locks. He huffs as he unzips the front of his backpack and hands Madam his carabiner clip. The cluster of jangling keys reminds him that he's just lost over a dozen clients, a major pay cut.

"There's no chance?"

Olga shrugs, the Chanel suit accentuating her broad shoulders. "No, no, no. I don't see it. Not a possibility." She puffs out her chest (yes, she could definitely be Greg's grandmother) as she slithers away. Her long legs, which do seem to be the remains of a fossilized Fosse dancer, trail one after the other toward the elevator. The doors open and close, whisking her away.

"Hah!" Sebastian yells toward the elevator. He sticks out his tongue and actually hisses, then cups his hand into a megaphone. "Gwen Verdon would've made a better exit!"

"Tough break, eh, Papi," says Miguel over the top of his newspaper.

Sebastian nods with a smile. He checks his watch. "Crap." And he's off. He sprints across Seventy-Second Street toward Lexington, then down to Sixty-Eighth for the 6 train to Grand Central. He's wary of a reprise of the number with the L. L. Beans but also titillated by the challenge it would be to dance around the preppy trio again.

.....

They gawk. As Sebastian darts past the wall-to-wall cubicle workers in his sweat suit and baseball cap, they appear as if in a filmstrip. He picks up the tempo. They still gawk. *Why the hell do I let these troglodytes make me feel bad about my clothes?* he wonders.

As Sebastian zips past the last cubicle and makes a right turn, the Prince of the Troglodytes meets him. A mere boy, it probably takes Brian three days to grow any of the wispy, dishwater-brown facial hair he sports. He wears a blue pinstriped suit and tortoise-shell glasses. He fiddles with the gold chain of his pocket watch.

"Sorry, Brian." Sebastian flings his arms outward and lets them strike the sides of his legs. "I know I'm late again."

"Follow," Brian commands, pivoting to face the opposite direction.

Sebastian furrows his brow. *Whatever.* He pivots, mirroring Brian's choreography, and follows him down the hallway.

The largest in the company, Brian's office channels Ikea. Apparently the Swedes convinced Brian to expand on their typical blond and white influences to include an opposing color scheme for his showroom: a large black desk, silver trash can, black coat stand, silver bulletin board, and silver filing cabinets.

"Sebastian, Sebastian, Sebastian. There are no part-time jobs, just part-time people." Brian, seated on a black knockoff Aeron chair, rolls farther away from his desk. He twists himself to one side, reclines slightly, then crosses his left leg over the right. Sebastian, seated in a black leather chair opposite the desk, grins at the sight of the little boy who asserts his power through such hackneyed choreography. Brian's a twenty-three-year-old forced into the role of a man at least thirty years his senior.

"Make me full time, then," Sebastian blurts out. "I'd be more dedicated." *Buck up!* he reminds himself; he must be his own Madam now.

"You mean you'd be more dedicated, for example, to dressing appropriately?" Brian's eyes trek toward the top of Sebastian's head, then down to his feet.

Sebastian's eyes tingle as he sizes up his boss in return. "Look,

I'm sorry about today's wardrobe malfunction."

"Sebastian, this isn't a stage play."

"I know." Sebastian takes off his baseball cap. He mumbles: "But sometimes I wish this all was a play, and not real."

"What?"

"Nothing. What I meant to say is that I'm terribly sorry about the way I'm dressed. I didn't have enough time to change between jobs. I figured it would be better to get here on time."

"You've been with the company six months, but it occurs to me that you don't truly value the opportunity we've given you."

"But I do. I need the money."

"If all this is—if it's only about money for you, you shouldn't be here."

"It's not just about money. I really enjoy it here." *Liar, liar pants on fire.*

"You don't enjoy it here. If you did, you wouldn't be chronically late." As Brian extends it, the chain of the pocket watch sounds like a ratchet; the crank of metal against metal makes Sebastian cringe. Bossy Boy pops open the gold case, raises his eyebrows as he checks the time, then snaps it shut with great force. Before he can catch himself, Sebastian jams his pointer fingers in either ear to drown out Brian's exclamation point.

"But I've only been late five—"

"Eight times in the last month. I have it all documented."

Of course you do. Sebastian forces an apologetic smile.

"And besides the tardiness, you still lack basic computer skills."

Sebastian clenches his jaw. Did Brian and Olga confer this morning about everything he lacks?

"Sebastian," Brian continues, "this is a small yet powerful company. Even with the recession our stocks are rising. By this time next year, with McCain hopefully in the White House, we'll be up, up, up." His pinched voice rises as he points a skinny finger toward the ceiling.

Sebastian glances upward. If Frank actually sees all this, he must be terribly disappointed in him for blowing yet another job.

"That is, with the right team in place. Progress is always in motion," Brian adds with one last jab toward the ceiling. "And we need to maintain that progress on every level of this company's structure. No matter what role an employee plays here at Drummond Software, he or she needs computer skills."

First Olga and now Brian has raised the curtain. Sebastian forces another smile. He's so damn lucky: free admission to not one but two matinee performances in one day. Should he applaud? And which performer deserves the Tony? It's a tough choice: While Olga's interpretation of her role as boss was at least bolstered by the fact that she had developed her own business, Brian Drummond III probably just attends board meetings and dutifully regurgitates what was said. It sounds, in fact, as if he's rehearsed this speech, waited for the right moment to break into song, directed to the appropriate member of the caste system.

Sebastian closes his eyes. The song comes: "Pick yourself up, dust yourself off . . ."

"What did you say?"

Sebastian covers his mouth. "Nothing. Sorry about that. Come on, Brian," he whines, hating himself for doing so. "Like you said, I've been here six months, and you knew I didn't have strong computer skills when I started."

"Don't get me wrong, Sebastian. You're a nice guy." He shrugs. "And you have a nice singing voice. But I'm positive you don't really think this company's the right fit."

"Fit?"

"Yes." Elbows on the desk, Brian steeples his hands. "This isn't the right fit for you."

The chorus boy nods, offers the principle the appropriate submissive response. After all, his financial fitness depends on this gig. Then another giggle rises up inside him at the absurdity of having to justify his fitness. Sebastian's reminded of Broadway chorus boy replacement auditions where they make you dance your balls off for hours, then ask your measurements. If you don't fit the outgoing chorus boy's costumes, it usually means you're out, no matter how talented you are.

"I realize you're getting older."

Sebastian huffs. "Older?" He feels his lips start to form a *P*, as in *prick*, but he bites his upper lip instead. How fabulous of Bossy Boy to remind his elder that he's aging by the moment. True; next to someone like Greg, Sebastian's too old. And he's probably too old to start up new love with Reid, isn't he? *Too Old for Everything: A New Musical Comedy.*

"But it's not too late for you to find something. I sincerely wish you luck with finding whatever job or career . . . whatever it is that you really want. And to show there are no hard feelings. I'll even pay you for tomorrow and Friday."

"Yeah. Sure. Whatever," Sebastian says under his breath.

"What was that?" Brian says, sitting even more erect.

"Nothing," growls the drama queen with what feels like the straightest face he can muster. "I'm fine."

Chapter

EIGHT

Sebastian's never stepped inside Green Earth, but now that he's here, words can't fully express his wonder. From the Tenth Avenue storefront, such a tiny door, he never imagined the garden shop was so expansive. Narrow, its aisles go on for what seems like forever. An ear-to-ear maze of foliage and plantings beckon. It's as though he's been transplanted onto Willy Wonka turf. *Talk about Technicolor.*

Sebastian focuses on the bucket of garden tools on the ground. "I'm fine. Really I am."

"It's their loss for firing you," Reid says.

"Thanks. I think."

"Besides, a stroll inside this place always cheers me up, even when I'm not looking for business inspiration."

"Sure you're not stalking me?"

"Maybe I am. Maybe not." Reid smiles, his dimples along for the ride. "Although this is our hood. Seriously, though, I'm glad I bumped into you, and that you agreed to join me."

"Sure." Sebastian chews his upper lip.

"Come on, who could resist such a heavenly oasis?" Reid juts his hand forward. "Shake on it."

"What do you mean?" Sebastian loops his fingers around his

backpack straps.

"You'll help me decide."

"I don't know." Still, Sebastian offers a quick handshake. It's hard to let go of Reid's warm palm, but he finally concedes, then tucks his hands in his own back pockets.

"Aw, come on." Reid squeezes Sebastian's shoulder. "I need you."

Sebastian folds his arms across his chest. "But why? You're the professional."

"Trust me, it'll be fun. Let go. Live a little." Reid jostles Sebastian's arms until they flop alongside his body, which induces a laugh from the Sebastian.

"Right." Sebastian chews his bottom lip. "Live, live, live. I assume you're also a fan of my favorite movie, *Auntie Mame*."

"Duh. What respectable, middle-aged gay man hasn't seen it a zillion times?"

Sebastian smiles. "You sound like my own Auntie Mame, Chloe."

"Is that a compliment?" Reid squints. With his reddish-gold eyebrows bunched together, he looks like a curious golden retriever.

"Of course," Sebastian offers through another smile, realizing that up close, Reid's dimples are crescent-shaped, not half-moons as he'd initially thought.

Reid palms Sebastian's lower back. "Over there."

Heat rises through Sebastian's body. He licks his lips. Why the hell did he agree to help some guy he met less than a week ago shop for plants?

Reid guides him toward the tables, which house a plethora of spring wonders. "What would you do?"

"Me?" Sebastian averts his gaze. The water fountain with a

lion's face, teeth borne in what looks like a yawn, reminds him of Arthur.

"Yeah. I'm talking to you, mister." Reid winks, then pretends to hold binoculars, twisting his torso side to side as if scanning the space. "I don't see anyone else in the joint, do you?"

"Nope." Sebastian looks toward the ceiling. He bows his head and offers what feels like, and must look like, his most sheepish grin.

"Okay then." Reid pumps his fists. "Let's do it. If you had to plan this, how would you lay things out?"

"But you're Dr. Garden," Sebastian persists. "Why do you need my help?"

Reid sets his bag on the floor and gestures for Sebastian to do the same. "Sometimes I just like doing things with another creative person."

Sebastian complies, sets his own backpack on the floor. "I don't know what I'd choose. It's been a while since I allowed dirt under my nails." He sneaks a whiff of his underarm. *Goodie, there's still a hint of cucumber-scented deodorant.*

"Come on, shape it in your head."

"Huh?"

Reid closes his eyes and taps on his forehead with his fingertips. It looks like the kind of mindfulness exercise Andrew would have Sebastian do. If Reid knew all the shit Sebastian struggles to articulate inside his head, he'd want to *run, run, run*, not *live, live, live* anywhere near him.

Reid unzips his backpack. "Check it out. Fifth Avenue co-op. Beautiful, isn't it?"

Sebastian takes in the rooftop terrace in the photo Reid hands him. "Sure is." *But what the hell does a boy from Margaretville really know about Fifth Avenue?*

"The colors, the flowers, Seb." Reid sucks in air, smacks his forehead. "Sorry, I mean Sebastian. How do you see it?"

"See it?" Sebastian winces. Great, when he really needs to visualize in Technicolor, his brain won't cooperate.

"The garden in this space," Reid says. "What do you imagine or envision?" He leans into Sebastian, who flinches. "May I? Promise I won't bite."

Sebastian exhales. "Okay." He offers a toothless half smile.

"Shut them," Reid says in a breathy baritone.

Sebastian surrenders, eyes closed. He feels the gentle tap of Reid's fingertips on his forehead.

"What do you see?"

Sebastian feels his mouth turn upward as he smiles into the gentle hint of peppermint on Reid's breath. "I see . . . maybe . . . white," he says in sync with Reid's final tap.

Reid whispers in Sebastian's ear, "Now you're in the zone."

Sebastian shakes away the tickle on his ear and blinks his eyes open. There's a shadow overhead. Is it the setting sun taking the stage, making itself known through the shop's skylight? Or is it something—or someone—else?

Reid brushes his hand against Sebastian's arm. "Okay. You said something white."

"Yes. White." A piano arpeggio fills Sebastian's head, along with the opening lines from Sondheim's *Sunday in the Park with George*, as spoken by the character George Seurat. "White," he catches himself saying out loud. "A blank canvas."

"A blank canvas?" Reid smiles. "Okay. That's cool."

"Yeah. White daffodils." Sebastian smells the cluster of flowers. "They're pretty."

"They are. Lovely." Reid writes in his notebook. "Resilient too."

"And maybe these." Sebastian checks the tag. "Hyacinths."

Reid nods. "Hyacinth, another resilient choice. I like the blue as well." He jots down something else in his notebook.

"And we need something sunny." Sebastian feels his heart race as he reads the tag on each bucket of flowers. "Yellow tulips, and red ones. Red would be nice, don't you think?"

"Perfect," says Reid. "You're a Technicolor guy."

Sebastian gasps. *Technicolor.* A tickle dances inside his chest. "And this. What do you call these?"

Reid holds up the tag. "Impatiens."

"Right." Sebastian bites his upper lip. "They seem like they'd be quite, as you say, resilient."

"I couldn't agree more," Reid says as he steps closer. "Impatiens fare well in the shade."

"Are you shady?"

"What?" Reid shakes his head. "I'm the perfect gentleman."

Sebastian lurches in place, as Reid's palm, now resting on his wrist, feels warmer than it was a few moments before when they shook hands. Heat radiates across Sebastian's face.

"See?" Reid continues sotto voce, as if revealing a secret. "You just tapped it out of your head. You employed your brilliant imagination to help me craft my garden. You've got an artist's intuition. I'm sure you'll finish the routine for the recital in no time."

Sebastian nods. Reid's gentle baritone induces an internal flutter, as if one of the shop's butterfly garden ornaments has come to life and slipped inside him. He releases his gaze and tucks his hands in his front pockets. He wants to believe Reid, but it's beyond frightening to trust someone new. After all, they've just met, and Reid's only been to one of his tap classes. Why the hell did Sebastian agree to follow a stranger inside this plant wonderland?

Reid extends an arm across Sebastian's body. Sebastian

flinches, pinned between Reid and the pot of impatiens.

Reid's face reddens. "Shall we?" He squares his shoulders and presses his chest against Sebastian's torso.

"Huh?" A wave of heat rolls through Sebastian's body. Reid's scent is a hint of sweat mixed with soap.

Reid whispers, "Shall we dance?"

Sebastian's throat vibrates with laughter as Reid's hand, cupped against his, causes another tickle inside his chest as he's given a single disco twirl. The dance partners' arms pretzel together, Sebastian's back concave and pressed against Reid's chest.

I shouldn't be doing this, Sebastian reminds himself. He commands the butterfly to go away and haunt someone else's nervous system. But it's too late: Reid's kneecaps spoon the back of Sebastian's knees. His breath, with its hint of peppermint, is warm against Sebastian's neck, his facial stubble cat-tongue rough against Sebastian's cheek.

Dizzy, Sebastian blurts out loud: "Don't you dare faint!"

"Excuse me?"

"Sorry, sorry." Sebastian pulls away. "I don't know."

"You all right?"

Sebastian cups his palms over his face. "I shouldn't. Too fast."

"No, it's not you." Reid stuffs his hands in his pockets. "It's my fault."

Is he pissed? Sebastian wonders. After all, when he showed up to his tap class, it was Sebastian who flirted in the mirror, trying to impress Reid with his skills. He also agreed to join him here in the garden shop. The truth is, after an entire year without another man's skin against his own, Sebastian likes that somebody wants to touch, let alone, dance with him.

Sebastian focuses on the darkened skylight. "I have to—I need to go," he says, shouldering his backpack.

Reid anchors the weight of his hand on Sebastian's arm. "Please, wait."

Sebastian shakes his head furiously. "Sorry." He bolts past the impatiens and out the door onto a dark Tenth Avenue. Thankfully, two blocks north provides the safety of home.

Chapter

NINE

A loud meow: it's as if the fur baby's been waiting at the apartment door for hours. Arthur bullies his weight against Sebastian's calf muscle, then tracks a figure eight around his legs.

"Whoa, boy." Sebastian wobbles with the loss of balance. The backpack makes a thud as he flings it on top of a pile of clothes. He grunts as he hoists and drapes the twenty pounds of Arthur over his shoulder.

Arthur allows two more strokes of his dancing tail, then he's off. The sound of kibble being voraciously gobbled is noticeable. Maybe Sebastian was right all along, that it's a bad idea to leave pudgy Arthur's food out. That was always Frank's vote, something they argued over constantly. But Sebastian still can't rally behind the psychology of self-control. After all, what if something happens to the parent, days go by, and the poor baby starves to death? Not a gamble he wants to take.

Exhale through your nose. That familiar inner voice, equal parts Mom, Dad, Andrew, Chloe, Arthur, and Frank, reminds Sebastian to breathe. Eyes closed, he burrows into the mass of blankets on the sofa. He checks the ceiling, then narrows his focus to Frank's image in the picture on the side table. The glass in the frame remains splintered in four sections, the husbands seemingly standing outside a window and looking in.

Sebastian whispers, "Where are you?" He catches himself midchew, spits out the nail chip, and brushes his wet thumb against his chest. He sits upright and scans the room. "Come on!" he yells toward the ceiling. "Where are you?" He closes his eyes and inhales on a slow five count: *one, two, three, four, five*. Exhale: *one, two, three, four, five*.

He continues the pattern with his hands cupped over his breast, as if prepped for a double-handed Pledge of Allegiance. But with each inhalation, his stubborn pulse runs counter to the breath cycle.

Frank. Who cares if it's irrational or crazy? If he's somehow present, Sebastian wants to see him. He wants to feel him. He needs his husband back—immediately!

He keeps his eyes closed and chants tenderly, "Frank? Frank? Frank?" Nothing. He opens his eyes. "Please, Frankie." Still nothing.

Outside in the hallway, a baby cries, startling Sebastian. He checks the peephole. He's never heard such sounds from the neighbors, nor seen a little one on his floor. If only he could cast himself as the understudy and substitute his own deafening inner cry for the hallway's abrupt quietude. But he can't. Utter silence. He shuts the peephole; whatever infant passerby there was must've gone.

The rusted hinges yell at Sebastian as he opens the medicine cabinet. He pops three Advil and slurps cold water from the tap to help wash them down. Suddenly, heat radiates over his face. *Is it Frank?* He once read an article in a Halloween issue of the *Village Voice* that stated that when ghosts appear, they can cause temperature change. He splashes his face with water. A few light, self-inflicted slaps, then he pats dry with a towel.

Wherever Frank is, he must find this situation far beyond Sebastian's usual melodramatic antics. "It's really absurd, all this, isn't it?" his husband would say, likely in the same dry tone he used with patients. *But if none of this is real,* Sebastian thinks, *why won't the feelings go away?*

He taps gently on his breastbone; thankfully, it facilitates a slower heartbeat. He drapes the towel around his neck and leans toward the sink's mirror. Wow! The bags under his eyes scream dehydration; the dark circles reveal the true consequences of both turning forty and his current sleeping habits.

A pointed knock, like a knuckle rapping against steel, comes from the front door. He grimaces; the sound, a series of double-time steps on his brain, intensifies his headache.

"Open up," Chloe's voice echoes from outside the front door.

"Hold on." Sebastian quickly pops three more Advil.

And before Sebastian can retrieve it, Arthur kneads and curls up on the towel, which has fallen on the floor.

The knuckle rap turns into fists banging, like tom-toms. He pictures Chloe as Tiger Lily leading the "Ugg-a-Wugg" number in *Peter Pan.*

"You got company?" Chloe's voice is muffled, as if her face is pressed against the front door. More tom-tom sounds. She's like a bratty child whose parents have put her in a time out.

"On my way," Sebastian yells as he heads into the living room. Arthur tags alongside as if on some invisible leash. Sebastian stops short of the front door, however, and reminds himself to make sure he's ready before he allows another player to enter the stage. But what should he tell Chloe? Do ghosts really exist? Maybe not, but something's definitely going on.

"Alone, Seb," Sebastian says toward Arthur, his sounding board. "Do this alone."

"Do what alone?" Chloe asks from the other side of the door.

"Uhh . . . nothing." Sebastian cups his face in his hands. "Hold on."

"Got it."

Sebastian pictures Chloe's eye rolls as she now, most likely, presses her head even harder against the gray steel door to hear whatever she thinks is going on inside.

"Excuse me," she continues with two more fist pounds on the door, "while I nearly faint out here from having my legs crossed so friggin' tight!"

Sebastian closes his eyes, then springs them open: *Showtime!* He forces a toothy smile and opens the door. "Keep your panties on."

Chloe looks him up and down. "You're chipper," she says, offering pecks on either cheek. "First of all, your buzzer doesn't work."

"How wonderful." Sebastian feels his mouth turn downward. "Something else that needs fixing."

"Nothing lasts."

Sebastian massages the headache from his temples. "Don't remind me."

"Second of all, what you said about keeping my panties on? No, no, no," she says, wagging a finger in his face. "Auntie Mame is straight-up commando, baby."

Sebastian scrunches his face as she breezes past. "How vivid," he calls after her.

"Third," Chloe yells from the bathroom, "my legs were crossed so tightly I probably scared the piss right back up the river."

"And fourth," Sebastian counters, shutting the front door, "maybe you've finally discovered the benefits of keeping your legs crossed."

Chloe's guttural laughter echoes throughout the apartment. "I don't think so. By the way, who were you talking to before you let me in?"

Sebastian leans against the bathroom's doorframe. The sound of Chloe's pee drizzling into the toilet reminds him of liquid being funneled into a glass bottle. He chuckles; goodness knows how much of her deposit is alcohol. But did she actually hear someone else inside the apartment? And will she still think he's crazy for believing Frank's ghost is here?

Sebastian catches his breath. "Arthur. I was talking to Arthur."

"Are you sure?"

Sebastian groans, presses the heels of his hands into his eye sockets. "A hundred percent," he mumbles.

"Say what?"

"I said, I'm glad you're here."

The whoosh of the toilet flush is unreasonably loud. Sebastian flees into the kitchen and Chloe follows. "You know, sweetie," she says, leaning against the table, "if you were talking to someone other than your little Prince Arthur, that would be fine."

"Really?" Sebastian pulls a carton of orange juice from the refrigerator and takes two glasses out of the cabinet. "If I were actually hearing or seeing things, you wouldn't think I'm cuckoo for Cocoa Puffs?"

Chloe pinches his cheek. "Get out of here."

Her touch induces a tickle in Sebastian's heart. But he doesn't buy it. "I appreciate your vote of sanity on my part," he continues, "but I know that—"

"What?" Chloe sits on top of the table.

Sebastian flashes another tense smile. "It was just my imagination, the whole ghost thing."

Chloe reaches for his hand. "Really?"

"Absolutely. No ghosts." Sebastian pushes the empty glasses toward her. "With my birthday and the anniversary of Frank leaving me." He closes his eyes. "I mean . . . his death, I just freaked out. You know me, good old drama queen."

Chloe jumps off the table and hugs him. "That's great. You had me worried." She rubs his back. "Not *worried* worried, but still."

"Not *worried* worried? What's that supposed to mean?"

"You know."

"Actually, I don't."

"Oh, honey." Chloe's brow knits together, her dark eyes look as though they might pool with water. "How things went down with your mom and dad."

Exhale. "Like I said, seeing Frank was definitely just my imagination." Sebastian feels his eyes grow heavy as if they'll also sprout water. He glances upward.

Chloe flicks her hand toward the ceiling. "What's up with that?"

"Nothing. Sometimes the people upstairs are loud." Sebastian laughs inside: *I guess when you turn forty, you learn how to fog the truth.* It sounds like something Chloe would say to justify her many half-truths.

"I see."

Sebastian rests his head on Chloe's shoulder. "My security. I lost them both."

"Your parents? Is that what this is about, sweetie?"

"No, that's not it. Well, in a way it is." He grabs their glasses. "It's the work situation. Adios to the dog walking and the office gig."

"Aww, crapola!" Chloe punches a fist into her palm.

"Tell me about it." Sebastian fills each glass. "The meager fee they give me for the tap class isn't going to hack it."

"Mmm. Orange juice, straight up. My favorite," Chloe says, her eyes wide in her best zombie stare. "So what are you going to do?" She licks her lips noisily, shakes her head.

"Not sure."

"I can spot you some dough."

"No thanks." Sebastian takes a sip, coughs. The juice seems unusually tart, almost metallic. He runs his tongue along the inside edge of the rim and gathers some of the flecks of pulp.

Chloe springs the vodka from the freezer. "Sorry, I tried, but I can't take this stuff without a little kick." She bevels her leg, cocks her head and hip, and raises her drink in the air. "Once a Rockette, always a Rockette."

"Hardy-har-har," Sebastian offers with a smile. In the past, Chloe's proven herself to be quite the chemist, but now she reminds him of a Houdini protégé. The vodka melds with the orange juice, gobbles up the floating pulp. She uses the magic wand, her index finger, and swirls the elixir around until it transforms into a sunburst hue. Propped on the edge of the table, she takes a sip of her new concoction and proclaims, "That's what I'm talking about." Eyes closed, she hums a low-pitched riff, like an oboe emitting the first notes of a lullaby.

"Can't you ever have any liquid without alcohol?"

"Smarty-pants. I only put in a splash." She scrunches her face. "To tell the truth, my taste for the sauce has been off lately."

Sebastian gasps. "Stop the presses!" He palms her forehead. "You coming down with something?"

Chloe flicks him away. "Calm yourself. I'm perfectly swell and just as in love with my libations as ever. I'm just a bit run-down. It's no surprise, considering all my date items." She clucks her tongue. "And you, Shirley Temple, need to lighten up."

"As soon as you tell me what to do, I will."

Sebastian's never noticed it before, but as it enters the space, the telephone's ring is like a xylophone struck at its middle section, a surprisingly comforting sound, like a gentle gong used for chanting.

"First," Chloe says, smacking her lips after another sip, "you need to keep up the air flow."

"I know," Sebastian says. "Keep the breath cycle moving." He exhales deeply. No easy inhale, however, because evergreen thoughts of Frank still haunt his every move. That he might be here, somehow present in his and Chloe's conversation, that he sees everything—including his random thoughts of Reid—is creepy. The xylophone ring continues.

"Second," Chloe says, "graduate from Shirley Temple to Shirley Temple Black." She reaches for the vodka and shakes the bottle at Sebastian.

"Fine. Hit me." It's not as if he's an alcoholic, so why fight it? Besides, he could use a dose of relaxation. He watches as Chloe's magic transforms his juice into a brighter, sweeter potion. He takes a swig. "Whoa." His eyes burn; he whistles, then raises the glass. "This'll knock your ass out," he says as he heads into the living room.

"Good. And third," she calls after him, "either turn on your answering machine, or get that annoying thing."

Sebastian shrugs. "I like the sound." He takes another sip before picking up the phone. "This is Mr. Hart," he says into the receiver. "Yes . . . Friday . . . four o'clock, Equity Audition Center. Got it."

Nestled on the chaise lounge, Chloe waves her arms in the air as if she's at a gospel revival. "What is it?"

"A callback."

Chloe taps her glass against his. "Halle-fucking-lujah!"

Sebastian chews his bottom lip. "Yeah, I guess it's a good thing." But Broadway or not, does he even want to do another show? Is the paycheck enough to make him once again play the all-American ethnic chorus boy, likely the only minority in the entire cast? And if Sebastian does accept the show, will he be selling his soul? *Bullshit! Maybe?* He takes another sip. The alcohol doesn't seem as strong this time, so he downs more. "I'm just not sure."

"Are you crazy? I mean . . . you know what I mean. You're not crazy. But it's great that you got a callback. You should be excited."

"Possibly, but . . ."

"But my tanning bed–bronzed ass, Mr. Hart. It's a Broadway gig! You get this one and it'll cancel out that last piece of shit show that wasted your talent. Make up for it."

Make up for it? Maybe that's exactly what Sebastian's done his entire life, tried to make up for lost things. But if that's the case, why did he begin dancing and singing in the first place? Is trying to be Fred Astaire, or sometimes even Gene Kelly, his way of keeping his parents alive? It's true that when he dances, part of him becomes that eight-year-old hopeful again; he's back home in Margaretville, bringing the musicals he shared with his parents to life. But nostalgia for childhood shouldn't drive his adult decisions.

Chloe pushes the covers aside and sits on the sofa bed. "Speaking of making up for things, maybe if you snag the show, you'll make up this lame excuse of a bed." She jabs her finger into the mattress. "Better yet, buy a new one."

"Yeah, yeah." Sebastian sits next to her and takes a cue from Arthur, who flips on his back. He strokes the cat's rabbit-soft belly.

"Some kind of motivation, you know?" Chloe props herself up against the sofa's headboard. "Really, Seb, do you ever make up this sack of cotton balls that's supposed to aid your beauty sleep?"

"Okay, Your Highness, I get the point." He rests his head on Chloe's shoulder again. "I guess you're right about the callback too. But . . ."

. . . . .

"But what?" asks Andrew, who stands with bare feet together on the purple yoga mat. He peers over the rim of his glasses, which have slid down his nose. He places his hands in prayer position and nods to Sebastian to do the same. "Let's exhale as you release. Inhale . . . raise your arms above your head . . . and exhale as the arms come back to prayer position. Now, you were saying?"

"I promised Chloe I'd go to the callback." Sebastian inhales without hesitation. He wonders why it's so much easier to do when instructed. "But aside from the money," he continues through another exhale, "being a forty-year-old chorus boy isn't necessarily the answer to what I need."

"And what exactly do you need? Let's transition again to our cross-legged position."

Sebastian does as he says. Andrew's a surprisingly good choreographer, the way the movements blend one into the next. Sebastian breathes into his hips, asks them to settle into their folded position. "Well, I need money, but I don't think that should be the deciding factor."

Andrew's eyes widen. "I don't follow," he says. "Allow your palms to rest on your knees."

"It's just—I'm okay with money. Sure, my savings will run out, and so will the measly unemployment check and my insurance. But I want to be something."

"And chorus boy isn't a worthy title?"

"It is, but . . . yes, I still love to dance. I really do enjoy performing. But—"

"Sebastian, there always seems to be a 'but' with you. Exhale."

Sebastian bites his upper lip. "I know." He releases the breath with sound.

"Excellent. Now back to your 'but.'" Andrew smiles and pushes his glasses up.

"Excuse me?"

"You said you still love to dance and perform, then added a 'but' to the equation."

"Oh." Sebastian clears his throat.

"What do you want?" Andrew's eyes narrow. "Other than being a chorus boy, what do you visualize yourself being?"

Sebastian feels his lips spread into a smile. He loves that his guru's more Jungian than Freudian. "I see myself . . . I want to create."

"You want to create?"

"Dance."

"You want to create dance."

"Kind of."

"Kind of? What's with that message you're sending out to the universe? You either want something or you don't. 'Kind ofs,'" he says, putting the words in air quotes, "don't make for progress, Sebastian."

"Yes. No. Definitely. Yes." Sebastian blows air from his mouth. "I'm positive I want to create. But it's not even working in my tap class, my ability to fully develop something of my own. That's what I meant about the whole money thing. Once I started dancing for money, it all changed; it almost took away my creativity. Almost."

"Almost or actually, which is it? Did dancing for money *actually* take something away from you?"

Sebastian nods. "Yes. Clocking in, dancing for money absolutely took away my creativity."

Andrew's exhalation is four counts long. "And how was that able to develop all these years? Why is something, or someone, else allowed the power to take away your creativity?"

"I don't know, but that's what happened." Sebastian allows himself the same four-count stream of air.

Andrew's mouth curls downward. "Specifics help." The stern tone, the frowning expression, is always the patient's cue to dig deeper.

"The chorus-boy thing." Sebastian sits up taller and feels his back muscles lengthen. He grimaces and makes jazz hands next to his face.

"I don't follow."

"The whole chorus-boy gig. To smile, be eternally young, jump through hoops seeking everybody's approval. That's not what I want for the rest of my life."

"Surely not every chorus boy sees himself in that light."

"Well I certainly do. That's just how I see myself in that role."

"Role?"

"Exactly. Like a perfectly rehearsed role."

"So maybe, as you suggest, it's possible for us to outgrow the roles we play in life. I don't know if you'd agree with me, but I also wonder if our need for things to remain a certain way may change depending on how we reimagine them. It's as if we constantly go into rehearsals for new roles, if you will, throughout life, in one new show after the other."

"I guess so." Sebastian exhales. "I think I get what you mean."

"Even though we don't forget each role we've played, we can still outgrow them. Better still, at least move forward in terms of our perception of all the roles we've played. Right?"

Sebastian rubs his temples. "Perception." *All this talk of symbolism and imagery. Now Andrew's seriously channeling Carl Jung, his own guru.*

"Exactly. Try it on for size. A thought: we can perceive things into reality that may not actually be reality."

Oh no: *Perception.* Beneath the Jungian psychobabble, Andrew probably "perceives" Sebastian's a nutcase. This is where it's all been leading? "You're right!" Sebastian blurts. "I also wanted you to know that all the talk about Frank still being here was just my perception. It was all in my imagination."

Andrew exhales noisily. "Okay. But if you did perceive him to be here, it's probably for a reason."

"He's not here." Heat radiates through Sebastian's face. "Like I said, I know now it was just . . . Frank's dead."

"Fair enough. Yet even if he is dead—"

"He is!" Sebastian's heartbeat climbs.

"Are you certain you've really put him to rest?"

To rest. Fuck! More symbolism. To rest. Such a clinical way to refer to a dead person. Sebastian imagines the laundry list of things others tell people about their deceased loved ones: "God bless him, he was laid to rest just yesterday." "She's at peace now." "At least she's no longer suffering." "He had a nice long life, for a cat." "She was a good woman, a wonderful mother." "Bless his heart, such a great man." "What a shame he didn't get to finish all the work he set out to do." *The language of death is so poetic, isn't it?* Sebastian clenches his teeth. "No!"

"Excuse me?"

"Wow." Sebastian checks his watch, follows with a knee-jerk prayer position. "Looks like our time's up."

"We can extend the session," Andrew offers, as his glasses once again slide away toward the tip of his nose.

"I really have to get to the community center. I can't afford to lose that gig too. And I have the callback after that."

"Mmm-hmm." Andrew smiles. "By the way, I think it's fantastic you added this extra session today. I'm proud of you. That's a good step forward in your healing. Knowing when to ask for extra help is brave, a gift."

Sebastian smiles, his heart warm from Andrew's words.

With his hands still in prayer position, Andrew bows his head. "Namaste to that, my friend," he says with another gentle smile. "And all the best at the callback. Break a leg."

"Thanks." Sebastian mirrors the bow. "Namaste."

Chapter

TEN

Sebastian leans against the studio mirror. Chloe sits to his right on a brown metal folding chair. Anchored on the piano bench, Mrs. Woo bucks and swivels as she drives the beat for the song "Anything Goes."

Millie, Hank, Kathleen, and Beau perform the steps. Every other set of eight, however, they're out of sync with the music. Sebastian harrumphs, because he daren't blame the group. After all, Fred Astaire or even the nimble-footed Gene Kelly would probably trip over the sequences this counterfeit choreographer has created for the aspiring hoofers.

Reid, adorable tap shoes in tow, rushes into the studio.

"You're late," Sebastian calls out over the music.

"Ouch," says Chloe through gritted teeth, as if channeling a ventriloquist.

"What?" Sebastian barks.

Chloe holds up her hands in mock defense. "Didn't say a word. Hey, Reid," she adds with a tug of his shoulder.

"I know. I'm a bad boy," Reid says. He rubs the space between Sebastian's shoulders.

Sebastian shakes away the shiver that climbs his neck. "I don't appreciate being stood up."

"Stood up?" Reid winks, his dimples a trio of eyes on Sebastian. *Don't smile.* "You know what I mean."

"Yeah, you know what he means, right, Schatz?" Chloe giggles, which elicits a pinch from Sebastian. "Oww." She rubs her arm, apparently drunk with laughter.

"Schatz?" Reid asks.

"Schatz is a German term of endearment," Chloe says. "It means 'treasure.'"

"Oh." Reid smiles. "I'll take that."

Sebastian huffs. "We need to get to work."

"Again, I'm sorry." Reid sits on the floor next to Chloe. "I had a consultation uptown that took forever. Terrace garden. The client couldn't make up her mind on anything."

Sebastian ingests every move: Reid loops the shoestrings around his thick, calloused fingers and ties them in two knots. No dirt under his nails after his garden consultation? What's up with that?

"I need your commitment." Sebastian shifts focus to the other students. They dance, or at least attempt the routine. But little do they know that their "aspiring" choreographer can't even come up with steps for the entire creative attempt. Or maybe they realize he's a sham.

Back to Reid, Sebastian says: "I need your promise. If you want to be in the recital, you must be here on time and offer your full concentration."

Chloe whispers: "Exactly. You want him to concentrate on you?"

"Cut it out!" Sebastian says. Then to Reid: "Just be here, present with me."

"Aye aye, sir." Reid salutes. "Present and accounted for," he continues, which prompts a chortle from Chloe.

Sebastian grits his teeth, stifles his own giggle. "Very well. We understand each other."

Reid joins the other students. And again Sebastian wants, but can't allow himself, to smile. It pisses him off that Reid thinks he can charm his way out of lost time. Drama queen or not, Sebastian's reminded of all those nights, and days too, that Frank was held hostage, their plans squashed because of last-minute work at the hospital. Single shift, double shift, overtime, peer reviews, journal article coffee clutches (*and Frankie hated coffee*), exams, extended Grand Rounds. *Blah, blah, blah.*

Chloe leans into Sebastian. "Looks like somebody needs a tampon."

Sebastian blows air from his mouth. "Very funny."

"Just chill, my little love."

Sebastian pouts. "I'm nervous about the callback this afternoon."

"You sure that's all?"

"Yes." *No.* Sebastian grunts, presses his back more firmly against the mirrored wall. "If Reid wants to be in this class, he needs to be on time."

Chloe slaps her hands together like a film production assistant with a clapperboard. "Take two." She cocks her head to the side. "The callback? You sure that's all you're worried about?"

"Absolutely," Sebastian squeaks from his upper register. He clears the tickle from his voice box. While Auntie Mame/Fairy Godmother's wishes may be well intended, Chloe pushes too hard. And there's no guarantee that Reid's such a stellar guy anyway. Coupled with the visual fiasco of the wannabe dancers who struggle through his disjointed choreography, Sebastian grows impatient with his inner monologue. Who cares if Reid's good or bad?

And look at the poor creatures Sebastian's supposedly mentoring in their quest to be the next Fred, or Ginger, or Kelly, or a consummate hoofer like Eleanor Powell—pathetic. Sebastian can't just circulate dance steps on them. He needs to set a complete number and to tell an entire story through movement. He craves a Technicolor vision of the bigger picture.

Blood rushes to Sebastian's head. He looks to the ceiling and begs the higher power, or Frank, or whatever that takes hold of him to back off. "Cut!" he finally orders above Mrs. Woo's orchestral magic.

They lurch; each student, including Reid, is a freshly scolded three-year old. A few more bars and the music peters out. Sebastian pushes away from his post against the mirrored wall. Moving as quickly as he does, he finds himself executing an unintentional grapevine as he heads toward the center of the room. "Millie and Hank, you're both too stiff in the legs. And the riff step you just did is in sequence A, not B."

"A equals the riff steps," Hank says, his eyes toward the ceiling as if determined to catalogue the information.

"And B equals the cramp roll steps," Sebastian says.

Millie jabs her husband's shoulder. "See! I told you the riff section wasn't in that sequence."

Hank blows air from his mouth. Sebastian pictures an older Ginger and Fred mid-fight on a sound stage between takes.

"And Kathleen—shuffles?" Sebastian stomps his foot. "Stay on your tiptoes. Tip, tip, tiptoes! Shuffle: Brush forward, brush back." His eyes widen. "Does that ring a bell?"

Kathleen's chubby face bunches up. She looks down as she brushes her right, then left foot forward and back, all the while teetering on the balls of her feet.

Mean. Sebastian knows it's unkind to hound her, but every

one of the students knows the most elementary moves, or at least they should. But are his steps to blame for the confusion? He isn't sure. *Still,* he reasons, *I should tell them when something's not working, shouldn't I?*

"Now Beau," Sebastian continues, his chest tight, "you must get rid of those scarecrow arms."

"Oh. I'm trying not to flail them so much." Beau drops his arms at his sides.

"Good," says Sebastian. With limited space inside for his tirade, he steals a dose of air for his lungs before he continues. The exhale that follows turns into a cough. "Now, you—"

"Yes, teacher?" Reid cuts him off with a wide grin.

Damn those dimples. "Besides being late, you still don't have the cramp roll sequence. It's—watch me! And that includes the rest of you." Sebastian points to his feet as he barks out the words and demonstrates the steps: "Flap cramp roll back flap, back flap . . . cramp roll, shuffle heel flap heel, flap step. Got it?" He wags his finger at Reid. "Tight movement, right under your feet. Do not push!"

Chloe mouths to Sebastian, "Biatch." Sebastian sticks his tongue out at her.

Reid aims his focus on his feet, bites his lower lip. "I'll work on it." The aqua blues appear a shade darker.

Is he pissed? Sebastian wonders, and then he dismisses the thought. "Excellent," he says to appease himself. *Let him be angry.* "All of you need to get over yourselves," he continues out loud, "and listen to each other better."

The students look sad, like those same little oafs who minutes before had done something to upset Daddy Seb.

"Until you all get these steps, I can't put the whole thing together," Sebastian further dictates. "And without the full routine, we can't start using the appropriate music." He wags his finger. "Without that, we have no recital."

"Ooh." Apple-cheeked Kathleen raises her hand. "We're not using 'Anything Goes'?"

Sebastian closes his eyes. "No."

"Well, whatever song are we going to use?" Beau asks. "Let's hear it already."

"We only have a couple of weeks left, Sebastian," says Millie. "I for one would like to get used to whatever song I'll be dancing to."

"She has a point," Hank submits in a gentler tone.

Chloe whispers into Sebastian's ear, "It is a little wacky the way you're teaching all this."

"I know," Sebastian forces through gritted teeth. Then to the students, "I understand how you all feel, but until you really get these particular steps down, including tighter rhythms, we can't move forward." Sebastian pictures himself in full Pinocchio drag, the suspendered shorts, Lederhosen, yardstick nose and all.

"Huh?" Kathleen squeaks.

"Yoo-hoo," calls the wise owl from the piano. She whistles. "Rhythm, anyone? I bang out the beat here," she continues with dark eyes magnified through the black rims, "and it's like all your ears are clogged."

"Thank you, Mrs. Woo." Sebastian smiles. "She's correct, you know? You're not listening, none of you. It's very simple. If you want to shine at the recital you need to learn not to push your own objective when you dance with others." He points. "And Reid, you're pushing it, really pushing it."

Chloe whispers to Sebastian: "And you're not being pushy?"

"No," Sebastian says quickly and loudly enough for his nasal cavity to vibrate.

"Am I really pushing?" Reid asks; his eyes seemingly are back to their normal aqua blue.

"As a matter of fact, yes . . . Reid." Sebastian closes his eyes. Part of him needs to hear himself say the name out loud. "You're forcing me—pushing your objective."

"Me?" Reid's dimples smile at Sebastian.

"Yeah, you." Sebastian places his hands on his hips.

"In that case, you should give me a private lesson," adds the dimpled one, accented with a wink.

Chloe moans. "Private lesson. Sounds good, eh Seb?"

The forty-year old heart pushes its tempo. Sebastian places his hand on his chest in an attempt to slow down what he pictures as an out-of-whack metronome. Winks, dimples, and all, it's difficult to tell whether Reid is angry or teasing. Maybe he's flirting? Frank, the psychiatrist part, might even say Reid's being passive-aggressive. Either way, it's hard for Sebastian to break contact with the aqua blues. *Beau-ti-ful.*

But what about Frankie? Sebastian pictures the letter A etched on his forehead: *Adulterer.*

"Or maybe, Reid, instead of a private lesson with me," Sebastian says, and then shifts his focus to his reflection in the mirror, "you could just pull back. Don't force the issue and you'll get the tempo and the cramp roll step in no time."

"Like I said: aye aye." Reid salutes Sebastian.

"Okay, then." Sebastian folds his arms across his center. "This is business. We understand each other. Business only." He sneaks another peek of Reid's aqua blues, then turns to face the other students. "Let's do it again."

Sebastian points to Mrs. Woo, whose nod includes two thumbs up and a triceps jiggle. He steps toward the mirror, where he can tell from Chloe's pursed mouth and raised eyebrows she's been watching Reid's (yes, probably) flirt fest. In turn, Sebastian hopes his best friend didn't smell reciprocal action on his part.

"Just remember, everyone," Millie says with a finger wag toward Hank, then her fellow students, "sequence B starts with the cramp rolls. Whereas sequence C"—she forms the letter with her hand—"starts with the time steps and moves us into the turns."

Sebastian nods. "Thanks," he says, impressed Millie is in the loop. The troop's collective blank expression, however, suggests confusion. Or, rather, translates as "We want to choke you!" And Sebastian's not sure whether to laugh or cry. Hell, if the tap shoes were on the other foot, he'd want to throw himself overboard. After all, he'd be just as confused—and, *frankly*, pissed off—being subjected to learning a routine in such a disjointed fashion.

Sebastian points to Mrs. Woo. Clapping in time, he counts down the start of the sequences: "And a five, six, seven, eight . . ."

The students begin, and to Sebastian's surprise, something's clicked—they're more precise in both steps and rhythm. Reid winks; Sebastian hesitates then offers a nod. "Good! Good!" he says.

"Seems to me," Chloe whispers, "you have a flirt-a-thon going on."

"Don't be silly. He's the one flirting with me."

Chloe snaps her finger. "Mmm . . . hmm."

Sebastian points to Beau. "Scarecrow!"

"Oops." Beau nods furiously and drops his arms to his sides.

Chloe leans into Sebastian. "Why were you nasty to him? If you don't like all the attention, why not just ignore him?"

"That's better," Sebastian calls out. Beau's response is all teeth, his Ricky Ricardo/Donald O'Connor smile. Sebastian turns back to Chloe. "He's being very arrogant."

"Beau?"

"No." Sebastian sucks his teeth. "Reid."

"Oh." Chloe chortles. "I wasn't sure." She leans over to whisper in Sebastian's ear, "But the arrogant routine is actually quite adorable on him, wouldn't you agree?"

"I'd agree that you're sick."

"Ooh! Sassy gal has entered the studio."

"I don't want him to think he can get away with it. Come into my life—"

"Come? You're thinking of coming with him?"

"Eww!" Sebastian elbows her. "I'm being serious here," he says, stifling a chortle.

Chloe clucks her tongue. "So am I. Dead serious. You need a release."

Sebastian waves at Kathleen. "Those shuffles are much better." Then back to Chloe. "He's . . . he's . . ." Sebastian pauses a moment, then looks toward Reid and closes his eyes.

"He's what, sweetie?" Chloe says. She rubs Sebastian's chest, and he's grateful for her help with an easy inhale and exhale cycle.

Sebastian bends his knees. "Hank and Millie, don't lock your knees." Then back to his interrogator, "I guess he's nice enough."

Chloe rolls her eyes. "Enough?"

"Yes, but—" Sebastian shakes his fist at the topic of discussion. "The timing is getting better!" Reid salutes him in response.

To Chloe, Sebastian adds, "I just don't know what I'm ready for. Maybe I'm not ready at all." He twists his wedding band.

Chloe cups his right hand. "You don't have to marry the guy, Seb. Besides, it might be a cliché," she continues, releasing his hand, "but they say time really does heal stuff."

"I appreciate your evergreen optimism, but I'm not so sure about that." Sebastian looks toward the ceiling. Time heals? Right. If that's true, why did Jerry Herman write that song from

Mack and Mable about being able to get through anything in life except erasing the love you hold so dear? *Time heals everything but loving you.*

He kisses Chloe's forehead. "You know, Auntie Mame, sometimes I wonder if you're the one living in a fairy tale."

This time Chloe goes inside, her eyes shut. Her chest rises with what appears to be a labored, if not forced, inhale. "Perhaps, my little love." Her chest expands; it settles as she blows air from her mouth. "Perhaps I am in Fantasy Land."

Sebastian shrugs. He joins the students as they continue the steps.

Chapter

ELEVEN

C laustrophobia might well be added to Sebastian's list of psychoses. It's 2008. Due for an upgrade, Actors Equity should blow out the ceilings of their rehearsal studios. Six foot isn't that tall, but every time he attends an audition here, he feels like a dancing hamster in a Habitrail. Better yet, the union should take back the *Fame* school down the street for its own private use. Although he's never been inside the building that once housed the legendary High School for the Performing Arts, he imagines the ceilings are limitless.

Sebastian winces. The studio reeks; overripe chorus boys that smell like sour milk. He checks his watch. Damn, they've danced for at least four hours. When he was eighteen, he could've done it. At thirty, it might've worked. But now, at forty, it's virtually impossible.

Sebastian massages his overheated, cramped calves. "Enough!" he catches himself saying out loud. He opens his legs in a wide V, straddles beneath a ballet bar, and stretches. He uses his unofficial good luck charm, a navy-blue hand towel, to pat his neck and face dry. He loves to catch a glimpse of the little red Polo Man stitched on the bottom. Frank gave him the towel on the opening night of another short-term gig as a vacation replacement on a national tour of *Thoroughly Modern Millie*; that was only three years ago.

He guzzles his third liter of the afternoon. As he twists to loosen his lower back, his belly feels pregnant with Poland Spring water, which he could swear he hears slosh back and forth. *So far so good.* No surprise appearances from Frank or thoughts of Reid to muddy his concentration.

Sebastian ascots the towel. Although it tickles a bit, he tucks it farther inside his collar. Yep, he's definitely the oldest person here. Twelve other men (boys, really) litter the space. Each twink he sizes up around the room primps more than the next. *God, was I like that when I started?* he wonders.

One such primped boy makes love to himself as he practices the routine in front of the mirror. It's astounding he still has so much energy after the powers that be forced them to pound their feet for the past four hours. Maybe it's because he's not a day over twenty, if that. Each beat of the four-corner movement—*left corner, right corner, left corner, right corner*—is accented with an extra swivel of his narrow, Barbie-doll hips. He alternates between toothy smiles and wide-mouthed exhalations. Sebastian chuckles. Lover Boy's reflection—a brown-haired, green-eyed, ultralean twink—is the recipient of a lap dance.

Greg, at twenty-seven, is at the higher age bracket of twinkdom but no doubt is the cockiest on today's roster as he struts from one hopeful to the next. He bobbles his neck from side to side and juts it forward and back. He blinks rapidly as he pecks out small talk with each boy. Ever the attention whore, he highsteps it, as if executing jazz walks in a Fosse routine toward Lover Boy, who seemingly still hasn't reached orgasm with himself in front of the mirror.

Greg's tap on the shoulder startles his pal's groove. Lover Boy's gasp is one of guilt, a younger troll caught in bed with someone else's man—*or actual husband.* Sebastian closes his eyes at the thought. *Don't go there. Not now.*

Lover Boy pushes Greg, who doubles over at the waist, seemingly drunk with giggles. Lover Boy adds his laugh track to the mix, then Greg whispers in his ear and points across the room.

Sebastian looks over his shoulder. *Oh no, he didn't!* Is Greg pointing to someone else? No, they're laughing at him. It's definitely the old "size up the aging queen" game. At one point Greg, his high-pitched cackle a dead ringer for Gertie Cummings in *Oklahoma!*, actually waves at Sebastian.

Sebastian's throat catches. He swallows hard. This is serious shit, and he can't help but retreat to that same place he's gone for over a year now: *What really happened that night between Frank and Greg?*

He downs more water and reminds himself he shouldn't take this crap. He's a forty-year-old man, one who's been in more shows than most of these boys' ages combined. He shouldn't feel inferior to any of them. He probably gives them too much power by playing their game. But isn't that what this whole crazy audition process is about—a game of survival to see who can snag the gig and win the prize money? Do chorus boys do it for the art?

Shame on me, he chides himself, if his reason for being at this callback isn't pure. Callback. Once upon a time he was a boy who only dreamed of being picked, let alone tapped for the final audition of a Broadway show. No agent then, no agent now, he's made Broadway a reality. That he can still push his expiration date in comparison to these less-than-ripe items (in age, *not smell*) must be a sign of his inner artist, if not financial savvy.

So here's his chance to make another once-upon-a-time come true and fill his bank account with steady funds. *Add another one to your resume*, the familiar, whiny voice inside calls. *Do it for the memory of dancing in front of the TV for Mom and Dad. Do it for Frank . . .*

Sebastian looks to the ceiling, then buries his face in the towel. What the hell's so wrong with being here, in this room, at this callback, one step closer to the union's highest-paying gig? Nothing. This is where he's supposed to be.

Sebastian looks up from the towel. *You're no longer allowed to look over there. Just ignore them.* He imagines sticking out his tongue at Greg. *Namaste*, though, he reminds himself. He sits cross-legged, palms rested on his thighs, and makes room for each four-count breath cycle to stream throughout his body. Andrew would be proud, Frank too—well, maybe not proud of the sticking out his tongue bit, but certainly proud of his ability to refocus and not obsess about Greg.

Sebastian peruses the decision-makers who sit against the wall opposite the mirror: a man and woman who were introduced earlier as the producers. Both are in their midfifties and dressed in business suits. There's also a casting director, early sixties, who wears jeans and a blue-and-white gingham button-down.

Marcus, midforties, stands next to the table with a stack of pictures and resumes. Sebastian freaked when he asked them all to make sure to footnote "special skills" on their blue audition cards. Nowadays, if you don't have a bag of acrobatic tricks at your disposal, you're at a disadvantage. The only trick Sebastian can fake is a cartwheel. He laughs at the absurdity: the more you can defy gravity, the better off you are in the land of the chorus boys, yet screwing with gravity becomes harder with age.

During the twenty-two years he's lived in New York, Sebastian's auditioned alongside Marcus at least a dozen times. And although they've never worked together onstage, he's seen the guy perform in at least a half dozen Broadway shows. Marcus's aura is assertiveness mixed with playfulness. It's no surprise, therefore, that he now holds the position Sebastian covets: director-choreographer. As Andrew might say, Marcus is both "present" and "in the moment," the exemplification of a man fully aware and in charge of his breath cycle.

Sebastian smiles. If only he could master the blend of boy and man that Marcus exudes—a spirit with forward motion who finds success in the world—then one piece of his own puzzle might be solved. A full-fledged adult at peace with the boy and man inside. *Yes,* Sebastian tells himself as he exchanges a nod with Marcus, *that must be what makes for a good choreographer.*

Marcus unearths four pictures from the pile and hands them to the casting director. The producers join the huddle and inspect the attached audition cards. *Must be cool to be in charge.* Sebastian squints as he watches Marcus gesticulate, his face animated with emotion as they study each potential recruit's theatrical vitae.

Another groan into his towel: Maybe Sebastian is cray-cray? Or maybe no actual ghost has been here after all? He shakes away the thought. No matter where he is, Sebastian's confident Frank will watch out for him. Somehow his husband's definitely here, in one form or another. In fact, he's probably behind Sebastian's ability, at the moment, to keep Greg out of sight.

Marcus points toward the herd. *Shit.* Sebastian hopes he won't be corralled with Greg when they dance in smaller groups. Goodness, now he's Cassie in *A Chorus Line*, an aging dancer who needs this contract to avoid being sent to greener pastures. He closes his eyes, tries to shake away the thought of it. Even if he doesn't really need the money from this potential gig, something deep inside still craves the attention, the spotlight.

A tickle shuffles in Sebastian's throat, and he coughs into his lucky towel. It's ridiculous: a love affair suffers when you're too busy looking for ways to fund it, he reasons. He landed his first dinner theater contract within two years of being in New York; flap ball-changed and screeched "We're in the Money" in ten productions of *42nd Street*, including the Broadway revival; and held dozens of other chorus positions over the last twenty-two years. Isn't it time to move on?

Sebastian massages knots from both shoulders. His stomach cramps suddenly; he hasn't eaten in six hours. He should just get up and bolt, commit to becoming a choreographer and not a dancer. Except there's no security in choreography either; it's probably just another level of bullshit. *Just take what you can get, Sebastian*, a familiar, pesky voice inside echoes. No doubt, it's Frank again, urging him to stay put.

Marcus commands the center of the room. He clears his throat. "One last time in groups of four. First up, let's see John, Bertram, Sebastian, and Greg."

Sebastian runs to the center of the room with the other three men; rather, *boys*. Greg, of course, arrives first and claims the center position.

Buck up! Now it's Frank's voice that reverberates inside Sebastian's head. This was the saying he always used on himself to deal with the pressures of medical school. And it works—whenever Sebastian hears himself say it, he snaps to attention and somehow gets things done.

"Okay," Marcus says, "Greg and Sebastian, take the downstage position."

Sebastian nods. *Fan-fucking-tastic*. It's one thing to be in the same group, but now he has to dance directly beside the troll. "Buck up!" he blurts out.

"Excuse me?" Greg squeaks.

"I wasn't talking to you," Sebastian says. *Lengthen the torso, tuck the pelvis under, and pull the tummy in,* he reminds himself. Otherwise, the extra meat around his waist—especially compared to the lean abs of the twinks standing next to him—might do him in.

"Whatever." Greg purses his lacquered mouth (is it lip gloss?), arches his back, and puffs out his already stacked chest.

Swampy, the space feels unbearably thick. Sebastian adjusts his position, anchoring himself farther away from Greg. He asks his own chest cavity permission for a good exhale. As usual, however, the full inhale doesn't come so easily; his torso hurts as he tries to take in air. *Better to keep pushing out the bad stuff.*

"John and Bertram," Marcus continues, "work upstage. Spread out. I want to see how you utilize the space."

Utilize the space? Sebastian rolls his eyes. Like Greg really needs to hear such a thing. Doesn't Marcus realize he's just given the rooster more cock for his comb?

"Let's hit it," Marcus barks and heads back toward the fellowship of decision makers.

Although Sebastian realizes the actual callback started the moment he walked into the room, he finds it hard to fake his way into a smile. *Come on, drama queen,* he taunts himself, *give them the old all-American ethnic chorus boy shtick.* After all, none of these boys seems challenged by nerves. Each one is plumed just so, ready for the prizefight.

"A five, six, seven, eight!" Marcus yells to the pianist, a rotund man who, with his thickly forested face, looks like he stepped off the set of *Blackbeard's Ghost.*

Sebastian holds his position, which feels, thankfully, miles away from Greg. The peppy beat of "Cheek to Cheek," another of his favorite Astaire tunes, finally induces the appropriate smile:

all teeth and raised cheekbones.

Greg edges closer. "They're only looking for one person, you know," he slips through his pursed mouth.

"And your point?" Sebastian says through gritted teeth.

"You're too old for this."

"Excuse me, Greg, but the last time I checked, we met when you were twenty; you're twenty-seven now and still haven't been cast in a Broadway show."

Greg blows air from his mouth. "Never as old as you, though."

Sebastian grimaces. "Thanks for the vote of confidence."

"You're welcome," Greg says full throttle, buttoning the quip with a smile.

As they begin the routine, no surprise, Greg overutilizes, hoards the space. He stops short on the chassé of the Lindy step. Sebastian nearly runs into him after he plants himself into the floor during a lunge. *It's Frank. It's got to be about Frank!* Sebastian tells himself. Greg can't deal with the fact that Sebastian got Frank and he didn't.

As the routine progresses, Greg juts his long, muscular arms to the sides, then swings them around during each movement. Sebastian grunts. *Buck up! And smile!* But it won't budge; his tight jaw won't allow for a cheek-to-cheek grin.

A chill invades Sebastian's body, then a flash of heat. *Frank?* He pushes out a breath, fights for a good dose of air in through his nose. *That night.* The image he's tried to squash for over a year haunts him again.

That night: Greg kissed Frank.

That night: Did they really?

That night: Sebastian started the fight. No, it was Greg's fault.

Sebastian's throat locks. It's harder for him to hold onto the breath than ever. He swallows hard.

That night: It was frigid. The air hurt and flash froze Sebastian's lungs, his words.

That night: It doesn't feel like it's been over a year.

Sebastian closes his eyes and opens them quickly. He offers a smile to Marcus and the other judges. Then, heat rushes through his body as if he's stepped too close to a fire pit. Dizziness comes. He shakes his head to exorcise the unbearable feeling. It seems to work; all teeth, he flashes the judges his best chorus cutie smile.

Suddenly, everything slows down: Greg's puffed-up chest ripples forward and back, his muscular arms flailing as he also loses his balance. His face and eyes widen, his lip-glossed mouth locks into a scowl, and his nostrils flare as he falls toward Sebastian.

"Ow!" Sebastian yelps. It's an unbearable yuck factor: Sebastian feels the heat of Greg's breath, which he had, once upon a time, exchanged with Frank when they kissed—and maybe even *that night*, the last of Frank's life.

Sebastian pushes Greg away, rolls onto his back, and takes hold of his right leg. It won't bend. He looks toward the ceiling for support. Is it Frank who gasps? The music stops. It's as if someone—for example, Greg—is dragging a knife up and down the length of Sebastian's leg. He pants: *exhale, exhale, exhale*. But his body doesn't cooperate. Where's Guru Andrew when he needs him?

For a flash, Reid comes to mind; a hug wouldn't be bad right now. And what will Chloe think? The leg hurts enough to make him cry, but Sebastian refuses—not in front of Greg.

Marcus extends his hand toward the poor, injured baby, but Greg takes it instead. *Troll*. Sebastian sucks in air through his gritted teeth.

"Are you all right?" Marcus asks, rubbing Sebastian's shoulder.

Greg giggles. "I'm fine," he says as he uses Marcus's other hand to stand.

Marcus turns to Sebastian. "And how are you?" His wide, greenish-gold eyes, which are pointed toward Greg, seem to say, *I'm looking at you, but I'm sure as hell am not talking to you.*

"You made me do this," Sebastian whines toward the ceiling. After all, he's never, ever hurt himself dancing.

"What?" Marcus asks.

"Nothing," Sebastian mutters, gripping his leg. "I'm fine." Now the knife has planted itself in the center of his shin.

Greg points to Sebastian. "You ran into me!"

"Go fuck yourself!" Sebastian bellows. He gasps, surprised by his own voice. He folds his arms and rests his head on his injured leg, his cheeks burning.

Greg lets out a hiss as he stomps toward Lover Boy. "Did you hear what he said to me?"

Sebastian bolts upright. "Yes, bitch! They all heard me." A chorus of twink mumbles fills the room.

"Calm down, now," Marcus says, reaching for Sebastian. "It was just an accident." He gives Sebastian's hand a gentle squeeze.

Sebastian's knees buckle as he tries to stand. "It stings. I . . . I can't move it at all."

"Somebody find an ice pack," Marcus says in a gentle baritone.

Sebastian commands his breath to do its job. He closes his eyes. His head swirls with thoughts of what his next step should be, because whether he wanted the gig or not, this fall just cost him the show. When Sebastian walked into the audition this morning he felt like Cassie from *A Chorus Line*. But now he's Paul, the kid with the bum leg. Sebastian looks to the pianist. Is this the cue for him to start playing "What I Did for Love"? Truth is, if Sebastian's any character in *A Chorus Line*, it's Sheila, the older, bitter chorine who needs to cut her losses and exit the line.

Chapter
TWELVE

Health insurance covers the bulk of Sebastian's visit. But how long can he afford COBRA? As for the "incidental fees" (six hundred dollars, which makes up nearly two weeks of his unemployment check), they find their way onto his Actors Federal Credit Union Visa card. He's fully aware this makeshift financing won't last. And when that day comes—no more credit, no insurance, no savings—what's the backup plan?

Hours ago, post X-rays, the ER doc tried to soften the blow: "It's a simple fracture," he said. Sebastian, however, pushed for the truth: "Your tibia's broken." *Fuck!* His right leg is his good leg; the right side of his body always more easily supports and initiates dance turns, even shuffles.

The papier-mâché cast starts just below his right knee, continues down the leg, and covers most of his foot. Though Sebastian can't feel them, he can see his toes peeking out the front. Two pillows support his bum leg while a third cushion, Arthur, snuggles next to him.

The door alert, a bell choir jangle, is a pleasant surprise; the handyman must have repaired it yesterday. Sebastian chuckles. Tonight, Chloe's off the hook, no knuckle solo on the steel door. He struggles to sit upright. "Hang on!" he calls. The cast isn't too restrictive, but the added weight throws off his balance. It's like carrying an extra hundred pounds. He swings his unfettered left leg over the edge of the bed—oh, how light in comparison!—to meet the mummified right limb. The doorbell chimes three more times. A four-count silence follows before another jangly reprise fills the apartment.

Ears rotated backward, Arthur breaks his fixed gaze on the door and leaps off the bed toward his filling station in the kitchen. What a life: sleep, eat, and repeat, all within the safe, cozy confines of their home. No worries about making money or defining and defending his identity—Arthur owns his feline status.

Another doorbell jangle. "I'm coming!" Sebastian shifts his weight onto the left leg. It's still hard to accept complete reliance on two metal appendages that look like they've been lifted from a gigantic Erector Set. The foam rubber on the handgrips and armpit rests, however, tickles something inside, reminds him of his six-year-old self and the Nerf football he used to throw back and forth with his father.

Sebastian checks the peephole. His throat locks, and he swallows hard. *Reid.* Could he ever get tired of saying his name? "Just a second." He exhales: *One, two, three, four, five.* He swears his chest crackles as he steals air inside.

Reid stands solid in the hallway. His crimped brow, which only highlights his dimples, forms a perfect expression of sympathy and pleasure to Sebastian, as soon as their eyes meet.

Shame on the wounded creature who inflicts such sadness upon a gentleman caller, Sebastian tells himself. He envisions the marquee—*The Gay Glass Menagerie: A New Musical.*

"Quelle surprise," Sebastian says in a breathy voice, and immediately feels like an asshole. Although he chews his bottom lip, he smiles inside; the bouquet of yellow roses and box of chocolates

Reid holds would make anyone's heart tap dance.

"You poor thing," Reid says. It sounds like he's sucking on a straw as he draws air in through clenched teeth.

"I'm fine, really," says the doll on a stand. Painful and comforting, the crutches dig into Sebastian's armpits as he uses one elbow to hold the door open.

"Chloe told me these were your favorite flowers." Reid presents his gifts. "And that you have a weakness for chocolate," he continues, his baritone echoing in the hallway.

Weakness is right. Sebastian likes what he sees. Reid wears cargo pants. Brown aviator Ray-Bans crown his head, the reddish-gold hair seemingly a lot shorter today. Sebastian cringes at the thought of his own mop, too long now and unruly as tattered roof shingles. He runs his hand through it. *Buck up!* He commands himself to anchor into the crutches, remain sure-footed.

"You lopped it all off!" Sebastian blurts out.

Reid's mouth turns downward. "You don't like it?"

"I do, I do." Sebastian looks toward the hallway ceiling. "It's adorable."

Reid emits a surprisingly raspy laugh.

"Really, it suits you," Sebastian adds through his own chortle, heat flooding his cheeks. Reid's cropped haircut reminds him of one of his favorite childhood friends, the redheaded Sea Adventurer G.I. Joe.

Reid runs his palm against the top of his head, which Sebastian imagines must feel like the bristles of a soft toothbrush.

Sebastian eyes the ceiling again—*Frank*—then quickly returns to Reid. He clears his throat. "Chloe should be back soon. She's rounding up Chinese takeout."

"Cool." Reid glances at the center of the apartment.

Sebastian scrunches his face. Maybe the piles of clothes

disgust him? He takes a snapshot of Reid's eyes, so different from Frank's. He closes his own and immediately sees Frank's face. He nods. *Unfaithful.* Sebastian shakes his head, commands the chill to leave his body.

"You okay?" Reid lunges forward, seemingly stops himself by firmly planting his feet in a wide second position.

"Oh. Yes. I'm fine. There's just a draft sometimes. You want in?"

"Pardon?"

"Inside." Sebastian shrugs. "Rude of me to keep you standing in the hallway."

"For a minute?" Reid wipes his feet on the black cat doormat.

"Of course." Sebastian counters left, allows Reid just past the threshold, and shuts the door.

"I snuck away from a client." Reid taps the box of chocolates against his chest. Grass and dirt stains pepper his white T-shirt, which he wears under a beige chamois button-down. "Hope I'm not ripe or anything," he continues. "I've been on this rooftop garden in the Upper East Side since five-thirty this morning."

As usual, Reid smells of fresh soap, like days-old cologne with a hint of sweat. Sebastian brushes a tickle from the tip of his nose. "Wow."

"Wow what?"

Sebastian smiles. "Nothing." He shifts his focus to the unintentional menagerie that bullies his home: the piles of clothes, the books, the CDs that litter the floor. "You left your job to come all the way here to give me flowers and chocolate?"

"FYI, I am the boss." Reid sniffs the bouquet.

Sebastian daren't look Reid in the eye; who knows what spell the aqua blues might cast? Still, he allows himself to settle into the sweet moment. It could be a scene from a musical, a gay version of *Easter Parade* or *An American in Paris*. Or better yet, one of the favorites from his teenage years, *Flashdance.*

"Yeah, I guess I could've had them delivered. But it wouldn't be the same."

Sebastian licks his lips. It seems Mr. Dimples definitely knows from Prince Charming. The giggly schoolboy feelings inside him are eerily familiar—this is how it was when he first met Frank. "It's very sweet of you to have taken the time," he finally says.

"My pleasure," says Reid as he steps inside the apartment.

Sebastian, understudy to *The Wizard of Oz* scarecrow, wobbles on his perch. He exhales and re-anchors himself on the crutches, pressing the full weight of his upper body into the spongy comfort of the rubber armpit supports. He works his way toward the sofa bed. Once there, he notices his guest, who now stands in the center of the room, is scanning the mess. Sebastian sucks air through his teeth. "Sorry. I'm not usually this disorderly."

"I wouldn't exactly call you disordered. Besides, you haven't seen my pad."

A half laugh rises from Sebastian's belly. He squirms at the thought of a formal invitation to Reid's self-described *pad.*

"You should let your leg breathe," Reid says. "Root yourself there. Dr. Garden's orders."

"Right. I should sit." Sebastian pushes air from his mouth: *One, two, three, four, five. Safe.* He rubs his heart—this man makes him feel grounded. Then he lurches as Reid places the gifts on the side table. Are they too close to his and Frank's photo? Sebastian scoots backward until he's flush against the arm of the sofa bed and rests against Frank's pillow.

Reid folds one of the blankets into a perfect square. "Best to keep it elevated," he says, placing Sebastian's bum leg on top. "Gee," he continues, "you're storing a heavy load."

Sebastian covers his brow. Reid didn't mean anything sexual

by "heavy load," did he? He runs his hand through his hair, banishes the gutter-minded thought from his head. As he settles his leg on the blanket, he wonders if the plaster cocoon feels as cold to Reid as it does to him.

Sebastian closes his eyes; taking in air is easy. The bouquet smells of his mother's rosewater perfume—not the cheap stuff. "Sensational," he says. And how easy it would be to continue onward and scribe his own rendition of Gershwin's "'S Wonderful."

Reid smiles, apparently tickled by the fur baby's tail as it rubs against his leg. "Hey, big guy," he says, stroking the top of Arthur's head. "He probably smells the grass all over me. I can put the roses in water."

"That's all right," Sebastian says. "Chloe can set them up when she gets back." And she needs to ring the front door soon. The roses, the chocolate, the aqua blues, and the dimples—it's becoming unbearable being so close to Reid. And then there's Frank. Sebastian's allegiance should be with his husband. *Always Frank.*

Arthur meows as he plops onto the bed. Reid's cell phone rings. Sebastian shifts his focus to the side table, to the picture frame with its damn cracked glass. He grunts.

"You okay?"

"I'm fine." Sebastian tucks his hands under his knees.

"If you need anything," Reid offers, looking at his phone display, "call me." He rolls his eyes. "Sorry. Let me get this."

Sebastian rubs his temples, hopeful his internal thermometer won't play any tricks and give Frank permission for an appearance.

"You'd better be kidding," Reid says into the phone. "I told you to stop calling," he adds through gritted teeth. "Like I said, it's not a good time. Not now. I'll—let me call you back." The groan of the cell phone's End button asserts itself in Sebastian's ear as Reid presses it into silence.

"That didn't sound good."

"It's nothing. Just a worm I'm dealing with." Reid's brow furrows. "I have to go."

Sebastian wants to, but is uncertain whether he should ask about this so-called worm. After a few long moments, he offers, "I'm really sorry."

Reid folds his arms across his center. "For what?"

"Yesterday." Sebastian resists the impulse to reach out to Reid. "I was so nasty to you in class."

"Aww, we're cool. I was doing my fair share of teasing too. Sorry if I was being too much." He tucks his hands in his back pockets. "Am I being too forward now, bringing you the roses and chocolate?"

"Not really," Sebastian says. He *really* wants to wrap his arms around his gentleman caller. But who knows where that would lead.

Reid's phone rings again, and Sebastian feels a chill. For some reason, this time around, the high-pitched beep sounds like Frank's beeper. Reid turns it off. "Spring's here. Everybody wants his or her babies to be the first to blossom. Yep, they always know how to get me back to the trenches."

The trenches? Sebastian checks the ceiling, closes his eyes. Frank always called his hospital work *the trenches*. And there were probably countless cases he never even shared with Sebastian, horrific casualties during his tours of duty. If he were here, Sebastian would tell him that now he understands so much better what it must have been like for him, his dear, sweet man, who braved the daily hospital war, tried so hard to save other people's lives.

"That call you just received, you sure you're okay?" Sebastian asks.

Reid looks toward the ceiling. "I will be."

Oh shit! Sebastian gasps. Does Reid also see Frank? He calms himself. "You seemed really upset."

"Nah." Reid anchors his hands on his hips. "Like I said before, just a difficult client. It's still early in the season, and he's trying to push me to plant an entire garden." He blows air from his mouth. "I should move along."

"Okay." Sebastian swings his leg over the side of the sofa bed.

"Don't get up." Reid rubs the space between Sebastian's shoulder blades. "I'll find my way out." And suddenly the gentleman caller's a little boy as he lumbers toward the door, scuffing one brown work boot after the other. "See you in class this afternoon," he says over his shoulder.

"You'd better," Sebastian says as he settles his leg back on the blanket. "We've got a lot of work to get that routine in order."

"It's a deal. You stay put until Miss Chloe gets here, and cross my heart, I'll make it to class on time." Reid winks. "You be a good boy."

"Wonderful." Sebastian gently rubs the center of his breastbone to alleviate the up-tempo beat. He waves goodbye to Reid with his right hand, the forever home of his and Frank's wedding band, their circle of life.

After Reid's gone, Sebastian shakes away the chill that runs along his spine. He catches another glimpse of the wedding band, and he cups his right hand over the left; the band's white-gold surface catches the sun that streams through the wooden blinds.

He's reminded of Mrs. Woo and the mystical, prismatic powers of her wedding band. But the apartment's dull overhead lighting doesn't facilitate such a rainbow-maker; there are shadows, shadows everywhere.

Chapter

THIRTEEN

I ts orange vinyl cover, maybe a ghost from the sixties, often makes Sebastian wonder how long the half-moon chair he nestles into has lived in the studio. Perhaps at least as long as the brown folding chair on which his papier-mâché leg, with its bully weight, is anchored.

It pleases Sebastian that Reid was on time for class. He's also grateful for Chloe's support. Assistant for the day, she commandeers the quintet that awaits, in staggered lines, their next round of orders.

Mrs. Woo reads the *New York Times* between the choreographer's starts and stops, his dancers, thankfully, fully along for the ride with his still disjointed methods.

Sebastian notices the paper's headline: *Afghan War Bride Saves Her Home, but Victory Is Brief.* No shit! And how shameful that the United States, even in 2008, still participates in the theaters of war in both Afghanistan and Iraq. He exhales. What kind of real victory is there with any brief accomplishment, especially in a circular game of *you hurt me, so I hurt you*?

"That was much better. It's come a long way," Sebastian says to his small troop. "It was tighter. Especially sequence A."

Kathleen raises her pudgy hand. "Can we start piecing together the steps anytime soon? I'm seriously nervous I won't be ready for the recital."

The collective wags their head. Sebastian wags back, his neck suddenly tense.

"Can we at least know what song we're going to be using?" Millie says. "And maybe do the steps to that music?"

Sebastian folds his arms. Yes, victory is brief; the troop was under his control a few moments ago, and now they've gone rogue. Even so, he doesn't want to tell them his choice—Fred Astaire's "Pick Yourself Up"—because he might still change his mind. "I promise," he says, "that when we meet again, we'll practice with the actual music we're using for the recital. Now, let's hit it. But this time, without Chloe. I don't want you to rely on anyone."

Chloe harrumphs. Her black, low-cut leotard calls attention to her narrow waist and silver tap shoes. She raises her arms into a V over her head, her dark locks bouncing as she curtsies to the class. They ooh and ahh, beg mercy from Sebastian. Chloe bats her eyes and places her hands in prayer position.

Reid flashes what might be the biggest frown ever: chin tucked, eyes looking upward, his mouth fixed in a pout that accentuates his sun-bleached, kissable lips.

Kissable. Sebastian slaps his wrist. *Don't go there*, he orders as he rubs away the sting. "All right," he finally says. "One last time."

Chloe claps her hands as if she's just won a spot on *The Price Is Right*. She pivot steps and hightails it toward the center of the room.

Sebastian winks at his best friend. Then to his troop, he says: "And this time, I want to see more pep and precision."

Mrs. Woo flips down the newspaper that covers her face. "Pep's my middle name," she hoots with two stubby thumbs up. She creases the newspaper in half and sets it next to her on the piano bench. She readjusts her wedding band so the diamond faces upward and rubs her doughy hands together. A final nod to Sebastian and she looks ready for action.

Sebastian takes a deep inhale. His chest puffed, hands on his hips, he scans his troop, making sure to lock eyes with each of them, ending with Reid's aqua blues. He smiles, redirects his focus on Chloe. He blurts out: "A five, six, seven, eight."

"Anything Goes" fills the room with the vigor of a thirty-piece orchestra. Four bars in, his troop's adherence to the steps seems on point. Sebastian watches Chloe execute a perfect riff step. *Fuck the Rockettes!* They were fools to not reinstate her spot on their roster. He shakes his head. *Just look at the speed of her taps alone.* Chloe's as fierce as Eleanor Powell ever was in her prime. BFF or not, Chloe's a winning performer. If Sebastian were choreographing a new Broadway show, or the Radio City Christmas Spectacular, he'd cast her. Sometimes when he looks at her, whether she's dancing or sitting still (a rare occurrence), he's still amazed she's also forty, only six months older than him. She doesn't seem a day over thirty.

Whoopee! Reid, the crew-cut trickster, finally nails the cramp roll section. "That's it!" Sebastian yelps, as if he's just witnessed a recruit scale an impossibly high wall at boot camp. His cheeks hurt from smiling: They've actually ingested his discombobulated orders. Each sequence coalesces better than he first imagined, his creation brought to life. If Frank's in the room, he's certainly proud. Sebastian checks the ceiling; hopefully his parents share the sentiment.

Surprise, surprise: Reid's riff step rivals Chloe's. And the wink he adds only cranks up Sebastian's desire to gently trace the dimples on his cheeks. Exactly a week before, when Reid gifted the roses and chocolate, Sebastian could've slipped from married man to adulterer. Now that they've known each other for two weeks, Sebastian's even more afraid he's falling. Still, he wants to know how Reid's weathered lips feel. Would they taste like peppermint? *No.* Sebastian shakes his head. *No!*

Eyes closed—enter Frank's scowling face. Sebastian scans the ceiling for another sign. Blood rushes to his head; that familiar dizzy spell calls him out. He tells himself to concentrate on the music, but he can't stop looking at Reid.

To double check, Sebastian shuts his eyes again. They burn as if he needs to pop an antihistamine. Eyes open, then closed again. It's no use, his husband won't budge—and not just his face. Frank screams at Sebastian, "Pick yourself up!"

Breathe. Instead Sebastian's chest locks. *Exhale.* He successfully pushes air outward—he doesn't want to faint again. *Inhale.* It hurts again as he tries to take in air. Heat dances toward his neck and filters downward, making his body feel heavy. *Victory is brief!*

Sebastian swallows hard. He presses his hand on his chest, tries to will his eyes open but can't. Instead, he surrenders to the music. But the piano is no longer a solo. Mrs. Woo must've flipped a switch, because she's always full of magic. Or maybe Frank's the conductor?

A jazzy trumpet solo wafts through Sebastian's head. "Anything Goes" is somehow replaced by a midtempo version of "Steppin' Out with My Baby." Sebastian, in black tie and tails, yet still with his cast, is on the Great Lawn in Central Park. It's nighttime; a brilliant spotlight helps the turf own its emerald splendor.

The spotlight cranes left to reveal Reid, who's also in tails, harnessed with a black garden tool belt. He twirls toward the center of the lawn and shoulders two gargantuan plastic bags from which he exhumes an endless array of baby greenery. Sebastian catches his breath as Reid tosses the preemies across the lawn, and instantly, like magic, they are fully aged garden creatures. A yellow rose bush, a Japanese maple, an oak tree, bamboo, ivy.

Reid shakes his head at Sebastian and gets down on one knee. Out come the gardening shears from his tool belt. With a few deft snips, Reid tears off the cast. The ripping sound, like Velcro being released, echoes inside Sebastian's head.

Sebastian removes his hands from his ears. He shakes off the cast, and it soars high above the spotlight and into darkness. He allows the music to carry him into a sway, his fingers intertwined with Reid's. With the aqua blues peering back at him, the shared winks and near kisses between dance steps, they're a same-sex version of Fred and Ginger.

But when Sebastian chassés away from Reid, he bumps into someone familiar—*Frank!* He wears his signature khakis, blue button-down, white lab coat, and a stethoscope around his neck. "Buck up!" he commands from beneath a furrowed brow. He shoos Reid away and twirls Sebastian toward him, pressing the stethoscope against his chest. "I can't hear anything."

"It's my heart, Frankie," Sebastian says. "What do you mean you can't hear me?" The music swells in his head, a deep, reedy sound.

Frank wags his finger. "Bullshit!"

"Sorry," Sebastian mouths silently.

Reid plants himself in front of his rival. He does a set of nerve tap turns, the sound and rhythm like a machine gun's rattle. He swipes Frank's stethoscope, brandishes it in his opponent's face, and places it over Sebastian's heart. "Incredible!" he proclaims.

"What?" Sebastian and Frank yell in unison.

And the music stops.

Reid booms, "Sebastian Hart, you have the loudest, steadiest heartbeat I've ever heard. And I truly am your treasure."

But within four counts, the music starts again. Frank reclaims his stethoscope and forces the once sure-footed Reid into a lurching hop step. A staccato beat accents the tug of war as the two men pull Sebastian back and forth. Sandwiched between them, Sebastian smiles at one and frowns at the other man in an endless loop. The music crescendos toward a climatic tremor, a piercingly dissonant chord from the orchestra's string section.

A final tug from Reid, and Sebastian settles into his arms. Frank tumbles to the ground in slow motion.

"No!" Sebastian screams. He helps Frank to his feet, back to his rightful place in the brilliant white spotlight. Then, with his chest raised, Sebastian places his right hand over his heart.

"Don't be afraid," Reid says. He opens the jaws of his gardening shears.

Sebastian winces, eyes closed. Eyes open: his wedding band is now severed from his finger. Reid flings it into the night air. The fractured circle soars up and over the spotlighted area, onto the lawn's darkened space.

Frank runs toward the darkness where the wedding band has fallen. The guttural moan he emits reverberates in Sebastian's head, a cacophonous sound. In the background, "Steppin' Out with My Baby" still plays, like a ghostly aria that goes on and on and on.

Chapter

FOURTEEN

Sebastian blinks his eyes open. No Great Lawn. No Central Park. No half-moon chair. He's definitely not in the dance studio.

"Sweetie?" Chloe waves her arms in front of his face. "Back with us, daydream believer?"

"Huh?" Sebastian notices his leg is propped up on a pillow. The bed he lies in, including the guardrail, is Milk of Magnesia white. He groans, massages the tension from his neck.

Reid gently rubs Sebastian's shoulder. "You checked out for another siesta."

"Damn." Sebastian pats himself down. Thankfully he still wears his T-shirt and slacks and not a hospital gown. "I didn't feel anything once I was out."

"Called your pal." Chloe places her hands in prayer position.

"Oh." Sebastian smiles, folds his arms.

Andrew nods. "I thought you might want to be reminded to breathe sooner than Monday."

"Why?" Sebastian asks.

"Hello?" Chloe snaps her fingers. "Your fainting spells?"

Sebastian sighs. "I'm fine."

"Well, I'm not." Chloe readjusts the pillow under his leg. "This is serious, Seb."

"Trust me." Sebastian smiles, tips his head forward with prayer hands. "I've been breathing just fine on my own."

A tall man in a lab coat enters the room. Brown skin, black hair, straight nose—he could be Sebastian's stand-in on a movie set. He smiles, points at Sebastian's cast. "You're getting to be a regular, aren't you?" he says in what sounds like an East Asian dialect. He refers to the chart he holds. "You're a tad anemic, but otherwise the blood work's normal. The brain scan you had on your last visit is also clear."

"That's wonderful." Reid rests his palm on Sebastian's shoulder and quickly removes it.

"But why didn't I come to for so long?"

"Well, Mister Hart," the doctor says, "it must be something in your genes. Some people faint harder than others, and thus fall into a deeper state."

"Yeah, too bad I have to faint to get some hardcore sleep."

The doctor, who can't be more than twenty-five, smiles broadly. His teeth are as pristine white as his lab coat. "Your friends tell me you've been under a lot of stress."

"I guess." Sebastian checks in with the three sets of orbs that scope him out: Reid, Chloe and Andrew. *That is, four sets of eyes*, he thinks, glancing at the ceiling.

The doctor hugs the chart to his chest. "Along with stress management techniques, make certain you get enough protein. That should help. You'll live a long life. You're good to go."

"Great." Reid shakes the doctor's hand. "Thanks so much for taking good care of him."

"I do appreciate it," says Sebastian to the doctor, who leaves the room. He asks the warm tickle Reid's concern brought on inside his chest to subside. "Chloe, how did you track Andrew down?"

he asks.

"Duh," Chloe says with a wave. "I've taken classes on and off for years at Exhale. Like I told you before, my energy's been down lately, so I upped the classes with him." She smiles and points to Andrew. "We've also met up for coffee a few times."

"Really. How long has that been going on?" Sebastian uses his knuckles to prop himself more upright on the bed.

Chloe folds her arms across her chest. "About two months."

"So much for confidentiality, Andrew," Sebastian says.

"Scout's honor," Chloe says. "Andrew didn't realize who I was to you at first."

"It's true." Andrew pushes his glasses farther up the long slope of his nose. "But she steadily opened up about her best friend and her concern for him. When she finally revealed his name, I put two and two together."

Sebastian rubs his temples. "And this two and two equals wrong."

"To be fair, Sebastian," Andrew says, "in our time together this past year, you've rarely mentioned Chloe by name. So, it's a simple misunderstanding." He smiles. "Look. You've given her reason to worry," he adds in a monotone bass.

Sebastian rubs the ball of heat isolated in his chest cavity. Now he understands what Andrew needs to better shrink heads, or whatever he does to help facilitate other people's wellness. *Two months? What the hell has she been saying to him all this time?*

"Here's the deal," Chloe says, as if reading his mind. "Maybe I subconsciously wandered into his yoga class more often because I knew the anniversary of Frank's death was coming up. And I knew I'd need backup to help you, my little love." She caresses Sebastian's hand.

Sebastian tries to relax his jaw. It shames him that Chloe

mentioned Frank in front of Reid. But the burden lifts temporarily when he pushes air from his lungs.

"Pardon me," Reid says to the group as a chime fills the room. "Yes. I get it!" he barks into his phone.

Chloe shoots Sebastian a look. He shrugs in response.

Reid steps into the hallway. "Never. All right?" he continues from outside the room. "I don't think that's a good idea. No. Absolutely not!"

Chloe cranes her neck toward the open door. "What's up with that?" she whispers. "His boxer briefs sound pretty twisted."

"No idea," Sebastian says. "Except that's the same tone he used earlier today on the phone with someone else."

"Look, Sebastian." Andrew tucks his hands in the back pockets of his chinos. "I can hang out if you want to talk now."

"That's okay. I'm out of here soon. I'll see you Monday. Thanks so much for checking on me."

"Thank Chloe," Andrew says. "She's the one who summoned me."

"Summoned you?" Chloe chortles and tucks her hair behind her ears. "I like having that kind of power."

Head tilted, Andrew looks over the top of his glasses. "Well, you did."

"Anyhoo." Chloe sits next to Sebastian and drapes an arm over his shoulder. "I informed him"—she smiles and points to Andrew—"in no uncertain terms that I'd kick his yogi butt if he didn't haul ass down here to check on you. Do you feel better, my little love?"

Sebastian nods. Andrew places his hands in prayer position. "Namaste," he imparts with a bow, then offers the same to Chloe. "Namaste."

Sebastian and Chloe reciprocate in unison: "Namaste."

Andrew shakes Chloe's hand before he departs. She turns to Sebastian. "Are you really okay with my knowing Andrew and taking his classes?"

"I guess. It just seems a bit much—my guru and all."

"Guru?" Chloe clears her throat. "That's giving him a lot of power, isn't it? Besides, he's told me he doesn't like that word. He's not a psychologist, Seb. He's not even a licensed therapist. He's a yoga teacher, a wellness counselor. You've said that yourself."

Sebastian feels his brow drop, chews his bottom lip. "I suppose. Still, I like thinking of him as my guru. And it seems a little shady, you going behind my back to take his classes and having coffee dates."

Chloe gently shakes his shoulders. "But we're family. I told Andrew that. I was afraid you might try to hurt yourself."

"Hurt myself? No, no, no. I wouldn't do anything stupid." He squeezes her hand. "And I'm completely grateful you're my family."

Reid lumbers back into the room. "You're probably ready to ditch this joint."

"Another irritating client?" Sebastian asks.

"Something like that." Reid scratches his chin. "I'll fill you in another time."

Chloe frowns. "I don't want to leave you alone."

"I'll babysit," Reid says.

"*Steppin' Out with My Baby.*" Sebastian cups his hands over his mouth as the song plays in his head.

Chloe clucks her tongue, then jerks a thumb toward Reid. "I like this guy." She checks her watch. "Ooh. Boss Man Gerald is probably getting antsy. I better get my ass back to the office." She chucks Reid under the chin like he's a toddler. "I trust you to get him home safely, a million percent."

Reid salutes. "A million percent it is."

"Adorable." Chloe pats Reid's cheek. "Yummy, yummy adorable." She drapes her lean arm around his shoulders. "Like I said from the beginning, this guy is a real treasure, a golden ticket. Don't you agree?"

Sebastian looks down. "Yep."

Chloe plants a kiss on Sebastian's forehead and whispers in his ear, "He adores you." She cradles his hand in her palms. "Be careful, my little love."

Sebastian looks toward the ceiling, closes his eyes. If Chloe trusts this treasure so much, why is she warning him to be careful? And so what if Reid adores him? *Adore* . . . the word vibrates in Sebastian's head as if sung under the strum of a harp's arpeggio.

Reid offers Chloe two pecks. And though Sebastian envies the cheek-to-cheek exchange, it probably wouldn't be a good idea for him to do the same with the man who presently has edged too close to him.

Frank . . . the name comes as if sung under a trumpet's four-count blast. Sebastian rubs his temples. The strain over his husband's return at any given moment of the day or night is becoming unbearable. One glance toward the ceiling and Frank appears. One rumination, lustful or not, about Reid, and Frank appears. Fear over what's ahead in his career as a choreographer and yet again, his husband appears. Then suddenly, Frank is gone, nowhere to be found.

Sebastian's chest expands and settles easily as he releases everything back into the world. The stakes of the game aren't really different than when Frank was, without a doubt, physically here. Night after night, Sebastian was left wondering when his husband would return home from the hospital.

. . . . .

Moments later, Sebastian and Reid head down Twelfth Street. Sebastian suggests they round the corner and take Eleventh Street to Sixth or Fifth Avenue.

Sebastian grips the rubbery crutch handles tightly. "So many trees, and row after row of brownstones. Just think about all the history and lives lived over centuries in these homes. I love this street."

"Me too," says Reid. "It's always so quiet and serene. I swear, in the fall, you can actually hear the leaves drop."

Sebastian gasps. "That's exactly what I've always thought when I take this route!"

Reid's dimples rise with his smile. "Our senses must be in tune."

Sebastian chews his top lip. "Maybe."

Reid hoists his backpack over one shoulder. "We should celebrate all we've accomplished with our work for the recital."

"I don't know."

Reid's mouth turns downward. Sebastian pouts too. *Those eyes.*

Halt! Sixth Avenue. Sebastian clamps down harder on the crutch handles and locks his shoulders. He jams each rubber cap on the bottom of his crutches into the pavement. His chest tightens as cars and taxis rush past and clusters of foot traffic mingle like zombies. The noise is deafening.

In a flash, Reid's off the curb. "Taxi!"

"Watch it!" Sebastian yelps.

"It's okay." Reid steps back onto the sidewalk. "No worries." He palms Sebastian's lower back. "I only wanted to hail us a ride."

"I'm sorry." Sebastian squeezes inward and downward at the same time, his armpits ground into the crutches' rubber pads. "I just freaked." No actual emergency vehicle passes—yet, just as it has for the past year, an intermittent siren highjacks his brain.

"Let's do something tonight," Reid says, his head tilted.

Adorable. If only Sebastian could say it out loud. *If only.* "I . . . I don't think so," he replies. "My leg. I shouldn't go out." His heart rate crescendos toward allegretto, not unlike the way it felt when he first met Frank outside Steps Dance Studio nearly seven years ago. That's the one good thing Greg has ever done for Sebastian: introduce him to his eventual husband.

"Your place. Let's do it!" Reid covers his mouth. "That's not what I meant. I didn't mean . . . it. Dinner. We can . . . you know . . . at your place. That's what I meant."

Sebastian coughs. "As you saw earlier, my place isn't really prepped for company." He shouldn't allow this man to set foot in his and Frank's home again.

"Okay then, a restaurant," Reid offers. The weight of his hand on Sebastian's forearm travels to the bottom of his feet.

"I'm still not sure." Sebastian rolls his shoulder back, which, thankfully, prompts Reid to remove his hand.

"Come on. Live a little! Isn't that what your dear Chloe always says?"

"Yes . . ." Sebastian closes his eyes. He could swear he senses a bucket of tears waiting in the wings. It's so sweet that Reid is so in tune with him.

"Then let's give it a try. We'll find a quiet place. Somewhere so peaceful you can hear a leaf fall from the ceiling." He walks his fingertips down the length of Sebastian's arm. "And gently tap the floor." He rests his palm on Sebastian's wrist.

Sebastian shakes off the flutter that dances throughout his body. "Sounds charming."

"Absolutely," Reid says. "You rest your leg, and we grab a bite. You get protein like the doctor ordered, and like a real gentleman,

I send you home in a taxi. And cross my heart, I'll look both ways before I hail your ride."

"But I can't go out with you." Even though it's been less than a minute since Reid touched his wrist, the warmth and weight of his hand still lives there.

"What do you say? A friendly token of appreciation."

"For what?"

"Your class, silly. In just two weeks you've helped me rediscover a little piece of my childhood."

Heat rushes over Sebastian's face. Dr. Garden's not only a landscape artist, but he's a poet. It's been forever since any man has given Sebastian credit for aiding in his self-discovery.

"I swear, Seb—sorry." Reid scrunches his face. "I mean, Sebastian. It's you, my friend. You've really helped me."

"I have?" Still, it's hard for Sebastian to fathom he's actually made such a difference in someone else's life, especially a man he barely knows. Of course he helped Frank with medical school, and also cosigned loans, but Frank was the real hero, not the other way around. After losing his parents (who had also saved him through adoption), and living for so many years deathly afraid to love anyone or anything, it was Frank who rekindled Sebastian's heart. And Chloe too—she's rescued Sebastian's heart all these years, along with sweet kitty Arthur and, of course, Andrew, the man he insists on calling guru. They've all helped him, as Andrew would say, work toward self-actualization. But what has he done to aid his various caregivers' development? Hard to tell; it's surprising. Therefore, that someone like Reid, a seemingly successful man, would praise Sebastian for his help.

"Yes. I mean it. You've helped me regain a part of myself," Reid says. "If only my dance teacher, Miss Sheila Jean, could see me now," he adds with a swivel of his head. "All that stuff from childhood just . . . you can't deny how it defines who you are today."

Childhood. No shit. Sebastian nods. Suddenly his stomach creaks. He didn't notice the hunger that lay dormant moments before.

Chapter

FIFTEEN

The Hourglass Tavern is as enchanting as Sebastian always imagined. The walls are peppered with still-life portraiture: sliced oranges, a vase overgrown with chrysanthemums, pumpkin squash. Aside from the shelves that border the room, there's also a built-in hutch that houses typical Greco-Roman tchotchkes: porcelain busts, tiny kerosene lamps, and clusters of marble grapes. The hollowed frames, which dot the magical space, showcase hourglasses of various sizes.

Sebastian feels transported to a café on the Greek Isles, or at least a scene from *Mamma Mia!* He laughs. Maybe the waitstaff will burst into song, serenade him with "Dancing Queen." Or better yet, "Gimme! Gimme! Gimme! (A Man After Midnight)."

It's quieter now that Sebastian and Reid have settled into dessert, but it still seems as if at nearly every table, couples stare into each other's eyes. Hand caresses, stolen kisses—talk about foreplay.

Sebastian readjusts his leg on the chair next to their table. He'd always envisioned himself here with Frank. Obviously the hourglass that gauged their marriage had different plans.

Sebastian rechecks the ceiling. He exhales. Frank's definitely offstage; it's just grapevines and leaves here, as far as he can tell.

He offers Reid a smile, proud they've engaged in the ultimate safe sex. At least until the suggestion was made, moments before, that they share a piece of tiramisu.

The table's candle highlights Reid's sun-bleached skin. A sweet face, open. Honest? Sebastian closes his eyes. On second thought, this ripe-for-romance setting might've been a mistake. Another tune from *Mamma Mia!* comes to mind: "S.O.S." But he shuts off the internal soundtrack, reminds himself it's been fine until now. No slips of the tongue or anything else, regardless of how many times he's felt the urge to touch those calloused hands, which are only two fingertips away. And just as Sebastian's noticed for the past two weeks, veins course in every direction on Reid's well-used hands. Reddish-gold hair sprouts from them, the same hair that peeks through the opened collar of his blue button-down.

Sebastian takes a sip of water. He imagines a reddish-gold harvest that blankets Reid's chest and his naturally enhanced biceps, that trails past his elbows and thickens until it meets his wrists, then stops abruptly once it reaches the base of his fingers. The grand finale: little tufts of reddish gold lightly planted as bookends on his knuckles, a beautiful complement to his cropped hair.

Sebastian rubs his eyelids. *Be present*, he commands himself, and downs more water.

Reid exhales. "And then he got on a plane." He dots his mouth with the napkin. "That was it. He moved to Rhode Island with the other guy."

"Ouch. That really sucks." Sebastian almost clinks forks with Reid as he reaches for a piece of the tiramisu.

"What he did. That he left me." Reid closes his eyes. "It was devastating after being together all that time."

"I can imagine," Sebastian offers tenderly, finding it increasingly difficult to maintain what he's convinced is a "don't you dare touch mine" *pas de deux* with Reid.

"I trusted him completely." Reid scrunches his face, dabs his eye with the tip of his napkin. "We even thought maybe, whenever it became legal in New York, we'd finally do it. The whole married thing."

"I'm sorry." Sebastian reaches for Reid's hands, but stops himself, cupping his own on the table. "I understand how that can stay with you. You still think of him?" *Dumb question, Sebastian.* Of course he can tell the guy misses his lost love.

"Um . . . not like I used to." Reid chews his bottom lip. "But there's more."

More? Oh no, is he sick? Sebastian scans Reid's body: the weathered hands, the sun-bleached lips. Skin cancer?

Reid folds his hands on the table. "Those calls I've been getting from the annoying client."

"Yes."

"They've actually been from my Rhode Island."

"Your Rhode Island?"

Reid knits his eyebrows. "You know, Rhode Island?"

"Oh. As in your ex." A rerun of *The Frank and Greg Show* flashes in Sebastian's brain. He massages his temples.

"He's been having trouble with his boyfriend. Well, fiancé— they're planning on heading to Canada to get married." Reid blows air from his mouth. "Anyway, he, my ex, has been calling me for advice."

Sebastian presses harder on his temples. "And this is a new development?"

"Not exactly," Reid says, his eyes narrowed on his cup of chamomile tea. "He's been bugging me for months with calls and emails." He glances at Sebastian, then back to the teacup. "It's very confusing."

"I get it." Sebastian takes a sip of his own chamomile. "I can totally imagine how confusing it is for you."

"I slept with him!"

The clink of Sebastian's teacup hitting the saucer makes them both jump.

"What?"

"Just after I met you." Reid's hands turn red as he clasps his fingers even tighter on the table. "I'm really sorry it happened."

"You're sorry you and I met?" Sebastian asks. He scans the scene; yes, lovers abound. Thankfully, however, the table next to him and Reid is empty. But less than a foot away, another pair, his skin brown, hers white. They're probably in their midfifties. They hold hands between sips of wine. Sebastian covers his brow. Do Mr. and Mrs. Loving hear everything going down right now between him and Reid?

"No, no, of course I'm not sorry that we met. I meant I'm sorry about last weekend with my ex. But it's not exactly what it seems."

No fainting allowed, Sebastian tells himself. He takes another long drag from his tea, but the familiar rush of blood to his head beckons him to take the plunge. He swigs from his water glass to counteract the tea's heat and twists his wedding band under the table. And with that, Frank enters, and with Frank comes Greg and the memory of *that night.*

Sebastian's never been punched in the gut, but this cramping sensation is probably what it feels like. He coughs to release the tension from his throat and belly, draws in air until his chest fills, and reiterates the internal command: *Buck up!*

Yes, Sebastian and Reid did meet just two weeks ago. *So what's the big fucking deal?* It's not as if they've consummated anything— certainly not physically, and most definitely not psychologically, Sebastian assures himself and the ceiling above. He doesn't have any right to be jealous of some guy in Rhode Island. But what about last Tuesday in the garden shop, when Reid seemed eager for a kiss? And what about Reid's behavior at Sebastian's apartment, the roses and chocolate? That was all real, wasn't it? Either way, the man who now cups his brow should've been honest.

The waiter, his dark, slicked-back hair shining from the candle's glow, suddenly appears. "Is everything all right?"

"Uh, yep," Reid says with a smile. "We're all good."

"Really?" Sebastian squints at Reid. But he also fakes a smile for the waiter, whose olive-skinned, aquiline profile shines just as beautifully in the candle's glow.

"More hot water for your tea . . . anything else, just let me know," the waiter adds.

"Thank you," Sebastian says.

The waiter clasps his hands in front of his white apron. "Sounds good." He smiles. "And don't be pressured by all the hourglasses. Take your time." His lean shadow fades from the candle's glow as he heads toward the Loving table.

Reid mumbles, "I made a stupid mistake." He shakes his head. "Stupid. Dumb."

Stupid. Dumb. That about sums up Sebastian at the moment. He stares at an hourglass mounted on the wall behind him. It's definitely curtains for the ill-fated *Gay Glass Menagerie.*

"It's not that he wants me back," Reid says. "He's engaged. It's just been hard for me to cut him off. I don't know why it happened. And it was one time, I swear." He heaves a sigh, making the candle's flame ripple. "I was confused because of all we'd shared. I didn't tell you because . . . I have no idea why I didn't tell you."

"But I haven't imagined everything, right? You've been acting as if you want something more with me."

"I do. Honestly." Reid scoots his chair closer to the table. "Everything I've said, all that I've done has been real."

"Not everything." Sebastian blows air from his mouth, which obliterates the candle flame and causes Reid's image to fade to black. "You lied."

"And it's still early. We've just met." Reid slides his hands on the table toward Sebastian.

"So what?" Sebastian twists his napkin. "You've acted as if we've known each other for months."

"It's hard, Seb."

"Sebastian!"

"Yes. Sorry. Sebastian." Reid grips the table's edge. "It's difficult to explain. But you of all people can understand loss, can't you? Because he's the one who left me." He gazes into Sebastian's eyes. "In a way, you and I are in the same place. I was abandoned a year ago, and I know it's only been a year since you lost Frank."

"A year, two weeks, and a day, to be exact!" Sebastian says. Then, in a quieter voice, "That is, if we're being truthful."

"Okay, then, let's be truthful: I've only known you for two weeks." He folds his arms on the table. "And a day."

Sebastian scrunches his face; he's irritated that Reid's obviously making fun of him. *It has been exactly two weeks and a day!* Aloud he says, "It's clear you still have feelings for Mister Rhode Island."

"I can't explain it. But no, it's not the same as before. Only that we shared a life together, just those sort of feelings. And I know it's done, over. I knew immediately after I made the mistake last weekend." He brushes Sebastian's arm, then quickly pulls away.

Sebastian cups his hands under the table, slowly twists his wedding band several turns in a row.

"I take full responsibility. I know I screwed up." Reid shrugs.

"Maybe I was just scared of my feelings for you. I think I went back to my ex to try to figure out if I was ready to move on. But I'm a thousand percent certain now that I want to try with you."

The word *why* forms inside Sebastian's head. He blows air from his mouth. "Like you told me, one second ago, we've just met. So how are you so sure about me?"

Reid huffs. "I know this is right." He thwacks his hand on the table, looks around, then softens his voice. "Aside from the confusion over my ex, which is done, I'm sure about you. I've been trying, but it seems like you're the one who's not ready. You give off mixed signals."

"Oh, now I understand. You can't get the guy you want—who again, you've literally just met—so you go out and . . ." He drops his voice to a whisper: "Fuck another man. Is that how it works with you?" He checks to see if Mr. and Mrs. Loving are looking. No, they seem content, their eyes locked on each other and invested in their wine.

Eyes closed, Sebastian exhales toward the ceiling. Was Frank really headed to the hospital *that night*, or to Greg's apartment?

"That's not what happened, Sebastian. You know it isn't."

"The night Frank died!" Sebastian blurts out. He immediately covers his mouth.

"What the hell?" Reid grits his teeth. In a low voice he says, "I wasn't talking about Frank."

"I need to go," Sebastian says. Reid's gone completely off script; he's not allowed to get angry. None of this fits his initial character breakdown.

Now it's Mr. Loving who glances their way. He shrugs, his dark eyes registering pity. Sebastian asks his heartbeat to slow down. It's definitely time to get out of here. There's enough dirty laundry at home, and he doesn't need to share any with the real lovers in this place.

"Okay," Sebastian says. He pushes a four-count exhale and four-count inhale. "I get it, Reid." He takes another swig of water. "The truth is this: you can't force yourself, or me, to be ready."

Reid nods. He murmurs, "I guess. Maybe."

Sebastian buries his face in his hands. If only he were ten again, when both his adoptive parents were still alive and no one, aside from his birth parents, had abandoned him. He wants to see Chloe and Andrew; they could help him breathe through this. And Arthur—he needs his little feline love, who knows how to behave like a good prince should. He needs Frank.

"I'm truly sorry," Sebastian says under his breath. *Sorry, sorry, sorry.* He's tired of hearing himself apologize. "Reid, I'm sorry your ex hurt you. And if I've been hesitant, or flirtatious, or whatever, I apologize." *That's an acceptable kind of sorry to feel for someone*, he reasons, though he resists asking Reid if it's okay. Finally, he whispers, "I should go. I really need to go."

.....

Sebastian grips the crutches on his lap. A Latina driver, probably in her early-sixties, helms the wheel.

"Told you," says Reid. He leans against the window, one breath away from Sebastian. "I kept my word. A short dinner and you'd be home . . . unescorted . . . before the stroke of midnight. A quiet end to the evening."

Quiet? Sebastian rolls his eyes and looks out the window past Reid. The sky glows with a full moon. It's warmer than last night, but with the cool breeze it feels exactly as it should for early April. Sebastian wants to speak, but there's nothing to say. He nods to the driver. The taxi hits a bump as they ease away from the curb.

Reid walks alongside the car. "See you in class?" he says through the open window.

Sebastian nods. *Breathe. Breathe, Seb. Breathe.* He twists his torso and looks out the back window. A quick pinch at the kneecap reminds him his leg's still cocooned in papier-mâché. Reid waves after the taxi. Despite himself, Sebastian returns the gesture.

"Looks like you got it bad," the driver says to Sebastian's reflection in the rearview mirror.

"You think so?"

"Mmm-hmm." She purses her mouth as she nods. "So, my friend, where are we headed?"

Sebastian has no idea. He's afraid, terrified even, if his racing heart is any indication. One of his favorite songs from *Evita* swells inside him: "Another Suitcase in Another Hall," a song about a mistress who's just been kicked out of her lover's home by his wife.

Sebastian twists his wedding band two full circles around, as if he were opening a combination lock, until the blemishes that are usually on top stare back—the object's tiny scratches that distinguish his and Frank's symbol of love. He exhales: *one, two, three, four, five.*

"Uhh . . . home," he says to the driver. "Forty-Eighth and Tenth. Please . . . home."

. . . . .

Within ten minutes, Sebastian is home. The subsequent four flights of stairs take fifteen to scale. Without support—no crutches allowed—Sebastian hobbles around and decontaminates the apartment. How the hell did so much fur find its way into the refrigerator vent? No wonder Arthur has so many hairballs. *Dust, dust, there's so much dust.* Wherever he wipes, the paper towel comes away black. He washes and changes Arthur's litter box. His wedding band gets caught on the handle of the hallway garbage chute and skins his knuckle. Close call, but the circle of commitment is still safe around his finger. With the tip of his tongue, a makeshift styptic pencil, he dabs his bloody knuckle until it's clean, then moves forward with the mission at hand.

Free at last, free at last: the decluttered desk is probably thrilled the papers are filed away. The DVDs and CDs are reunited with their neighbors, the books, and all are finally returned to their home on the cherrywood shelf. The metal sofa bed frame, like an out-of-shape dancer's skeletal system, pops and squeaks as Sebastian manhandles it and tucks the mattress inside. After a year (and two weeks plus a day's time, to be exact) the sofa is finally just that: a place to sit until its evening transformation into a sleeping pod. The unruly mounds of comforters and blankets are now folded and neatly stacked in the hall closet.

After four hours, the one-man cleaning crew plops on the sofa and pecks Arthur on the bridge of his nose. Now kitty can't reprimand him for bailing on domestic duties; furthermore, there's nothing random for the rambunctious feline to knock over in the middle of the night. Or will he miss all the clutter that's defined him and Sebastian for so long?

.....

On Monday morning, Sebastian vows to make this day, this week, a different one; he's uncertain how it will happen, but he pledges transformation. Wherever Frank is, he needs him to understand that moving on is the right thing to do. And while Reid has lied about his ex since they've known each other, he was right about one thing: Sebastian's also told half-truths—and Frank would second the opinion.

It's deceptive, Sebastian now realizes, to think a man he hardly knows could replace the love of his life. He exhales loudly. A welcome release of air trapped in his chest helps guide him into a standing position. With the crutches' aid, he hobbles from the living room to the bathroom.

Arthur cocks his head as if to say, "You're nuts, man," and runs into the bathroom. Sebastian trails him inside, then turns on the water. Kitty hops onto the sink's rim and swats at the waterfall, which runs down his face. Sebastian chuckles: Arthur doesn't flinch when he's on a mission. He takes a half dozen more licks beneath the faucet, shakes away the wetness and leaps out of the bathroom. Hell, maybe Arthur's right, and Papa's certifiable after all. Sebastian grows antsier by the minute, highlighted by involuntary twitches of his own paws. Supported by the crutches, he huffs and flicks the tension from his hands.

In the kitchen, Sebastian teeters above Arthur, who chows on kibble—thankfully kitty's finally on the diet formula and only gets a cup a day, or else Sebastian might have to say another goodbye. After some time, however, he's too winded to continue the hobbleography. Dizzy, he moves to the sofa. Suddenly, he feels that familiar sensation, a rush of blood to his head that might signal another fainting episode.

A creaking sound comes from the floor above. Sebastian scans the room. *Am I hearing things?* Looking upward, Sebastian sees a giant hourglass on the ceiling; its black sand oozes quickly from the top into its bottom bulb. Yes, it's been one year, two weeks, and four days since Frank's death. He swallows hard to release the scratchiness in his throat. Will the voices, visitations, and sometimes vexations happen this same time every year for the rest of his life? And if so, can he handle it?

Sebastian looks at Arthur, who's finished his meal and joined him on the sofa. "I don't understand," he says to his purring baby. Then to his husband's image in the photo, "I don't know what to do." *Move on. Finally move on?*

He closes his eyes, afraid to ask Frank—or himself—if they should finish this. Eyes alert, he refocuses on his husband's image, willing Frank to give him a sign. But silence is all that exists. Sebastian grunts and presses his forehead against the cold pewter frame. He groans; he can't move toward anything, anywhere, or anyone else without knowing exactly what happened *that night.*

Enter stage left: Greg. He'd flirted shamelessly the entire evening with his Frankie, not the other way around—no matter that they'd only dated for two months, just before Sebastian was in the picture. Sebastian hugs the photo frame. Maybe he wasn't enough after all, and Frankie wanted to go back to an earlier time, to someone younger, to Greg.

Sebastian lays back and rests his head on one of the sofa arms. Once again blood rushes to his head. "No!" he commands. This time, no one's allowed to faint. He sits upright and slams the photo frame face down on the side table. "Fuck you, Frank!" he yells. *That night . . . where were you going?*

Chapter

SIXTEEN

March 20, 2007. Sebastian had always hated when his special day fell on odd numbered years. *Buck up*, he told himself, ready for his thirty-ninth. *At least you're not forty yet.* Maybe he and Frank weren't in the appropriate attire compared to the rest of the Madonna, Boy George, and Depeche Mode wannabes in the joint—but it was his birthday! Sebastian was entitled to go against the grain. Sporting a black suit and a multicolored tie with flecks of black, purple, and red, his dancer-thin body was speckled with white dots of light from the disco ball above. He was in heaven that night, celebrating with Frank and Chloe.

A banner above the stairwell read "Temptation: The Ultimate '80s Dance Party" in purple, cubed letters. In the right-hand corner of the sign was a fluorescent yellow triangle. Inside the geometric figure was a cartoon eye—sparkling blue iris and long lashes—and the host venue's name: The Pyramid Club.

The East Village spot was hopping. Being trapped among hordes of people had never been Sebastian's strong suit. And when the hell had he ever ventured to Avenue A? But because the joint played all the tunes from his teen years, the trek was an easy sell. Plus, it was a double-whammy celebration: his birthday and Frank's freedom. No hospital, no homework. Med school was kicking Frank's ass, and he desperately needed a break.

Sebastian pulled Frank closer. How amazing to be with his angel in a black suit, accented by a burgundy tie with yellow teardrops. It was packed, yes, but it was as if at that moment no one else in the room existed. Culture Club's "I'll Tumble for You" played over the sound system. Sebastian laughed when, more than once, Frank nearly tripped over himself as they mamboed to the music.

Sebastian rubbed Frank's chest. "You're so cute when you try to dance."

"Oh, I only try to dance? You think it's funny?" Frank squeezed Sebastian's butt.

Through giggles, Sebastian said, "Not at all. You're adorable . . . for an old-timer." He pulled Frank by the belt loop until their hips wed.

"Okay, kiddo," laughed Frank. He rocked his hips from side to side.

Sebastian closed his eyes and pressed his pelvis more firmly against Frank's. Maybe it was the booze, or perhaps it was George Michael's voice over the speaker belting out "I Want Your Sex." Either way, their bodies, pressed together like that, made Sebastian instantly hard. It felt better than good since they hadn't touched each other in weeks.

Frank blew on Sebastian's ear. "Don't get smart, little mister."

A shiver; Frank's warm breath tickled, but signaled to Sebastian that (at least he hoped) sex would be on tap later. Frank brushed his five o'clock against Sebastian's cheek—*heaven!* Then wetness: another shiver arose in Sebastian as his ear lobe was seduced. And Frank wouldn't release him, squeezed his husband tighter against his own body.

Frank whispered: "You calling me an old-timer with two left

feet? Before you know it, drama queen, your clock'll strike forty."

"Well that's still a year away," Sebastian said, unable to stop his mouth from turning downward. "Don't push it." He shimmied out of Frank's waist grip.

Frank pecked Sebastian's forehead. "I'm just teasing you, Seb."

"I know." Sebastian allowed a smile to peek through. Still, it saddened him; under the circumstances, jokes from Frank were almost cruel. No doubt the Freud-meets-Jung protégé had the struggle of being the oldest medical student and then resident in his program on the path toward becoming a psychiatrist, but what could be worse than being a beyond-the-expiration-date chorus boy that Sebastian had become at thirty-nine?

Their fingers interlaced, Frank spun Sebastian toward him. "Not a bad move," said Sebastian, his ear pressed against his husband's chest, where he felt his heart's thump. A peck on the mouth, Frank tasted of the citrus concoction and vodka that made up their Sex on the Beach drinks.

"Okay, Fred Astaire, let's make a deal," said Frank, his arms harnessed around the middle of Sebastian's back as they swayed to Madonna's "Into the Groove."

"Bring it on," Sebastian whispered in his ear. And to his surprise, Prince Charming's footwork, moment by moment, was actually becoming better.

"Here's how it'll work." Frank twirled Sebastian around again. "You give me a proper dance lesson, and I'll give you a proper physical."

"If you insist, doctor," Sebastian said in a lower register, focused on Frank's brown eyes; then the darker colored, wavy hair; and, of course, his trademark tiny half-moons on each cheek, which he doubted, as he'd done on several occasions in the six years they'd been together, that he'd ever find on anyone else.

"But only a physical. No analysis." Sebastian licked his lips. "Let's try keeping Freud and Jung out of the exam room for the rest of the night." He kissed Frank's neck, which tasted like a fresh slice of grapefruit. *Yum! The Obsession cologne?*

"It's a deal," Frank offered, his cheek pressed against Sebastian's.

And Sebastian was dead serious about not letting Freud, Jung, or any other psychobabble upstage their night. No drama allowed, he insisted to himself. And in support of his celebratory spirit, the music, like magic, shifted to Madonna's "Holiday."

Frank cradled Sebastian's neck, the tickle a welcome sensation. And while usually self-conscious about PDA, Sebastian initiated a long kiss. Wet, very wet, and warm. The full-bodied taste of Frank was like drinking another Sex on the Beach.

As he and Frank hugged, Sebastian noticed Chloe weaving through the crowd. She carried an open bottle of champagne and three glasses. "Okay, hubbies, break it up." She offered a round of European pecks on the cheek, then handed Sebastian two glasses. "The music sucks, but I still think this was a cool spot I chose, huh, boys?"

Sebastian elbowed Chloe. "You done good, Auntie Mame."

"Damn straight." She propped her hand on her hip. "But can't we get the DJ to play some real disco?" Wide-eyed, she morphed into a Valley girl: "Oh my God . . . like, I know I'm supposed to like totally love all our Gen-X music, but . . ." She shifted into her real voice. "Shit, man. I'd even settle for that creepy eighties cover of 'Puttin' On the Ritz.'"

Sebastian laughed and tugged on Frank's lapel. "He cleans up nice, huh, Chloe?"

"Yes, ma'am. Both of you do." Chloe filled their champagne flutes. The bubbles glowed translucent purple from the disco ball and lights. "Here's to the handsome couple." They clinked and drank on cue.

"Mrs. Woo told me yesterday that Mr. Woo sent me a birthday greeting," Sebastian said. He took another sip of champagne. "Always nice, that Mr. Woo. He said that 2007 would be a banner year of good luck for me."

Chloe arched her eyebrows and transformed into Norma Desmond from *Sunset Boulevard*. She pinched Sebastian's cheek. "Whatever colors you choose from the crayon box, my little love."

"Here's to the ghost of Mr. Woo?" said Frank, a hand cupped over his mouth that muffled his laugh.

"It's not funny!" Sebastian yelped.

"You mean Mrs. Woo's hallucinations that Mr. Woo visits her from the dead?" Chloe rolled her eyes. "All jokes aside, that's just off, honey."

"Maybe she isn't crazy." Sebastian took a big gulp of champagne, a rare act for him. He cleared his throat and continued. "I believe her. I think it's totally possible Mr. Woo stays in touch."

"You believe in fairy tales, Seb." Chloe planted a kiss on his forehead.

Sebastian closed his eyes. "And there's nothing wrong with that." His brain flooded with past conversations: Neither his husband (whom he wished had more often channeled the Jungian, instead of Freudian, parts of his brain) nor his best friend showed the appropriate sensitivity after Sebastian revealed everything— fantastical as the details might've seemed—of what ultimately forced him to say goodbye to his adoptive parents so many years before. It wasn't a huge surprise; if Frank and Chloe thought Mrs. Woo was crazy, they must've considered Sebastian's father certifiable.

"That's one of the things I . . . we both love most about you." Frank rubbed Sebastian's chest. "Your willingness to believe in things is exactly what makes you so special."

"Not irritating?" Sebastian ran his hand through Frank's wavy hair, rested it on the base of his neck.

"Perhaps. Sometimes," Frank added with a wink.

"Absolutely, positively. But like Frank says, that's why we love you." Chloe topped off their glasses, then raised her own. "Hear ye, hear ye," she continued. "To the soon-to-be licensed head shrink and soon-to-be award-winning choreographer."

"Whoa, girl," said Sebastian. "The verdict is still out on the choreographer thing."

Another clink. Chloe downed her entire glass in one long swig. "And as for me," she said, "fuck the Rockettes and the sequined horse they galloped in on." She snapped her fingers and refilled her glass. *Five, six, seven, eight*: Sebastian clocked the time it took her to make the champagne disappear, as if he were counting down the start of a dance number.

Sebastian raised his glass. "And as for the producers of that shit-for-brains show I was wasted in, fuck them too." He gasped, covered his mouth. Until now, he hadn't realized how much rage he'd harbored since the show's closing night, all the pent-up feelings about working in yet another short-lived project. *Ugh!* This time next year, he'd be turning the dreaded forty. After zillions of experiences in the trenches, wasn't it finally time to move onward and upward? He took another hit of bubbles. *Geriatric chorus boy*; he let the thought soak in. He told himself to remember to discuss all this age-related anxiety with his therapist, Mina; that is, if he decided to continue their work together, because she was definitely more Freud than Jung.

"I'll double that, my dear Seb," Frank said, his smile revealing his dimples. "That last show was unworthy of your talent and beauty."

"Ooh." Chloe waved her taut arm. "I don't have any good pictures of you guys." She pinched Sebastian's arm. "Dummies. Everything happened so fast that day in Boston, other than that one crappy shot from the courthouse photographer, we never got a decent pic after your wedding."

"I know." Sebastian tapped his forehead. "But it's all up here, forever. Right, Frankie?"

Frank smiled. "And here." He tapped his heart.

Chloe grabbed her black Prada handbag and unearthed a Lilliputian camera. "Isn't it adorable?" she said. "I just got it for the trip to Cancún."

"What time's your plane?" Sebastian asked.

"Auntie Mame's got hours, yet." The twin bangles clanged like expensive silverware as Chole flicked her wrist.

Sebastian rolled his eyes. Knowing Chloe, she would hang out for as much fun as possible until the very last minute before her flight check-in.

"Okay, boys, show me those beautiful smiles."

After the flash, Sebastian planted a firm kiss on Frank's cheek. The champagne he then siphoned from his husband's lips tasted like forever. The feel of Frank's five o'clock against Sebastian's own, a low-grade sandpaper texture, cemented the deal. They needed to be home—now. *Besides,* Sebastian chuckled to himself, *it is my birthday.* A return to his original birth state wouldn't be out of order, he reasoned. No jackets, ties, shirts, or briefs allowed, only bare caramel against olive skin.

Chloe interrupted his reverie. "Yoo-hoo! Get a room, lover boys," she said, bobbing her head to Duran Duran's "The Reflex."

With Frank's breath warm against his ear, Sebastian was hard again. He whispered, "Let's go home." Then he spotted Greg, standing across the room at the bar. *Fuck!*

"Eww," Chloe's alto voice reverbed inside her champagne glass. "Troll alert."

Sebastian scanned Greg's extraordinarily fit twenty-six-year-old body: a massive chest enhanced by a tightly fitted hot pink shirt and black pants. "What's he doing here?" Sebastian hissed. He turned to Frank; even though the club was dark, he could tell his husband blushed, dimples and all, as his eyes followed Greg across the dance floor.

"Are you kidding?" Chloe said. "He comes here every week."

Frank smiled. "That he does."

"How would you know?" Sebastian asked, and commanded his heartbeat to slow down.

"Well I—I just remember that this was always Greg's Sunday night haunt."

Sebastian looked back at Greg. "Can you believe the way he flaunts himself?"

"He's always been that way," Frank said. He noticeably checked out Greg, who slowly and deliberately, as far as Sebastian's perception was concerned, sauntered toward them.

"Aww, shit." Chloe downed more champagne. "It's back."

Even though he was mad at himself for being what his mother would call a *jellyfish*, Sebastian couldn't tamp down his envy. Some memories were too difficult to dial back. Frank and Greg had history; it was brief, but they had dated. Who knew what trouble they could get into if he wasn't there?

Kiss, kiss. With the back of her hand, Chloe wiped off both of Greg's lip-glossed pecks.

"My darling Chloe," Greg said, "I'm so sorry about the Rockettes thing. But you know how it goes." His beefy shoulders wiggled as he spoke. "I was only the assistant to the assistant, but I tried to convince Terrence to convince Lidia not to pull the plug on you after the second callback."

"Yeah, yeah. I got the memo. Apparently thirty-nine's too old to maintain twenty-four counts of high kicks." She blew air from her mouth. "That's some bullshit! Because I can outkick all those younger bitches, anytime, anywhere."

"That's the truth," Sebastian said.

"Well, we all have our fifteen minutes." Greg unfastened the top three buttons of his shirt. *Did he get pec implants?* Sebastian wondered.

"Absolutely. Fifteen minutes. About as long as you'll be screwing Terrence until you move on to yet another assistant. Or better still, you'll just latch on to a full-fledged director. Right, Greg?"

Frank sighed. "Okay, gang. Why don't we change the subject?"

Sebastian sucked his teeth. "He started it!"

"Come on, Seb." Frank rubbed his lower back.

"Very good, very good," said Greg, shamelessly eyeing Frank.

"Fabulous idea, Doc," Chloe said. Then to Greg, "Don't call us, we'll call you." She saluted him. "I see someone over there who owes me a hello." She instituted a military pivot, then, over her shoulder said, "Catch you in a few." She gave them an air smooch and headed toward a man in a plaid miniskirt and Doc Martens sporting a Flock of Seagulls coif.

Greg tapped Sebastian's shoulder. "And you, poor thing. I just wanted to say how sorry I was to hear about your show closing."

Sebastian pulled away, readjusted his jacket. "Yeah, I'm sure you lost sleep over my loss."

"Seriously, though, how embarrassing to get what might be the last Broadway show of your career, and it closes after three performances." Greg smoothed the front of his shirt. "It's not like you're aging backwards, Sebastian."

"And some people, also not aging backwards, no matter how

many 'roids and creams they apply in an attempt to stay twinki-fied, are just stuck, and will never earn maturity."

Greg rolled his eyes. "Whatever." Then he kissed Sebastian's husband on the lips. "Frankie."

"Frank!" Sebastian snapped, surprised by the lower register at which the words came out. "Not Frankie."

"Hmm." Greg squinted, his glossy lips pursed. "Not Frankie?"

"No," said Sebastian. "Never Frankie. Not to you." His chest tightened. He'd never been prone to dizziness, but in that moment it felt as though a wave of blood flooded his entire body. He shook his head briskly and the lightheadedness faded.

"Very good, very good," he said, looking Sebastian up and down. With his arms folded, Greg's boulder pecs nearly popped through his shirt.

Sebastian felt transported back to the fourth grade. Greg's sneer, that familiar look from other chorus boys he'd struggled to deflect at every audition, made him feel as if he were on the playground, narrowing his eyes at a dodgeball opponent.

Sebastian interlaced his fingers with Frank's. "Let's go."

"Take it easy," Frank responded with a gentle squeeze. Sebastian loved being reminded that Frank's hand was slightly larger than his own. Generations of his husband's patients would appreciate a doctor with such strong hands even if, as a psychiatrist, he'd never touch them, he told himself.

Greg winked. "Aren't I entitled to say hello to my ex-beau?"

"You weren't his beau. You hooked up for, what was it, two months? That's all it was: an eight-week gig." Sebastian flung his hand upward, and a bit of champagne escaped his glass. He continued: "Two months does not make you Frankie's ex-beau."

"All I know is that however long we 'hooked up,' as you put it, it was the best sex he ever had." Greg ran his tongue over his teeth.

"Isn't that right, Frankie?"

"Asshole!" Sebastian shouted, surprised he said it out loud. A chill filled his body; quickly, like a switch, heat radiated from his toes to the top of his head. That Frank had kissed Greg—and done whatever else with him for two months—meant Sebastian had also had indirect carnal exposure to that troll. "You're disgusting," he added.

"Whatever," Greg said. "Just remember, I was the one who first introduced you two . . . husbands." He drew the last word out, as if testing its veracity.

"We *are* husbands, douchebag!" Sebastian raised his fisted hand, his wedding band aimed at Greg's face.

Greg blew air from his mouth, folded his arms.

"That's right, bitch," Sebastian continued. "Legally and in every other way, forever and ever. No matter what you or anybody else says. We are married, so go fuck yourself!"

Frank wrapped his arms around Sebastian's shoulders. "Easy."

"Tell him to take it easy!" Sebastian barked.

Journey's "Don't Stop Believin'" blared over the sound system, and Sebastian's heartbeat took on an up-tempo cadence to rival the song. He rubbed his chest and took another sip of champagne. The truth was, as much as Sebastian hated it, that Greg was right: he was ultimately responsible for Sebastian meeting the love of his life. But still.

"Good night," Frank said to Greg in a low voice. "Nice seeing you," he added with a smile.

Greg shrugged and pursed his lips; it was a wonder he could keep them closed with all the lip stuff he'd slathered on. The word *saunter* came to mind as Sebastian watched Greg sashay toward a crowd dancing to "Don't You (Forget about Me)." Yes, *saunter* was the word Sebastian always thought of when he imagined someone like Greg hijacking his husband's attention. And this troll definitely had some kind of power, some "thing" going for him. It was hard for his rival to admit, but Greg, at least physically, was a sex cloud wafting through the crowd: chiseled jaw, green-blue eyes and, 'roids or not, a beautifully sculpted, tanned body.

Sebastian, still holding tightly onto Frank's hand, cringed at a sudden realization: even if Frank and Greg's thing was six years ago, and only lasted two months, it was probably hot. Is he as good in bed as his rival? Did Frank miss Greg's *saunter*? Had Frank touched Greg the same way he touched Sebastian? And why the hell weren't Sebastian and Frank already home doing the things husbands do in private?

Sebastian resituated his hand so his fingers threaded with Frank's. Even so, as Greg *sauntered* away, Sebastian swore Frank's eyes lingered on him longer than was necessary.

Yes, *jellyfish*. Sebastian heard his mother's high-pitched, Glinda the Good Witch voice ring in his ear. It was Mom's word for a person whose jealousy was like the poison of the free-floating sea creature. *Remember, Sebastian, a jellyfish stings if you cross its path.* Since childhood he'd wrestled with such thoughts. Toys, friends—not that he had many—and both his parents, for that matter: with all things, and all people, Sebastian found it hard to share. Through the years, he'd fallen into becoming the jellyfish for the rest of the world; if not, he always figured, the world would abandon him. Unfortunately, however, the jellyfish inside ultimately forced people and things to say goodbye. But not Frank, not their cat, Arthur, and certainly not his Chloe—they'd be with him forever.

The all-too-familiar blare of Frank's pager broke into his thoughts. Frank silenced the mechanical nuisance and examined its screen. "Shit! They need me back tonight."

"Really, right now?" Sebastian gripped Frank's hand.

"Sorry, babe." Frank caressed Sebastian's cheek. "You know I have to."

Sebastian massaged the space between Frank's thumb and index finger. "Aren't you a little lit to be on duty?"

"No, I'm cool," Frank said. "I can catch a snooze in the doc's lounge if I need to. Why don't you hang out for a while?"

"Oh sure," Sebastian said in his most sarcastic voice. "I can just stay here all night and let Greg insult me."

"Oh, Seb, don't start in again about him."

"No, really, it's fine." Sebastian gazed at the crowded dance floor. "It's not like it's my birthday or anything."

"Okay, already!" Frank held up his hands. "If that's the way you need to act."

"I'm not *acting* anything." Sebastian snapped. "It's the way I feel."

Frank looked toward the ceiling. "I need to hit the bathroom. Meet you out front?"

"Aye aye, captain." Sebastian offered a salute. The heat that invaded his face suddenly dissipated; he couldn't help but be charmed by the sight of rugged-shouldered Frank steering through the crowd in sync with yet another eighties one-hit wonder, Noel's "Silent Morning."

Chloe came up to him with a guy in tow. He looked about twenty-three, and he was clearly drunk. "What up?" Manboy warbled, sounding as if his tongue had been clipped. His eyes were bloodshot eyes, seemingly half awake. He spoke again: "What up, boss?"

"Uhh . . . not much," Sebastian offered.

"Okay, then." Manboy's head teetered atop his skinny neck, making him look like a bobblehead doll. He wore a blue Coldplay

T-shirt. His torso slumped forward, and the tip of his tongue peeked through his trout mouth.

Chloe pressed Manboy's shoulder blades together and cocked him upright on a nearby bar stool. "You're sweet, but you need to calm yourself," she said. A frown; the overgrown baby looked as if he might start sucking his fingers at any moment. "On second thought, you need a break." Chloe gently tapped the base of Manboy's neck. He complied, folding his arms and resting his head on the bar.

Her babysitting duties fulfilled, Chloe fished inside her purse and popped what looked like a red pill, then gulped the rest of her drink.

"Should you be taking that with all the alcohol you've downed?"

"First of all," Chloe said with a classic eye roll, "I know exactly what I'm doing. Don't forget, my pharmacist daddy-o raised me to know what's what about everything I put inside me." She popped another red pill. "And second, my little love, you need to mow your own front lawn."

"What?"

"Just saying." Chloe swung her rail-thin arm around and pointed across the room.

Sebastian sucked in air. An all-smiles Frank stood close to Greg, seemingly spellbound by the whore's show. Greg flailed his arms as if he were in a Vogue Ball dance competition. *Category: Asshole!* a voice inside Sebastian growled. What kind of person needed to work so hard to always make everything about himself, to be so self-involved?

Right on cue, Greg fulfilled the role Sebastian had cast: he cackled as if he were the only one in the club, and ran his hands down the front of his fitted shirt.

Chloe snapped her fingers to regain Sebastian's attention.

"Third, my little love, you shouldn't be so sensitive about Greg. While he does qualify as, let's face it, a hottie, the package is half full." She held Sebastian by the chin. "It's just like I've told you time and again about mindless trolls like him."

"And what exactly is that?"

"Some people just like to suck their own dick."

"Eww." Sebastian buried his face in his hands.

"Oh, please." Chloe said. "Now listen very, very carefully. Your husband, your Frank, adores you. Beyond, beyond, beyond digs you. Get it, Drama Queen? You need to trust all that shit that floats your boat: I'm talking a Frank plus Sebastian inside a heart kind of thing. In a sickeningly sweet, monogamous, fairytale way, he totally hearts you. Got it?"

"Does it really seem like I'm jealous?"

Chloe arched an eyebrow. "Do I really need to answer that?"

Sebastian cupped his brow. "Forget it."

"I thought not." Chloe smooched an air kiss at Sebastian.

Sebastian motioned across the dance floor toward Frank. "Come back to me," he murmured. He couldn't help but think of the song from the musical about reincarnation, *On a Clear Day You Can See Forever*, which was titled just that: "Come Back to Me."

Frank pried himself away from Greg's hug. He nodded to Sebastian, albeit with a troublesome smirk on his face, reminiscent of a boy who'd just been reprimanded. Still, he waved goodbye to the "thing" and began to make his way across the floor. Sebastian felt Greg track his husband, twisting and jutting his thick neck forward to follow Frank's every move.

Sebastian draped his arm over Chloe's shoulder. "Be careful tonight, huh? And safe travels."

"You know it. I'll send you the Cancúniest postcard I can find."

Just as Frank nudged against Sebastian's leg, the eighties remake of "Steppin' Out with My Baby" filled the room.

"Hey!" Chloe pumped her fist in the air. "There's your song, guys."

"Yeah, perfect," muttered Sebastian. "Some stepping out I'm doing. Out the door, into the cold, and home alone on my birthday."

"Drama queen," Frank and Chloe said in unison.

Manboy lifted his head. Chloe shushed him and guided him back into his snorefest, his head rested on the bar top.

"It's true." Sebastian felt his eyes grow heavy. "I'm being left alone tonight."

"What about Arthur?" Frank said.

"Yeah, your fur baby," Chloe offered in her finest baby talk.

Sebastian warmed to the thought. Yes, at least his sweet Arthur was always there for him.

"You'll be fine." Chloe's eyes flickered as if they were conveying Morse code. She offered a wave, her arm rotating from the elbow, on par with a member of the Royal Family. In a British accent, she said, "Good night, my little love."

"Smartass," Sebastian said. *And goodbye to Manboy*, he thought, because in a few hours Chloe would likely be in a taut red two-piece by the pool, sucking down margaritas and doing the salsa with some guy in Cancún.

Sebastian smiled. "So fresh."

Chloe countered, "Better fresh than stale." She pecked Frank's cheek, cleared her throat, and pulled Manboy in for a round of deep kisses.

"Carry on, your majesty," Frank said through a laugh. Sebastian loved seeing them so close, his only family now, this wild, elegant gazelle woman and this gentle yet territorial leopard man.

And then, unbidden, images from earlier in the night flooded Sebastian's mind. Not just the hug Greg forced on his husband, but everything else: the *sauntering*, the pawing all over Frank's body, to which Frank seemed to pose no objection.

·····

The air was clear of snowflakes. Avenue A was dressed in black ice. No taxis in sight.

Fan-fucking-tastic, something else to mess with his birthday. Not funny, Mother Nature. It was March twentieth—this was supposed to be the first night of spring?

Sebastian and Frank shuffled uptown carefully along the glazed sidewalks. Heaven forbid either of them suffered any broken appendage. Frank might be able to, even in a cast, handle the emergency room loonies. Sebastian, on the other hand, would be barred from chorus gigs, and where would that lead them? Aside from every other financial commitment, they had to contend with the cosigned med school loans.

Sebastian nearly slipped on a sidewalk corner, but with the help of a *Village Voice* kiosk, he kept his footing. "You still have a thing for Greg, don't you?"

"Shit," Frank said. "We'll never get a taxi. Let's try Tenth."

"Did you hear what I said?"

Frank re-tucked his hair underneath his knit hat. "I was just being polite."

"Polite?" Sebastian said through gritted teeth. He scrambled to catch up with Frank, who had veered into Tompkins Square Park. "Greg was a total asshole to me."

"You weren't exactly an angel yourself."

Sebastian tightened the wool scarf around his neck. "What's

that supposed to mean?"

"Come on, Seb." Frank stopped. "Sometimes, a lot of times, you treat the world around you like it's a musical, and you're the director and choreographer."

"It's how I see things. It's not a joke."

"I didn't say you were joking, and I understand it's who you are." Frank's words came with clouds in the cold air. "But sometimes it's hard to deal with someone who always jumps to conclusions and claims to see everyone and everything so clearly before he gets more evidence."

"Sorry if you think it's crazy, or childish the way I see the world. Anyway, Greg's the one who crossed the line. He made fun of us, joked about us being married. That doesn't bother you? Don't you care how I feel?"

"For fuck's sake, will you ever get it? Look. I'm sorry. Sorry I failed, once again, at not being aware of your precious feelings."

Sebastian gripped the park's semicircular fencing. "Don't patronize me."

"I'm serious." Frank lost his footing, grabbed onto the fence too. "But just because some of us don't wear our feelings on our sleeve doesn't mean we're less evolved."

"I don't wear my feelings on my sleeve."

"But you do, Sebastian." Frank ground his gloved hands into his forehead. "Greg and I had a thing six years ago, which to me is ancient history; a very, very minor thing. Big fucking deal. I'm yours, completely." He took off his glove, flashed his wedding band. "Okay, sure, we had to go to Massachusetts to make it legal. But someday soon, I'm certain New York will recognize us, and so will the federal government. Either way, we're married. I'm your husband, and I love you. And I'll never, ever leave you. Why isn't that enough?"

"I know what we have," Sebastian said. Yet despite himself, the whine flowed: *Why the fuck can't I have faith in what Frank and I share? Why do I always assume my feelings are truer than others'?*

Pathetic. That's what Sebastian thought each time he heard such things come out of his mouth or swirl in his head. His neurotic inner monologues, jellyfish thoughts. From his earliest recollections, that was the way things worked. Any person, place, or thing he showered with love would eventually wake up and say, "You know what, Seb? You suck, big-time. You're a major fucking loser, and I'm out of here!" That's the route his biological parents took. That's also what his childhood cat, Mister, did. And that's the door his adoptive mother and father also chose to walk through when they died.

Frank cupped his gloved hands over Sebastian's. "Listen to me clearly: Greg's an infant."

"Yeah. A wicked witch's infant."

"That's the spirit. So maybe it's time to drop it?" Frank smiled as he playfully shook Sebastian's shoulders.

Frank's touch sent chills throughout Sebastian's body, and he wanted more, not less of his husband at that moment. But the pager, whose shrill alarm filled the brisk air like a truck backing up, overruled him.

"Shit." Frank silenced the menacing object again. He took off his gloves and Sebastian's hat and ran his hands through Sebastian's hair. From his downturned brow, Sebastian felt the eagerness with which Frank wanted to convey honor, loyalty, love.

Frank offered, as tenderly as a lullaby, "Let Greg's stuff be his own problem." His face relaxed, dimples at rest, and he pressed his lips against Sebastian's. Frank tasted quite intensely of strawberries—the champagne. "You don't have to take on the whole world," he added softly. "Or pretend you know what everyone's feeling."

"I disagree." Sebastian put his knit hat back on. "I'm onto people. I know their shit."

A cloud formed as Frank blew air from his mouth. "Breaking news," he said through gritted teeth, "people are onto your shit too." He slipped his hands back into his gloves.

Ouch. Sebastian felt a knot form in his belly. "All I know is that without being in touch with how things and people make me feel, I might as well not be alive."

Frank adjusted his overcoat, fastening the top button. "Then from where I'm standing, part of you is stone-cold dead."

"What the fuck does that mean?" Sebastian reached toward Frank.

Frank slammed his fists against his legs, the sound echoing through the park. "I'm sorry to tell you this, but sometimes you treat the world as if it owes you something because of everything that your parents didn't have the chance to give you."

Sebastian gasped as the knot in his belly felt like it doubled in size. "Go on then, leave me already!"

Clouds of frosted air lingered between them.

"Wait. I'm sorry." Frank grabbed Sebastian's arm. "I—about your parents, that didn't come out right."

Sebastian harrumphed. "Your message was Technicolor clear to me." And although it seemed wrong to do so, Sebastian released his arm from his husband's firm yet gentle massage.

Frank checked his watch. "I hate this. I don't want to say good-bye. And I really don't want to say goodbye with us mad at each other."

"Better run." Sebastian flicked his hand. "Hospital's waiting."

They finally reached the other side of the park, East Tenth Street. One taxi, and another, yet neither indicated they were for hire. Frank's chest rose; he pushed air from his mouth, took an effortless breath that made Sebastian envious.

"All right," Frank said. "Your imagination isn't always off. I know I'm not always in touch with my feelings. Hell, Doctor Burns calls me on my bedside manner all the time during grand rounds. Want to know my secret fear?"

Sebastian nodded. "Of course."

Frank aimed his focus on the snowy pavement. "Sometimes it scares me what kind of psychiatrist I'll ultimately make. And, as you've said before, you like it when I'm more in touch with my Jungian rather than Freudian worldview."

"Yes, and?" Sebastian tilted his head back, his nose pitched forward. *Damn.* He felt the snooty tone induce a wave of shame. His throat locked: *What a royal fucking bitch!* Still, he allowed the drama queen its power, couldn't let go of it—whatever *it* might have been at that moment. After all, why couldn't Frank tell the hospital no for once, just for one special night? It was Sebastian's birthday. Couldn't Frank have pretended to be sick? And more importantly, why had his husband let that solicitous thing, Greg, hang on him like that inside the club?

"What I'm trying to admit is that I know, as hard as my ego gets in the way of my doing so, I sometimes cut a part of myself off from you."

A smile wanted to overrule, but Sebastian's down-turned mouth held steady. "I'm glad you can take responsibility for that."

"But aren't you guilty of the same thing, Seb? Isn't it possible that sometimes you cut off a part of yourself from me because of your need to have too many feelings?"

A gust of frosty wind, Sebastian would swear, came as if on cue. "I'm sorry, Frankie." He tightened the scarf around his neck. "There's no such a thing as having too many feelings. And wouldn't your guru Jung, or maybe even Freud to some extent, say that exploring your feelings is important, and they're symbolic of what's truly in your soul, some kind of markers toward your future and self-actualization?"

Frank shrugged, his eyes closed.

Sebastian's smile exited the stage again, his mouth turned downward. He knew they were deadlocked. The pager offered a reprise, alerted Sebastian that it definitely was time for him to say goodbye to Frank.

"Finally." Frank turned off his pager. "Let's snag that one." He whistled toward the taxi across the street. "You can drop me off at the hospital, then continue home."

"I'll take care of myself." Sebastian tucked his hands in his coat pockets. "I'll catch the subway at fourteenth."

"C'mon, Seb. Don't be mad at me. It's too cold for you to walk further."

"No." Sebastian balled his fists in his coat pockets. "I need to be alone."

"Fine." Frank pecked Sebastian's cheek. "I should—I guess I'll see you. After my shift."

"Great. Whatever," Sebastian said to a cluster of snow on the pavement. "Just go already."

Frank stepped off the curb toward the taxi's lights.

Black ice.

Frank slipped.

Another set of lights came.

Frank's head stuck the curb.

The taxi swerved and plowed into an adjacent building. The merging of light and sound could only be compared to what Sebastian internalized after watching a film about the atom bomb in fifth-grade history class.

Yet, in the flash of time, Frank didn't utter a sound; he obviously didn't have time to scream. Sebastian never imagined silence could be so deafeningly loud.

Chapter

SEVENTEEN

The Frank summit takes place in front of 890 Broadway, the legendary building at Nineteenth Street, home to the American Ballet Theater rehearsal studios. A gaggle of bunheads sweep past with their signature waddle, hips and toes turned out. They maintain a V pattern and rush inside the building.

Bountiful sunshine; Sebastian embraces the warmth against his face, especially with the chill brought on by this meeting.

"And you hobbled your ass all the way down here, on crutches, to ask me that?" Greg juts his stout neck forward, hands on his hips.

"I need to know the truth." Sebastian's jaw pops as he opens wide to release the tension.

"Apparently." Greg uses the edge of his shirt to polish his gold Versace sunglasses, obvious by the Medusa logo on each arm.

"Look." Sebastian teeters on the twin metal enablers. "That night. I saw."

"You saw what?" Greg props the sunglasses on his head.

"You tried to play Frank that night. Even Chloe noticed."

Greg rolls his eyes. "Of course she did."

"You were rubbing yourself all over Frank that night." Sebastian presses his right palm against the building's surface.

The lukewarm brick, although scratchy, sends a welcome tingle through his body.

Greg adjusts his black messenger bag across his torso. "Damn, I hope I find that kind of love someday," he says with surprising tenderness.

Sebastian inhales deeply, revels in taking his time for silence. "Maybe you will," he finally offers. Somehow today, Greg seems less wicked.

"Trust me." Greg closes his eyes, purses his meaty, gleaming mouth. "Cross my heart: as much pleasure as it would've given me to share the private company of your fine gentleman, nothing happened—or would've ever happened—between us that night."

Sebastian cups one hand over his brow to shield his eyes from the sun. "You sure?"

"Scout's honor." Greg offers a peace sign with a side of chortles.

Sebastian juts his torso toward Greg, nearly loses his balance on the crutches. "It's not funny!" Surprised by his own aggression, he allows himself another deep inhale.

"Whoa, calm down." Greg pats Sebastian's shoulder. "I'm not making fun of you. I just think it's interesting you've tortured yourself about this for so long."

Sebastian clamps tighter onto the crutch handgrips. "If the tables were turned, you might've done the same."

"Sheesh. It's been over a year. You could've asked me a long time ago."

"Maybe." Sebastian sneaks a peek at the blue, cloudless sky. The sun's burn in his eyes isn't as harsh it felt moments before. He exhales. "But you were coming on to Frank so much that night."

"And he was so much in love with you. Idiot!"

"Excuse me?" Sebastian massages the sudden tension in his left jaw.

"Listen, I wouldn't volunteer for the gig, but somebody needs to tell you how warped you are."

"I am not warped." Sebastian pushes down hard, his fingers clamped around the handgrips, until his full weight grinds the crutch tips into the pavement. "I know what I saw."

"Sorry, okay?" Greg sighs. "I was probably wrong, or inappropriate, or whatever. But let's not forget, I'm the one who introduced you to Frank in the first place. Correct?"

"Of course."

"Then how do you think I felt at the time, being dumped after only two months?" Greg asks. "Not only does Frank tell me he's not into me, but also that he's in love with you. I felt like shit."

Sebastian looks Greg in the eye. "That's really how you felt?"

Greg licks his lips. "I am human," he says. "And can I tell you the honest truth?"

Sebastian's heartbeat crescendos. "I guess."

"Shame on you." Greg clutches the straps of his backpack. "Honestly!"

"Pardon me?" *What the hell does this troll know about honesty?*

"I mean it. Shame. On. You," Greg says. "Frank would never, ever cheat. Not the way he was wired. And you should've known that."

"I did—I do know him."

"Obviously not. Because if you did, you'd know Frank was wrapped around every part of you. He was yours, you dummy, fully fledged yours."

Gershwin's "My One and Only" fills Sebastian's head. Eyes closed, and Frank enters the scene. He's never offered Sebastian such a smile in all the times he's appeared these past few weeks. But now, an actual dimple-inducing grin spreads across Frank's lovely face.

Greg claps his hands. "Hello?"

Sebastian shakes his head, releases Frank's image. "You're right. All I can say is thankfully, I knew my husband well."

"It seems you did, Sebastian." Greg nods with a smile. "It seems you did."

No tension this time as Sebastian expands his torso, then releases the breath from his lungs back into the warm air. "Congratulations, by the way, on the new show."

"Yippee!" Greg throws his arms in the air. "I got it. My first Broadway show."

Sebastian nods. Too many apologies to extend: He wants to say sorry to Frank. He wants to say sorry to anyone he's ever doubted, including himself. "Thanks for helping me clear my head of all that," he offers.

"Oh, please." Greg waves his hand. "You know, some old drama queen once told me maturity has its privileges."

Sebastian doesn't even try to squash his smile. *Maturity.* He's amazed Greg actually retained what he said to him over a week ago.

"Anyhoo, ciao for now." Greg puts on his sunglasses, puffs up his hulking chest. He waves over his shoulder as he saunters down Broadway.

Sebastian shakes his head. *Surprise, surprise.* He finally relaxes his mind into reality. Maybe Greg's similar to Chloe in his need for a certain kind of harmless attention. Sebastian sucks his teeth. How dare he judge either of them? He's preached to them about being mature, but all this time has allowed his childhood fear of abandonment to sit at the head of the table for so long, especially after Frank left *that night.*

The clear, Technicolor-blue sky draws his attention again. He stares directly into the sun's glare. *Greg is right,* he thinks.

Sebastian never should've doubted his husband's commitment or how he was wired—Frank's true nature was to love Sebastian till death.

Chapter

EIGHTEEN

———————

A warm breeze rushes inside, encourages the wooden blinds to tap dance against the window frame. The *clickety-clack* steadies Sebastian's heartbeat. His nightly scene with the sofa bed, and starefest with the ceiling, upstages sleep. Just as he thought moments before, his usual appetite for a mound of bedding has dissipated. It would be aggravating now to have the comforters as they once were merely weeks before—twisted together in plies, smothering him under their weight. Instead, he opts for two blankets, which are neatly draped over his body and spill over the sides of the bed.

He twists his head on the pillow to admire his sweet bundle of fur, whose front and back paws are crossed. Adorable: the tiny mouth curled upward, the dancing whiskers. He's a miniature, pudgy black panther in slumber. It must be true, Sebastian convinces himself, that cats have nine lives. Among this three-man family, it seems Arthur's the only one embracing the art of moving on.

Be grateful for what is now. A voice, not recognizable as his own inner voice, echoes inside Sebastian. Perhaps it's one of the Golden Oldies in disguise: his mother, his father, or Frank? It's difficult, now, to distinguish one from the other.

Sebastian rolls toward the atonal beeping that vies for his attention from its place on the side table. "Yes?" he says into the phone. He blinks, squints: the red numerals on the clock tells him it's 3:00 a.m. "What?" He bolts upright, which startles the sleeping fur prince, who grumbles and leaps off the bed. "I'll be right there!"

Thirty minutes later, déjà vu: "You're Getting to Be a Habit with Me," from *42nd Street*, plays in Sebastian's head as he's accosted by the medicinal smell of yet another cramped Saint Vincent's hospital room. Reid might've been subpoenaed as backup, but that would've been too forward.

Sebastian's grateful none of these unexpected visits to the hospital have required him to report to the ER wing for the "emotionally unstable"—otherwise, he might've run into any number of Frank's old psychiatrist colleagues.

A creaking sound comes from above. Sebastian once again seeks consultation from the ceiling. If Frank's somehow responsible for stage-managing all these visits, then bring down the curtain already: *Show's over, Frankie!*

Talk about nine lives. Laid up in bed, her normally olive skin a bit pale, Chloe seems even younger than usual. Her dark waves are gathered in a ponytail. "Picture me vomiting up my guts at Pedro's," she says in a groggy voice. "Funny, huh?"

"Yep. You should've been a comedian, because this whole thing is really fucking hysterical."

Chloe smooches the air. "Feisty."

"Who the hell's Pedro, anyway?" Sebastian pictures himself folding Chloe's slender body in half, throwing her in a front loader, and setting it to the spin cycle to wring out all the bullshit.

"Look, I'm sorry, my little love. But it's not what you think." Chloe shuts her eyes. "I was just scared. So I thought it best to get my butt to the emergency room and make them give my gut the old pump routine."

"Seems to me too much of the old pump's your problem."

"Ooh," Chloe sings before trailing into a ghoulish laugh. "Good one."

"Does my face tell you I find this whole thing funny?" Without using his hands, Sebastian swings his cast leg off the extra chair he's been using for elevation and scoots closer to the bed. He sits back on his chair, rests his leg on the floor. "Getting drunk with some guy named Pedro?"

"Wow." Chloe clears her throat of what sounds like a gallon of phlegm. "You're really in charge of that thing now. Good boy. Not letting it stop you for anything."

Sebastian channels Captain Hook in *Peter Pan* as he shoots back in a guttural voice, "And you're not a kid anymore."

"Excuse me, but I'm only six months older than you. So speak for yourself, Mister 'I'm Getting Too Old for the Chorus Boy Thing.' Stop aging yourself."

Sebastian rubs Chloe's hand. "You can't keep using that stuff to escape. No matter what your father put you through."

Chloe gasps. "Touché, my little love, touché," she says under her breath.

Perhaps it was cruel to bring that up, especially since he's probably the only person she's ever told about her father's abuse. But Sebastian wants Chloe to wake up and not let the past dictate her future.

Sebastian's chest vibrates in unison with a guttural exhalation. A friend can't fill the void of romantic love, but certainly a solid friendship can teach him about the capacity to love. And in massaging Chloe's hand, he hopes she'll trust that she's worthy of being loved for who she is on the inside; hopefully then, she'll order a ceasefire and stop running around with one random guy after the next.

"I do love you, Seb. Absolutely, positively, you're my best friend. But sometimes you're D-E-A-D wrong. And to tell the truth . . ." She sighs heavily. "You're really fucking judgmental!"

"I'm not judgmental," Sebastian says as he reaches for his best friend.

Chloe cups her hands over her belly. "All I'm saying is that things aren't always what you imagine them to be." She gazes directly into his eyes. "I told you I nixed all the crap."

"So what's the deal with—"

"Let me finish!"

"Sorry." It feels as bashful as Sebastian means it to sound.

"Here's the truth." Chloe pushes herself more upright on her bed pillows. "Aside from one or two mildly spiked drinks, I haven't had the appetite for any shit for the past couple of weeks."

"Seriously?"

"No more booze. Done with the pills. Dry." Chloe shuts her eyes as if in meditation, and gently rocks her head on the pillow.

Sebastian pats her hand. "Well, that's good."

"Unless, of course, it's a pill I really need." Chloe winks. "You know, for medicinal purposes."

"Okay." Sebastian rests his elbows on the edge of the bed. "But what about tonight with this Pedro guy?"

Chloe laughs. "Pedro's, my darling, is a Tex-Mex joint on Eighth Street where I pigged out on too many enchiladas. Yada, yada, sensitive stomach, go figure. Actually . . . I've been blowing chunks since last weekend." She looks away from him. "I'm preggers."

"You're what?" Sebastian's cast thumps against the floor.

Chloe does jazz hands. "Tada!"

"Getting pregnant isn't exactly a magic trick I thought you'd ever perform."

"Yep. Auntie Mame is seven weeks along." She rubs her belly. "Apparently lordy lordy forty isn't too old for some things."

"Holy shit," Sebastian says. "But you've never been—isn't a first-time pregnancy risky at our age?"

"Well, my little love, after totally freaking out over this whole thing, I realize it's meant to be. It's a sign."

"A sign?" Sebastian rubs his forehead.

"Come on, Seb." Chloe gently taps his arm. "You always believe in signs."

"I do?" Sebastian folds his arms.

"Please, Mister Technicolor, don't you know yourself by now as well as the rest of us do? All that fantasyland, movie musical stuff you crave, all that crap where things happen magically. You can't resist it, so you allow yourself to go along for the ride every time." She clucks her tongue. "That's you in a nutshell, my little love."

"Oh." Sebastian chews his bottom lip. "All that nutty stuff." He's never thought of his quirks in the way Chloe suggests, as something his loved ones particularly admire about him. Sebastian continues, "But I thought—or at least always hoped—you'd be more careful."

"Maybe something in me skipped the pill and wanted the condom to break." Chloe shrugs. "So, here's my plan." She rubs her hands together as if trying to warm them. "I'll be a damn better parent than either of mine were to me." Then tenderly, "I'm going to make up for the baby I lost."

"Aww . . . beautiful. I'm so proud of you." He rubs her arm. "You're going to commit to really doing it right, taking care of this baby?"

"Not exactly. I mean, yes, I'm definitely taking care of this baby.

But I was more so referring to Mick."

"Mick?"

"Mick the Dick? You know, that older married guy I met when I was still in college? I've mentioned him before."

"That jerk who 'rescued' you from your dear old predator dad?"

"Yep." Chloe shuts her eyes. "That's the one I'm talking about. And in many ways Mick did rescue me. But what the hell did I know? I was only twenty-one; he never would've left his wife and kids."

"You told me that part. And that's exactly what made him such a dick, using you that way."

Chloe hugs one of her pillows. "Well, I didn't tell you what the fuckwad made me do the morning after I graduated."

"What?"

"Have an abortion."

Sebastian cups her hand. "Why didn't you ever tell me?"

"Would you tell your best friend—your best friend who, by the way, was dumped at birth by his biological parents—that you got rid of your own baby?"

Sebastian's belly cramps. Chloe's probably right: it hurts him to think of anyone knowingly abandoning her or his baby. Still, the friend before him, who has truly nurtured him for so many years, deserves a pass, doesn't she? "Listen to me," he says. "It's not your fault some older, manipulative fuckwad made you do something you weren't sure was best for you in that situation."

"Either way, I'm still responsible." Chloe shakes her head on the pillow. "I can't change the fact that I made that decision."

"I understand." Sebastian rests his head on her shoulder. "I'm sure it was hard. How could that ever be an easy decision?"

Chloe nods and whispers, "But this time it's right." Her eyes scan the ceiling.

Sebastian looks upward. "Do you see him?"

"What?" Chloe looks toward the ceiling. "See who?"

"Nothing." Sebastian shakes his head. "No one."

"Actually, I did see something in my head. I was thinking how crazy things turn out and everything comes full circle. I never imagined I'd want it, but now I can really have a family. You know what I mean?" She places her hands over his. "In addition to what I've always had with you, and with Frank, of course. You know I also loved him like a brother, right?"

"I know. Thank you," Sebastian says, glancing at the ceiling. "Now, I don't mean to be rude." He sucks air in through his teeth. "But do you know who the father is?"

"Of course. And unexpectedly, unplanned, it just happened." Chloe bites her upper lip. "And please don't hate me for it, but I'm really in love."

"In love?" Sebastian asks. "Why in the world would I hate you for finally allowing yourself to fall in love?" His heart races with the best kind of anxiety, joyful that Chloe has finally committed to one person.

"The thing is . . ." Chloe clears her throat. "I haven't been romantically involved with Gerald; the same is true of all those other guys. Of course Gerald's been fabulous with teaching me everything about publishing, and he's been my rock with some of this stuff going on, with the baby and . . . and Andrew."

"Andrew?"

Chloe smiles. "Him."

"*My* Andrew? What's he got to do with it?"

"Well, you know I've been taking his yoga class a lot recently."

"Yes, you've both told me that over and over."

Chloe looks down at her hands. "Then there's usually coffee. You know, right there at the studio café and . . . my big mouth, you know, I beg Andrew to talk about you and your breathing. Because I get worried, right? Well, we don't just talk about you, not really. Just on the level of are you fine, blah, blah, blah." Chloe rests her palms on top of her pillows. "Anyway, I've learned a lot about myself while having coffee with him."

"Good. I'm glad he's offered you guidance. And I'm sorry I've been so much in my own headspace and not here for you more."

"It's okay. I know it's been hard for you." Chloe reaches for the pitcher on the nightstand, downs a full cup of water. "It's been hard for me too. I've been worried about you. So worried."

"I'm fine. Day by day, I think I'm getting better." He looks toward the ceiling.

"The father of the baby."

"Sebastian," a familiar man's voice calls from the doorway. It's Andrew. Sebastian looks at Chloe, who raises her dark eyebrows as if to say, "Hey, it's just one of those things."

"Really?" Sebastian shakes his head briskly at the ceiling. "Frank always said I was the last in the room to get a joke. I'm such a fucking idiot." He grunts. "I'm certifiably stupid."

"Seb." Chloe reaches both arms toward him. One of her pillows drops to the floor. "We've been together like, seriously, for three months."

"Disgusting!" Sebastian barks.

"Please don't blame Andrew," she adds. "Like we told you the other day, he didn't even know who I was to you at first. I held off on telling him." Tears stream down her face.

"She's telling the truth," Andrew adds quietly.

Chloe's face floods with more tears. "I swear, Seb, it was a month before we figured it out." Her breath catches. "And I begged him to let me tell you about us."

"You fucked my guru!" Sebastian clutches his hair. "Out of all people in the entire universe, you couldn't choose someone else?"

"Sebastian, my friend," Andrew says, his brow furrowed, "you know I've never used the word guru."

This can't be ethical, Sebastian thinks. Even if Andrew isn't a therapist, and technically calls himself a yogi, a wellness coach, or whatever the hell he is, it's just wrong. It feels incestuous, like his big sister and brother, his protectors, have copulated. And now they'll be having a baby together.

"We can explain," Chloe and Andrew say in unison, their tone like a sax and oboe blowing a dissonant chord.

Sebastian points to Chloe. "Fuck you!" He points to Andrew. "And fuck you!" He hoists himself onto his crutches and heads out the hospital door.

Chapter

NINETEEN

The taxi ushers Sebastian home in a half hour. He doesn't care about the expense. After stepping on Chloe and Andrew's minefield, he needs safe shelter as quickly as possible. Funny how a place called *Hell's Kitchen*, his neighborhood for the past seven years, can offer such comfort.

No messages on the answering machine, not even from Reid. *Everyone's a traitor. Everyone lies!* Some imagination he has—he should've noticed Chloe and Andrew's *pas de deux* from the wings.

Television and DVD player set, he cues "Pick Yourself Up." He presses the Pause button, freezes on the image of Fred Astaire and Ginger Rogers just as their palms touch, initiating their dance.

An image of himself dancing next to Reid immediately fills his head. Crazy, isn't it? All this time Sebastian's wondered where Frank is, and now, for whatever nutty reason, he wonders what Reid is doing at this very moment.

Without warning, horns trumpet the song's opening notes, and Fred and Ginger's dance fills the screen. Sebastian checks the ceiling. Did Frank start the movie? Sebastian shuts off the DVD player and asks himself to concentrate on being present. "Create" vibrates throughout his body as he says it, his hands cupped over his face. He rummages through his backpack until he finds the recorder and presses play.

Mrs. Woo's voice booms from the recorder. "You ready, Mr. Hart?"

A giggle. "Yes, ma'am," Sebastian's voice replies. "A five, six, seven, eight!"

"Pick Yourself Up" starts. Sebastian closes his eyes as he listens to Mrs. Woo's pianoforte, his heartbeat in sync with the song's moderate tempo. He taps out the beat with his left foot as he hums along. A few bars in, he shuts off the recorder.

"No!" Sebastian calls out. He slams his hands on his thighs; the sting, there, snaps him back to attention. He can't bullshit himself, or his students, any longer. Inspiration, yes, but no more literal copycat Fred or Ginger or Gene or Eleanor or any other dance idol's moves.

He presses play on the tape recorder. Eyes closed, his arms crossed over his eyes, he lays down on the sofa, allows Mrs. Woo's rendition of "Pick Yourself Up" to run its entirety. But his brain freezes as soon as the song finishes, panicked at the thought of filling up choreography its full cycle. He grunts, strikes fisted hands onto the sofa. "It's only a two-and-a-half-minute song, you dope!" he yelps into his palms. And it's ridiculous because he knows full well that his capacity to create dances, at least before Frank said goodbye, is unlimited. *Is it the song?*

He sits upright on the sofa. Now, he sings the song "Pick Yourself Up," and while doing so, with the palms of his hands, he taps out the rhythm of each step (at least the so-called sequences of steps he has thus far) on his thighs. Still, no! Somehow, all the steps he's been hounding the students with don't seem fit. *Am I forcing something?*

He groans as he pushes upright from his elbows and literally picks himself up to standing from the sofa. Without the crutches' help, he hobbles toward his desk file drawer. Taking them out of their secret folder (he's never even shared this particular set with Chloe), and just as he's done a zillion times before, he flips through the stack of dance notes and sketches, the words and images he's been creating for years, moving before him like a filmstrip. He hugs the stack against his body, then stuffs them back into their folder and the desk drawer.

Another grunt. Sebastian lies on his back in front of the bookshelf. Without notice, the wind is taken out of him as Arthur pounces onto and kneads his belly. A tickle runs through Sebastian's body. "Hungry again?" he asks. Arthur coos and jumps off the sofa; he bats at the DVDs and CDs in the bookshelf.

"Hey, sweet thing," Sebastian says through a laugh. "You wanted a clean home, and now you're trying to muck it up?" He strokes the underside of Arthur's neck.

A low-pitched meow, which spans at least four counts, rises from Arthur. He lunges toward the bookshelf. A handful of DVDs and CDs tumble onto the floor.

Sebastian sucks his teeth. "You little monster," he says with a smile. "I've got to work," he continues as he re-files the DVDs and CDs.

A quick meow, then Arthur settles there, all purrs, in front of the bookshelf, reminding Sebastian of one of those Fifth Avenue darlings, a lion sculpture at the entrance steps of The New York Public Library.

Sebastian notices his own writing on the face of one CD case. He remembers, now, that this is another of Mrs. Woo's recordings from about a year ago: "I Want to Be Happy," from *No, No, Nanette*, one of Sebastian's favorite shows. At the time, she'd asked him why he'd liked it so much. And looking at the CD now, he reminds himself what he's always said: He loves that the ingénue, Nanette, fights everyone around her for independence. She wants to change and move forward, and her friends, who serve as a kind of Greek chorus, have actual back and forth dialogue with her, through song, acting as her ethical and moral conscience as she navigates growing pains. For Sebastian, then, although he was part of a chorus when he performed *No, No, Nanette*, at least he felt integral to the plotline, the story's forward movement.

Arthur rubs against Sebastian's cast leg and doesn't flinch as Sebastian cups his head, locks eyes with him. "You want to be happy?" Sebastian asks, widening his stare into Arthur's greenish-gold eyes. Arthur meows, breaks their gaze, and jumps on the sofa.

Sebastian lies flat again on the floor, the CD case cupped over his heart. He closes his eyes then springs them open, focused on the ceiling. "I want to be happy," he says. "And if I want to be happy, I have to try something new."

Every tap step he can imagine and all the sequences of steps he's given his students flood his brain. He pictures them entering with eight-counts of flap ball changes, moving into a single- then double-time step sequence. He sits upright. "It'll work!" he says. He taps those opening steps out with the palms of his hands, on his thighs, follows up with the cramp roll sequence he'd drilled into his students. He hobbles over to the desk and writes down the steps.

Mrs. Woo's honkytonk vibe drives her recording of "I Want to Be Happy," as well as Sebastian's heart and soul, and leads him toward each new step. It takes four hours, yet despite the cast leg he finally choreographs and notates the entire routine, his wingman Arthur, between naps and trips to the kitchen for food, watching from the sofa. By the time Sebastian settles on the last four bars of steps, it's eight thirty in the morning. The final routine evokes elements of Fred and Ginger with a taste of Gene and Eleanor, and every other movie musical dance legend he's loved, but in its entirety, the choreography is all Hart. And something inside is eager to share his newborn creation with Reid.

.....

Steam rises. The only light in the tiny bathroom comes from an unscented votive candle. Its flicker, encased in cobalt-blue glass, creates a shadowy glow. Fog clings to the oval mirror, calls to mind one of those ghostly sepia portraits—a faded collage of a clenched-jawed Ma, Pa, and their boy and girl offspring seated in a Victorian parlor. The cucumber aroma from the last two capfuls of Frank's bath gel calls to mind a tropical island. Long ago, the couple considered beating a retreat to Ibiza, but that was once upon a time. Like many other dreams he'd hoped to share with Frank, that particular journey was aborted. He wipes his brow. *Be present.* He's still here, not someplace else.

Naked, Sebastian grips the towel bar for support. He sidesaddles the salmon-pink tub and summons his arm strength to help guide his body, still carrying the weight of the cast, into the foamy water. He stops briefly; the temperature is just shy of painfully hot. With a deep sigh he slips farther in, surprised it's not as hot as he first imagined. He props his cast leg on the edge of the tub.

A smile comes. He's amazed the gel has maintained its potency for over a year. It still smells of freshly picked cucumber and makes a foamy bubble bath. The tub is deep, long, and has a slanted back, one of the reasons Sebastian and Frank chose the apartment; it always has been the perfect place for an after-rehearsal, or post-show relaxation tank. And now it feels bottomless as he finally settles into the water.

Inhale. Exhale. It feels like less of a command now. He sits upright, runs his fingers through his hair. Funny; for the past several weeks he's obsessed about his unruly mane. Now, it feels like it only needs pruning, a touch-up. He reaches over the edge of the tub and grabs his digital recorder.

"Create," he says into the recorder. He continues the mantra, hopeful it's not merely a dream but reality. "Create." No time for one-hit wonders. "Create." He's successfully completed the tap number, but that's not the only thing he needs to birth. How happy he'd be as a fulltime choreographer.

Sebastian visualizes the *RKO Movie Musicals* book. The massive volume no longer hogs the desk but is safely tucked away on the shelf with his and Frank's books. All the vibrant pictures and stories in *RKO* are pure magic: behind-the-scene tales of how one musical or another came to fruition onstage, onscreen, and in the souls of drama queens like Sebastian—*and maybe even Reid?* He wonders how many spells have been cast over the years by these musical fairy tales.

Sebastian rubs his eyes with his free hand and sings into the recorder, "I want to be happy." He shakes his head. "Fuck!" He shuts off the recorder and plops it onto the bath mat. He uses his upper body strength to slide along the slanted back wall of the tub until he's horizontal, his cast leg is propped up against the tiled wall, and his head now submerged under the bubble bath's surface. It's warm, not at all hot, especially beneath the dissipated bubbles.

He holds his breath underwater and counts four measures, not to any song, just eight counts of four measures: One, *two, three, four, five, six, seven, eight* . . . Two, *two, three, four, five, six, seven, eight . . .* Three, *two, three, four, five, six, seven, eight . . .* Four, *two, three, four, five, six, seven, eight.*

His chest tightens. The water sloshes as he pushes against its weight to a sitting position, his cast now rested again on the tub's edge. He spits out the suds, wipes away the foamy mask. Something inside him wishes he were a fish and is grateful for the sudden ability to master the breath.

No problem he's drenched or the area rug might be ruined. In one swift movement, Sebastian's flat on the sofa. Arthur, startled by the flecks of water that graze his coat, jumps off and runs toward the kitchen.

"Sorry, boy." He looks at the framed picture of him and Frank. "Enough!" he shouts. The weight behind his eyes pushes forward, and tears rush down his face. "It's not fair," he says to his husband's image. In his heart, he hears Frankie's response: "No, Seb. But you've got to do it. I want you to be happy. It's time."

Chapter
TWENTY

That night. Posthospital and Frank's dead-on-arrival verdict, Sebastian lumbered about their apartment. He paced in the kitchen where It picked at kibble, looked up, and mouthed a hello. While endearing, It irritated Sebastian all the same. He should've returned the comfort; after all, the poor thing had also lost Frank. But despite himself, Sebastian couldn't be bothered with It, the damn needy thing. He daren't scoop up the warm sack of fur. The body against his own—every breath, purr, heartbeat, and meow—would remind him too much of Frank.

The ER doctor told him the impact of Frank's head striking the curb wasn't the culprit. Instead, the murderer was a brain aneurysm that preceded the fall. Sebastian was convinced It blamed him for Frank's death. Yes, It hated Sebastian for taking away the security blanket It loved so much.

Sebastian nearly stepped on It as It weaved through his legs, yowling incessantly. It stopped to butt Its head against first one shin, then the other. Still, Sebastian fed It again, dumped kibble into the bowl until It stopped the aria. Kibble, kibble, kibble! The bottomless pit was fed four times *that night.* It finally ran out of the kitchen and announced Its satiety with a lower-pitched mew, then gifted Sebastian with a barf trail.

Sebastian breathed through his mouth to avoid inhaling the smell of bile as he wiped up the mess, pissed he was forced into the role of housekeeper. Either way, however, the obnoxious thing was braver than he, because It kept moving forward; this only heightened the irritation that permeated every corner of Sebastian's mind.

Sebastian paced around the kitchen for hours. He could've screamed, but he knew that if he did, he might not be able to stop the ultimate crescendo toward full-forced wails. Finally, he harnessed the strength to leave the kitchen and took up residence in the living room. And the pacing continued: toward the window, around the sofa, next to the nightstand where an empty picture frame—a birthday gift from Chloe—stood waiting for the right occupant. Sebastian was suddenly grateful she was so insistent on capturing the still life of him and Frank earlier that night. Maybe somehow Chloe foresaw it would be the last picture ever taken of them together.

That night. The screams finally began inside Sebastian's head, though he still couldn't verbalize any of his feelings to the walls, the window, the phone, or the obese sack of fur perched on the sofa. Should he call Chloe? *No.* She was probably still at thirty thousand feet in her sky cabin. His continued pacing carried him into the bathroom, which held him hostage for yet another hour. But he couldn't stop, even with his then sore back and feet. He began cackling like a madman in a horror flick, his tummy buckling and chest locking as he sucked in air.

The medicine cabinet? Zilch—he'd hoped to find the pills that were prescribed two months earlier for leg spasms he'd experienced after dancing his ass off at an audition for yet another box office bomb. "Fuck!" he shouted. He checked again; nothing! He slammed the cabinet shut. This was Chloe's fault; she'd probably taken the bottle of muscle relaxants with her to Cancún.

It meowed again from the living room. The piercing sound reminded Sebastian of those things in heat during childhood summer nights in Margaretville. He saw his mother's roundish face, then his father's, gaunt from too many puffs of smoke. The image of his sweet ginger cat, Mister, passed before his mind's eye. *Mister.*

Sebastian covered his ears. Any more meows from It would've been unadulterated torture. "Shut up!" he yelled out the bathroom door, despite knowing that he probably was being cruel to the poor thing. It stopped briefly, but started up soon after, louder than before.

An escape route sprang to mind: there was vodka in the freezer. Sebastian shook his head. *No. Absolutely not!* Vodka would only remind him of the Sex on the Beach cocktails he and Frank shared so many times. So he slumped there, where he was, onto the closed toilet lid. With arms folded as a pillow, he rested his head on the sink. His body, heavy with trying to bully himself and everyone else into silence, had grown too tired to pace.

A police siren wailed from the street, finally smothering the tomcat cries It insisted on projecting throughout the apartment. When a rush of frosty night air whooshed against Sebastian's body, he bolted toward the open window. A stronger gust of wind came. The smell of snow, clean yet violent, swept inside the apartment and forced a chill from the bottom of Sebastian's feet to the top of his head. As he stood there, letting the frigid air blast him full in the face, he felt the warmth of It pressed against his leg.

"No more!" Sebastian screamed. The voice that arose from his bowels vibrated in his head, a guttural emission like the dissonance of an orchestra's warm-up sequence. He visualized his innards spilling through his belly button: bile, piss, and shit all releasing until his body was turned inside out. *What's the body, anyway: Flesh? A slipcover?* Exhausted, Sebastian finally collapsed onto the sofa.

In the ensuring silence, the damn thing curled up next to him on the sofa. It purred loudly, and the greenish-gold eyes seemed to say, "I am not an It. I am not a *thing.*"

"Oh, sweet Arthur," Sebastian heard himself say. "My baby, my baby, my baby," he continued as he blotted his tears and drew in a long, slow breath. He rested his head against Arthur's and checked his wristwatch: 3:30 a.m. Hands on his belly, he released a four-count breath through his mouth.

His focus aimed toward the ceiling, Sebastian finally realized where he was: Onto the next day, from *that* day, from *that* night before. *Life goes on for everyone, except Frank,* he thought. *Life fucking goes on and on . . .*

Chapter

TWENTY-ONE

Naked, still, Sebastian's face and body remain wet with the tears and the bathtub's potion. He twists his wedding band slowly until it lodges against his knucklebone and reveals a tan line. Sad, but true: the phantom ring around his caramel-colored finger will probably fade in time.

Sebastian pictures himself on all fours, no cast, no forty years of skin. He's six, maybe eight months old. He straddles the edge of a blank wall-sized canvas. As if wielding a rattle, he grips an oversized aqua-blue crayon. He forms a large, cloud-like figure in the center of the canvas. Within it he etches *S + F*.

"Sebastian and Frank," he annunciates as he draws lines at five points around the cloud's perimeter. Without warning, the cloud morphs into a brilliant yellow sunburst, the *S + F* still contained inside its body.

Forty-year-old Sebastian's eyes grow heavy. He touches his wedding band, fingers the spot just above the knucklebone where it still won't budge. For close to seven years now, Sebastian's body has been this symbol of love's home. He looks toward the ceiling. "It's okay. I love you," he says, wiping his face with his bare arm. "I'll always love you," he murmurs to Frank's image in their framed photo. He tugs hard until the white-gold circle finally surrenders to his will and slides off. Sweaty, his body shakes with the onset of tears.

Sebastian takes a deep inhale and rises from the sofa, uses a steady breath cycle as he moves to retrieve his treasure box from the bottom dresser drawer. The small wooden box was a birthday present from his parents, a total surprise for their twelve-year-old son. Apparently, his father cut and glued all the dovetailed pieces, and his mother added the moss-green felt lining. The lid's tableau is a trio of loons—his father created one, his mother the other, and finally, they etched the third figure together.

When they handed Sebastian the box his father said, "The loons, Seb. Both parents incubate the eggs and raise their chicks together." His mother kissed his forehead and said, "It doesn't matter that we adopted you. We're all just as tight as loons. Daddy and I will always be your forever family." They'd written on a card inside: "Always keep this box, please do. Beneath its floor, our treasure to you."

Although the card they'd written on was lost long ago, Sebastian remembers those words as if his parents had offered them yesterday. Until tonight, however, he hasn't visited the reason for the words in twenty-two years, not since the day he arrived in the city.

The treasure box cradled in his arms, Sebastian moves to the floor. The rug under his bare ass tickles. He scoots backward, using the bottom edge of the sofa frame for support. He groans and extends his cast leg forward, bends the other leg inward to form a triangle. He places his wedding band on his knee.

Sebastian takes a whiff; he could swear the treasure box still smells of lemon polish after all these years. Stiff hinges, but it opens easily enough. He squints; the felt that carpets the bottom interior is lifted at the sides, and flakes of dried glue are noticeable around the edges. From beneath the treasure box's lining, a sheet of paper sticks out. He peels back the corner of the felt and tries to force the paper free. As he tugs harder, his wedding band falls off his knee and lands on the carpet. Reaching high, he places the band next to the picture on the side table.

He continues his tug-of-war with the paper. Finally, he bullies the felt bottom into surrendering, sending a cloud of dried glue particles into his face. To his surprise, he unearths five pieces of paper, folded in half and stapled along the top edge. When he unfolds the pages, he gasps. It's a deed that he never knew existed. After both parents were gone, he was told the land on which the ultimately burned husk of his family's home stood was owned by the bank. He didn't question it. At eighteen then, with no more ties to Margaretville, all he wanted was to get to New York City and never look back.

At the time, there had been no lawyer or kindly relatives to help the legally adult yet utterly sheltered teenager. Both parents' funerals, only six months apart, were quiet affairs attended by the pastor and a handful of their teaching colleagues. It pissed Sebastian off, but that's the way it was. Yes, his parents were both teachers—his mother taught kindergarten and his father third grade—but the Harts weren't particularly popular in town. Over the years, Sebastian had heard the whispers at school—that his parents were crazy, and that he must be too if they'd adopted him. Sebastian moans at the memory of it all. He doesn't believe his parents were mentally ill, just too paranoid for their own good. They kept to themselves, the trio of so-called loons that made up the Hart family.

Before Sebastian left Margaretville, the manager at the local bank informed him that his parents had an account that contained seventy-five thousand dollars. He wasn't sure back then how they'd saved so much from their small-town teachers' salaries, although it was apparent to Sebastian from his earliest years that hoarding was their second career. Of the money his parents squirreled away for him, Sebastian only used half to help fund his first year in New York. The rest he deposited in a savings account; regardless of the bills he accumulated in subsequent years, Sebastian tried to survive without tapping into those funds. Now, twenty-two years later, zilch is left of his initial inheritance.

Sebastian shakes his head. Why didn't his parents tell their only child about the deed? He looks toward the ceiling, then whacks the top of his head. "Dummy, dummy, dummy!" he yells. Of course his parents told him about the deed. It's just that for all these years, he hasn't listened as carefully as he should have.

He fingers the loons on the treasure box lid and hears his parent's voices: *Always keep this box, please do, beneath its floor our treasure to you.*

Chapter

TWENTY-TWO

Flying is out, even though it's been almost seven years since those infamous hijackers changed the world. Along with worries of dying in a fiery crash, Sebastian's also terrified airport security or other passengers might see his brown skin as a threat. Chloe has told him time and again he's warped for thinking racial profiling exists, but since that day in 2001, he's more certain than ever of its existence.

Being lifted off the ground by artificial means is not Sebastian's idea of fun, anyway—at least when executing a dance feat such as a grand jeté he's the controlling force of his own body. Therefore, Port Authority bus terminal and Adirondack Trailways will have to suffice. All the more poetic, he reasons, because that's the mode of transport that first ushered him into New York City over two decades before.

It's nine o'clock when the bus chugs down Main Street, a circuitous path toward the drop-off point. Sebastian's surprised they stay on Highway 28 instead of winding through the village. Maybe the man at the wheel craves the beauty of the scenic route as much as Sebastian does.

And the journey provides a sweet view. Norman Rockwell might've painted the village of Margaretville, which proudly displays its Victorian stateliness along the main route. Some structures are taller than others, some older; each, however, has its own character. To Sebastian, it's as if the founding mothers and fathers carefully selected a rainbow chorus for its village (*nontraditional casting?*), knowing each house would fight to win the most applause from townsfolk and tourists alike.

Even though Sebastian's been AWOL for twenty-two years, the street shops maintain their dollhouse charm. In the glow of a half-moon, their candy-colored exteriors still elicit childlike tickles in his now-adult gut. Each shop, in its everlasting, Technicolor splendor, appears like stage scenery, backdrops wedded to one another.

Sebastian widens his eyes. "It's gone?" He grimaces and sits upright as the bus whisks past the lot on Bridge Street, the spot where one of his favorite places, the Bun 'n' Cone, once lived. It was—he hates to think of it in the past tense—a local diner and ice cream parlor that, until its death, probably still closed nightly at seven o'clock. The Hart family trio had a standing date here every Thursday at five. Mom and Dad insisted it be their late-week treat: burgers, fries, and a vanilla-strawberry ice cream cone for dessert. Sebastian presses his hand against the glass and sighs. *Another piece of my childhood dead, all gone.*

Yet the streetlights, blending with the reflection of the East Delaware River along its path, are the ones he remembers from years past. He counts each light, twenty in all, as they charge toward the thoroughfare that finally signifies their entrance into Margaretville's town limits.

The bus stops in front of the Hess gas station on Highway 28. Its next-door neighbor is Delaware National. To Sebastian's surprise, the banking institution's former name escapes him, unlike every other dwelling in his hometown. In any event, whatever it was dubbed at the time of his departure, its representatives had obviously misinformed him about the deed to his family's property.

Sebastian's off the bus and onto the crutches in less than five minutes. He heads toward the Margaretville Motel. The evening's place of rest—or unrest, whatever the case might turn out to be—boasts low ceilings and white walls. It's a typical ranch-style highway stop, with a dorm room–sized microwave and refrigerator to boot.

The nineteen-inch television, circa Sebastian's college years (that is, had he actually gone to college), doesn't appear current, although, to its credit, Fred and Ginger would look stellar on its black-and-white picture. A second take and oops—his perception is off once again. It's actually a more advanced model than he first thought: TRU-COLOR, so reads the aluminum tag catty-corner to the TV's channel selector. And bonus points indeed for the establishment: free HBO.

Another smile—the leaf-patterned bedspread and sky-blue shag reminds Sebastian of the Motel 8 he and his parents stayed in when they visited Disney World in 1973. The highlight of that trip wasn't Mickey Mouse, but the rerelease of *The Sound of Music*, which they saw at a drive-in theater in Kissimmee. He wanted desperately to be one of those children Julie Andrews nurtured and eventually adopted. He related most to Liesl, especially when she sang and danced in "Sixteen Going on Seventeen."

He sits on the edge of the firm bed and hoists his cast leg on top of a slatted chair. *Ugh!* While the papier-mâché vice has seemed lighter the past few days, it obviously still plays the heavy. He calls the front desk: "I need a taxi."

"Who?" The woman at the front desk squeaks. She sounds as if she could be a relative of Mrs. Woo. "In Margaretville, at this hour, son? *Where the ham?"*

Sebastian giggles. Where the ham? It sounds like something his mom would say. "Family," he says. "I have a family visit."

The taxi driver, who's somewhere around sixty years old, also registers surprise on his long face when Sebastian slips into the backseat at such an apparently too-late hour. "Area's changing leaps and bounds up there," the man says, flashing a gap-toothed grin. His pin-straight hair, raven black and gathered in a rubber band, is reminiscent of a My Pretty Pony figurine.

The taxi reeks of Sebastian's first eighteen years of life. *It's 2008!* He shakes his head at the thought. *Isn't smoking banned in all public places throughout the state?* If so, why doesn't this guy use the opportunity to beat the addiction?

"Rebuilding and such going on up the hill, you know," Mr. Pony continues. "City people gobbling it up by the square inch, daily. Framing for new homes. McMansions—that's what they call them thingies—is really what they're harvesting up in here. Although some people do try to keep refurbishing the old ladies still standing." He chokes out a phlegmy cough. "For the most part, though," he adds, clearing his throat, "it's just land up there for days on end: Land, land, land."

Sebastian nods. "I know." He instructs Mr. Pony to take Walnut Street up the hill. And as they proceed, neither says a word for several minutes, which suits the prodigal son in the backseat just fine.

It's just as Mr. Pony said: many have staked claim to the abundance of earth that Margaretville provides. Pockets of such bare acreage are few and far between each dwelling. While every other home maintains the Victorian style Sebastian recalls from childhood, many others are sprawling, modern monstrosities.

From their starting point in the village, it only takes ten

minutes to reach the familiar yet somehow foreign territory of his old neighborhood, the same amount of time it took Sebastian and his parents to drive down the mountain every morning for school. Even though it was (and still appears to be) rough terrain, Sebastian loved to walk into town, joyful he could make the journey just as well on his own two feet.

"Whoa!" Sebastian yelps.

"Ooh," says Mr. Pony as he brakes hard. His face in the rearview mirror is ashen and raw, like Sebastian's father's was at the end of his life. He looks out the window, looks back at Sebastian with pursed, weathered lips.

Sebastian checks his watch. It's 9:30 p.m. "I'll only be a few minutes," he says. He gets out of the car and steadies himself on the crutches; a scarecrow perched in the middle of the now empty lot of his childhood home. The taxi headlights give him a peripheral view of the grass—or are those weeds that dance against his leg? Either way, whatever grows here seems much taller than he remembers. *Over half of my entire lifetime, to this point, has gone by since I last stood here.*

Whatever foliage the yard whistles with, by way of the warm breeze, its odor is the subtlest hint of licorice. He cranes his neck, inhales. Maybe it's another acquaintance from way back when: *Susan?* After all these years she must still be here in the mix. When his parents first mentioned such a flower—black-eyed Susan—a then six-year-old Sebastian was convinced it was some battered woman they knew. He takes in more air though his nostrils.

Namaste. Though he can't distinguish everything in the darkness, he thinks his other childhood friend, Queen Anne's lace, her pale hint of gardenia—at least that's how he catalogued her scent—still sprouts among the wildflowers. He tightens his grip on the crutches and trudges further into the foliage. The half-moon appears to have made a costume change from a luminous white to a grayish suit. He asks the sky why everything here, like everything else he encounters outside the place where he now stands, changes yet stays the same: his biological parents; his first cat, Mister; his parents, who raised him and nurtured his heart and soul; his Frank.

Sebastian closes his eyes. He's tired of judging whether or not his ruminations, his "warped" perception of things, qualify him as certifiable, or as a drama queen—or, perhaps, all of the above. He knows everyone who left unexpectedly is up there in some kind of heaven, watching over him.

He inhales. Yes, while it may not be as strong as it was in his childhood, the air still smells of licorice mixed with gardenia. He exhales, convinced now that this return visit congregates all his loved ones in the same place and time. His past, present, and future merge in this moment.

He rubs his tummy just above his belly button, where a slight burn asserts itself. At eighteen, he bolted out of Margaretville quickly, perhaps too quickly to deal with the forced abandonment by so many loved ones. Maybe he's just too chicken to let go of the victim role he's played all these years. He lowers his chin toward his chest, with cupped hands catches the groan that rises from his gut. He wonders just how much of a straw man he looks, propped up on the crutches.

Sebastian waves toward the taxi. "I'm fine. I just need a bit more time."

Mr. Pony leans out the window, nods. Sebastian lowers himself onto the ground, a spot where he danced once upon a time, and even made snow angels. He closes his eyes. While the foliage that encases him still induces a tickle, he breathes away the sensation, surrendering to the environment. Whatever surrounds him now claims his childhood landscape as its home. Sebastian, and every other Hart, has long since abandoned this address.

. . . . .

Aside from the farewell Sebastian obviously doesn't recall—when his parents left him as a newborn in a hospital ER—his first official goodbye (or was it the second?) occurred when he was ten years old. Mister, his ginger tabby cat, stopped eating. Sebastian's father held him by the scruff of the neck while his mother gripped Mister's head and tried to shove kibble into his mouth, but the innocent creature only arched his spine and refused.

Sebastian's face flooded with tears. But his parents wouldn't listen to what Mister's body was saying. *These fucking human beings*, the poor feline must've thought of the two who lorded their arrogant control over him (and Sebastian).

"Stop!" his human brother yelled, the sound coming deep from within his belly, which finally made both parents pull away from the cat. But before Sebastian could recuse him, the poor feline's entire body convulsed: Mister went limp, his blue eyes fixed on Sebastian. In the terrorist attack, Mister's heart must've seized.

Sebastian looked up and realized his parents were both crying. But neither said a word, *Murderers!* Even if it wasn't intentional, even if it was because they thought force-feeding would save his life, his parents had applied capital punishment. And the crime Mister's selfish, human guardians accused him of committing? Reaching the end of his intended life cycle at only nine years old.

Sebastian scooped up Mister, ran into his room, and wrapped his papoose in an aqua-blue towel. He refused help from either parent as he buried his sweet brother on the front lawn, in the sunniest spot he could find.

That night, in shorts and bare feet, he roosted on the front porch and watched as the Crayola midnight-blue sky above a beastly hot night transformed itself. It rained as hard as his own tears had that entire day on Mister's makeshift grave.

The next morning, as soon as his parents left for the day (not before each of them reminded him to do something productive instead of pining away for the cat), Sebastian scrounged up all the money he'd collected in his ten years of life: dollars from birthday cards, empty peanut butter jars of change he'd filled by combing through the seams of his father's moss green recliner, and some-times spare change his mother allowed him to keep after chore runs to the market.

His beat-up Radio Flyer wagon in tow, he found his way to the nursery two miles away from home. Along the way, in honor of Mister, whom Sebastian often recruited to play Toto to his Dorothy, he threw in a few "we're off to see the wizard" skips. Once he crossed Agway's threshold, he spotted the perfect trea-sure. The tree looked like a baby version of one he'd seen in front of Gasho, the Japanese restaurant where his social studies class dined on a field trip. Yes, with its iridescent reddish leaves, Sebastian knew the Japanese maple was the perfect tribute to his fur brother. He planted it directly over Mister's sunny spot on the front lawn.

Eight years later, in the middle of Sebastian's senior year of high school, his mother developed lung cancer. She never smoked, but his father had for decades. Upon diagnosis, the doctor explained it was his father's hand-me-downs that had finally caught up with his mother.

Within two months' time, Sebastian was forced to say goodbye to his family's weekend evenings together. He could no longer fling his body around, kick his legs, or do pseudo tap dances that would provoke gales of laughter from his parents. Gone, at least temporarily, were the movie musical idols his parents had introduced him to: the debonair Fred; the flowing, ball-gowned Ginger; the dapper Gene Kelly; the nimble-footed hoofer Eleanor Powell; the cute yet sassy Debbie Reynolds; the comically endearing Donald O'Connor. *Goodbye to all that.*

The day after they scattered his mother's ashes in the mountains, unspoken house rules gradually took effect. Smoking was now forbidden, as was watching musicals on the RCA. Even Sebastian's solitary pleasure, watching videos on MTV, was no longer allowed.

On top of this, his father's behavior grew increasingly erratic. While the Harts attended services at the Presbyterian Church every Sunday, they never were what Sebastian would call religious. Yet suddenly, his father turned into a self-proclaimed zealot. He eventually lost his high school teaching job because the parents didn't appreciate Mr. Hart's scaring their children with fiery biblical passages and apocalyptic speeches. Homebound, Sebastian's father read the bible for hours at a time, oftentimes out loud behind his locked bedroom door. Thankfully for Sebastian, he never, ever professed anything derogatory or cited passages that were supposedly against homosexuality.

Over several months, the older man became unrecognizable. He lost at least twenty pounds from skipping meals, and his son began to wonder if lung cancer had finally staked a claim on his other parent. But he couldn't convince his father to seek medical help. Every so often, Sebastian thought he smelled tobacco on his father's clothes. But he brushed such thoughts away, convinced it was only his imagination. Delusional or not, his father had surely learned his lesson from his wife's death, hadn't he?

The night before his high school graduation, Sebastian was awakened by his father's voice. The old man was screaming, reprimanding his reflection in the bedroom dresser mirror.

Sebastian hugged his rail-thin father. "Daddy, what is it? Another nightmare?" He guided him to sit on the bed.

The old man simply smiled and said, "Dreams aren't real, son."

"I don't know, Daddy," Sebastian said.

"Not asking you, boy," his father continued. "I'm telling you the truth. Your mother sat right at the kitchen table and told me we were all doomed." He coughed up a glob of mucous and wiped his mouth with his bare, ashen arm. "End of days!"

Sebastian squeezed his father's bone-dry hand. "Calm down, Daddy. Mom's gone. She's in heaven. Remember?"

The old man shook his salt-and-pepper head vigorously. "She's here. That's the truth." He narrowed his hazel eyes at Sebastian. "And she told me to make sure you listen up good. Told me she's real proud of you and that she wants you to keep dancing. It's the end of days, yes, but don't you dare stop dancing until the end." He shook his fist to punctuate his words. "And she'll be at graduation tomorrow night. You hear me, son?"

"Yes, Daddy." Sebastian wrapped his arms around the old man's bony torso. "I understand." He kissed his father's forehead and tucked him back in bed, murmuring assurances that all would be well and that they'd celebrate his graduation the following day in honor of his mother.

But the next evening, his father refused to rise from the bed. Sebastian called for the old man repeatedly but only got a muttered dismissal from behind the bedroom door. Sebastian was left to lie about why he had to traipse in cap and gown across the stage of Margaretville Central School alone. Both Harts were abandoned: a parentless son and a father home alone.

Later, in the aftermath of what happened, Sebastian would be plagued by suppositions. *If only he were there*, he could've awakened to the smell of smoke. *If only he were there*, he could've made it to his father's bedroom, fighting his way through the purplish-red flames, and pulled the older man out. Hand in hand, they could've race toward the front door, toward safety. *If only.*

But that's not what happened. The truth is, Sebastian came home twenty minutes after his father's final curtain call, just in time for the cleanup crew to strip bare the rest of his life. Immediately upon arrival, a fireman handed him the loon treasure box. As Sebastian stood there, the fire-truck wails mingled with the slow crackle of the dying fire. He imagined his father being crushed by the same wall of sound as he allowed the flames to swallow him.

This particular goodbye, which ended in yet another cremation of a parent's body, led Sebastian over a hundred miles southeast to New York City, a place where he'd later learn the right way to do his movie musical idols' dance steps (and a few of the ones from the MTV videos he'd watched). But even after he moved to the city, even after he met Frank and lived with him for nearly seven years, a sinking fear he'd turn out to be just as crazy as his father always lurked in the pit of Sebastian's stomach.

A loud honk comes. "You all right out there?" Mr. Pony calls from the taxi.

Sebastian lifts his head and waves. "Fine, just a few more minutes." Up and onto the crutches, he trudges through the thick foliage toward the edge of the property. The freshwater pond captures the moon's reflection. He's amazed at the sight: steep mountains sprinkled with shiny bulbs of light. He widens his eyes. The scene reminds him of a Lite-Brite pegboard. True, it seems the area really has been built up since he left. He glances at the pond again. *Nope, definitely no loons this time of year—maybe never, if they've permanently migrated elsewhere.* He smiles to himself—he can almost hear his mother, father, and Frank whispering in his ear. He's certain that if he stares long enough, a trio of loons might glide past.

Chapter

TWENTY-THREE

The clear sky over Union Square Park is a perfect backdrop for the early April sunshine. Sebastian and Chloe claim a bench along the dog run, the crutches propped against the black wrought-iron fence. The farmer's market, only a patch of grass away, is busy as ever, the park filled with die-hard New Yorkers hungry for the finally consistent springtime weather.

Two middle-aged men stroll arm in arm toward the main attraction. "Aw," says one as he tugs his companion's arm. They lean on the fence, ogle the furry tricksters inside the dog run. Each canine appears euphoric to be alive in the shared experience of gallops, drools, and fetches.

A mother-and-child pair passes by, making Sebastian grin. A twentysomething father, in perfect sync with his toddler boy's gait, glides past a line of strollers with a speed that would rival a feline's best sprint. On a nearby bench, an elderly couple nestle into each other, the old man grumbling (and smiling) as his wife blots the perimeter of his jaw, perhaps to whisk away any remnants of their shared sandwich.

An image comes to mind: Mrs. Woo plucks out a piano rag as a parade of couples strut past him. They lurch in a signature cakewalk style (arms hooked at the elbow, torso tilted backward, one knee raised, pause for eight counts) as they make their way around the park. Sebastian buttons the image with a toothy smile. Yes, twofers abound in the glorious park, and they all should grab what they can, while they can: good weather, good time, good loving.

Sebastian closes his eyes. Another snapshot fills his head: seated on the bench, his fingers interlaced with Frank's, their wedding bands clasped together in the middle of all this life. He sighs. *Husbands.* Yes, they had a long run, but another day for other chances is here.

A cough pulls him out of his trance. "Seriously?" Chloe asks, apparently choking on her tea. "All these years you didn't know they'd set up a trust?"

Sebastian nods. "The bank was surprised with that one, too."

"And that much for only five acres?"

Sebastian sucks his teeth. "A hundred and fifty thousand dollars doesn't exactly make me a millionaire. Well, that's minus the closing costs for the property, and also the yearly real estate taxes they've been taking out of the trust for the past twenty-two years."

"Amazing, Seb," Chloe says. "Even in death your parents are still with you, taking care of you."

Sebastian smiles. "I know. They really loved me."

Chloe leans forward, her face serious. "Now that you have a bit more financial security, would you please finally get a damn cell phone?"

Sebastian reaches into his backpack. "One step ahead of you."

"Say what? Oh . . . yippee!" She cradles his palm-sized cell phone. "You've finally stepped into the twenty-first century." She high-fives him.

"Yep." Sebastian adds, laughing. "I'm ready for whatever's ahead."

"That's the truth," Chloe says. "But do you miss Margaretville, think you'll ever want to go back?"

Sebastian shrugs. "Someday, maybe. But I'm good for now. Either way, it'll always be a part of me."

Chloe's mouth turns downward, her brow pinched. "And your wedding band?"

Sebastian smiles. "Safe." He pictures himself cradling the wooden treasure box. Until he placed his wedding band inside and found the deed to his family's home, nothing else had called the place home. But he's confident the box, and the loons that adorn it, will protect every *schatz* he decides to house in its sacred walls.

Chloe chews her upper lip. "I'm really impressed, Seb." She wipes the moisture from her eyes. "So damn proud of you."

"Aww ... thanks," Sebastian says, his own eyes tearing up. "I'll second that." It's the first time in a long time he's shared her sentiment. "Although I'm still annoyed with you," he adds, rubbing her arm.

"Uh-oh." Chloe sucks in air through her teeth. "You're still mad?"

"Just the teeniest bit irritated." Sebastian indicates how teeny with his fingers. "Not really. I was just disappointed. The way you went behind my back with Andrew. To get him."

"Get him? No, no, no, my darling Seb. There was no *getting* Andrew. I found him, and he's definitely the one. Thanks to you, my dear friend, I found Andrew. It's magic."

"You believe in magic?" Sebastian raps lightly on her forehead. "You sure you haven't popped anything into your system?"

"Yes, ma'am," Chloe says. "System's clean." She gently rubs her tummy. "I'm all about the little one."

"Of course," Sebastian says. He never thought he'd use such a word to describe Chloe, but she's definitely *giddy*.

She hugs him. "And I feel especially clean now that you forgive me."

Sebastian whispers in her ear, "Drama queen."

"Maybe yes." She tugs his ear. "Maybe no."

"Well, well, Miss Thing. And to think you didn't believe in all that Prince Charming, fairy-tale crap."

"All right, all right. I get it." Chloe's eyes dance in a four-corner pattern: sky right, sky left, ground right, ground left. Then, with half-closed eyes, she says, "I guess we all have a bit of a drama queen inside."

Sebastian gives her a knowing look. He'd love to put her words in his treasure box for keeps. "Look," he says through a cough, irritated that it's still difficult to ask for things. "I need a favor."

Chloe drapes her wrists over his shoulders. "Anything."

Sebastian unzips his black backpack, which sits on the pebbly ground. "I'd like to share my stuff with you," he says in a shy, pinched voice.

"Ooh!" Chloe's dark eyes widen as she claps her hands. "Goody-goody!"

Sebastian casts his eyes downward and hands her the over-sized manila envelope. "Help me organize these numbers?" he mutters. "They're all mine. I've had them for ages."

Chloe shakes her fists like a child on Christmas morning ready to tear into Santa's gifts. "Originals?"

Sebastian nods. It makes his stomach cramp to admit he actually created something from his own heart and soul. "I thought maybe the community center would let me use the space to rehearse. I could get some dancers . . . maybe make an audition video of my stuff."

Chloe pinches his cheek. "You little shit!"

Sebastian feels his mouth turn upward. "And I finished the number for the recital."

Chloe gasps. "You did?"

Sebastian nods briskly with a smile. "New song: 'I Want to Be Happy.'"

"Oh my word, *No, No, Nanette*! That's like one of your favorite musicals."

Sebastian nods. "You know me well." He says toward the brilliant blue sky, "I Want to Be Happy."

"Damn straight, that makes me happy, too," Chloe says.

"Help me teach it to the class?"

Chloe squeezes his arm. "You know I will." She shakes the hefty envelope. "And we all know these numbers you've been hoarding are brilliant."

"But you haven't seen any of the actual dances."

Chloe sticks out her tongue. "I'm a zillion percent sure," she says. "If it comes from you, I know it's brilliant."

Brilliant. It seems like such a big word. Sebastian blows air upward from his mouth to cool his face. "Thank you, Chloe." He clears his throat. "It means a lot to hear you say that."

"My dearest friend, my little love," Chloe says, putting her hand over his heart. "I absolutely, positively never say anything to you I don't mean."

"Guess I can't argue."

"No, you can't," Chloe says, standing up.

"Where are you going?"

Chloe lowers her chin and widens her eyes like a coy schoolgirl. "Andrew and I have the baby's sonogram today." Her face splits into an ear-to-ear grin. "I'm sure Andrew wouldn't mind if Uncle Sebastian joined us."

Sebastian smiles back. "Uncle Sebastian would love to, but

there are a few things he needs to take care of."

"Such as?" Chloe asks.

"My first order of business is a trim for my locks," Sebastian says. " And after that there's . . ." He closes his eyes and licks his lips. "Something I need—I want to do by myself."

Chloe smiles brightly. "Reid?"

Sebastian half-smiles. "Just stay tuned, Auntie Mame."

"Whatever you say." She pecks his cheek. "I'll let you know what happens with the sonogram." She turns to leave, then walks back. "And course I'll let you know what happens with the dances." She hugs the envelope and blows him a kiss over her shoulder as she heads into the farmer's market crowd and out of the park.

Sebastian scoots backward, cradled by the slatted bench. He tells himself to make room for the sounds of the inadvertently choreographed mayhem on the makeshift stage whose marquee reads *Union Square Park*. Such incredible feats of color and sound on the other side of his closed eyes: people laugh and whisper and shout; birds chirp, their sound echoing the air; a cluster of kiddies chortle; dogs bark as they gallop and skid within the pebbled playpen.

Sebastian places his hands in prayer position. *Namaste.* Yes, he tells himself, these people, his fellow humans, play a welcome symphony for his soul. Their words mixing together, relying on one another to build and amplify, calls to mind the song "Make Our Garden Grow" from the musical, *Candide.* Among all this life, his breath cycle can only be described as surround sound: every inhalation whooshes inside and satiates his lungs as easily as each exhalation flows outward, until the next wave's intake.

He opens his eyes. Thinking of growing gardens of course makes him think of a certain Dr. Garden. He pictures it: Reid in a moss-green button-down, the sleeves rolled up just below his elbows, the reddish-gold hair on his arms gleaming in the sun. Sebastian rubs the tension from his forehead. *But can I trust him?*

Sebastian grabs his crutches, rises to his feet. He can sit in the shadows, alone and pining for the past, or he can dig in the dirt to create a new garden. *Let the dirt fill your lungs, Sebastian*, he commands. *Choke on it, roll around in it; spit it out until, once again, you're fully open to every available breath.* Why the hell not at least try?

Chapter

TWENTY-FOUR

Two hours later, it feels as if twice as many have passed. After a quick trim from his barber, Sebastian heads toward the office on Ninth Street. He parks himself and his trusty backpack on an ivy-patterned bench and props his crutches against the gray stucco wall. He cradles a small bamboo plant tied with a red ribbon.

Soon, the man he's been waiting for steps out of the building's white-framed entrance.

Sebastian points to the building's awning, which reads *Dr. Garden* in gray block letters. "Very impressive, Doc," he says.

A pinkish hue spreads across Reid's face, and he bows at the waist. "At your service."

Sebastian giggles. Just as he imagined it, Reid sports a variation of his signature costume: moss cargo pants and a beige button-down worn open like a jacket, the sleeves rolled up to the elbows. Once again there are noticeable smudges of grass and dirt on the front of his white T-shirt. Sebastian's lips dance from trying to contain a smile.

"I see you got your ears trimmed," Reid says. "Looks great."

"Thanks." Sebastian's face grows warm as he finger-combs his hair, a bit of length on top, the sides shorter. "Just a touch-up."

"Cute," says Reid, as he sits next to Sebastian. He points to the bamboo plant. "Did you arrange that yourself?"

"Not exactly." *Reid.* Even inside, Sebastian loves to say his name. "Korean deli, Twelfth Street." He adjusts his cast leg and sits up taller on the bench.

"I see." Reid's dimples deepen as his mouth turns upward.

Sebastian looks to the sky, then directs his eyes on the patch of grass in front of the bench. "Chloe's well." He exhales, hoping to release the tightness in his chest. "She asked me to send her love."

"The feeling's mutual. You know, I'm really glad she's okay. She'll do just fine with the baby. We'll all help out."

Sebastian grips the edge of the bench. That Reid cares as much for Chloe makes Sebastian want to kiss him. "And the other thing is—"

"Is what?" Reid offers in a breathy, lower register than his normal baritone.

"I . . . I don't know." Sebastian closes his eyes. Something dances inside him. He looks to his left, focuses on four tall, rectangular boxwoods so green they appear as if they'd live forever. "Actually, I do know." He clears his throat. "Just like me, you also have a weakness for certain things." He retrieves a small box of chocolates from his backpack.

"Oui oui, monsieur," Reid says in his baritone. "This is the good stuff." He sniffs the brown box. "La Maison du Chocolat," he adds, reading the label.

Sebastian's breath lurches, trapped in his throat. "And this is for luck," he says, raising his other gift. "Here's to good things all around."

Reid takes the bamboo plant. "I don't know what to say." He ducks his head shyly. "I'll treasure it, Sebastian."

Sebastian shrugs. "Seb is fine."

"Seb?" Reid leans toward him. "Really? You don't mind?"

Sebastian nods. "Cross my heart." His chest rises with ease and satiates itself with the warm spring air. Along with the boxwoods, daffodils, and daisies, impatiens also live gracefully in the terra cotta enclosures that border *Reid's* house of design; coupled with other sensations, they form a cacophony of smells.

"Well, Reid," he says. It feels fantastic to say his name out loud.

Reid sets the box of chocolates and bamboo plant on the bench. "Yes, Seb?" he offers with a wink.

Inhale. Exhale. Sebastian coughs the frog from his throat. "I'm here because I want to know that you . . . I need you to understand." He scoots forward on the bench. To his surprise, Reid's eyes actually are steel blue, not the aqua color he thought they were. Sebastian shakes his head; people aren't always exactly what imagines them to be—and certainly not always what he tells himself they are. He chuckles at the thought: *Maybe Technicolor is sometimes overrated.*

"You okay?" Reid asks.

Sebastian looks down at his hands. "I know it's only been three weeks that we've known each other."

"Time's relative."

Sebastian catches his breath; the hand that caresses the base of his neck sends an un-choreographed jitterbug through his entire body. He opens his eyes. "I'm fantastic."

"Yes," Reid says as he gently massages the base of Sebastian's neck, "you're definitely fantastic."

Sebastian's torso buckles as his body pitches forward. He stops the fall by gripping onto Reid, who, in turn, loses his balance. They nearly wipe out but seemingly, in unison, regain their footing. Sebastian feels certain of his grip around Reid's shoulders, and Reid's bear hug, too, as they guide each other toward the stucco wall.

"Shall we dance?" Reid says.

Sebastian chuckles. "Who's Fred and who's Ginger?"

Reid shrugs. "I'm versatile."

Sebastian raises his brow. "So am I." He places his palms on Reid's shoulders. A round of devilish giggles spread from the center of Sebastian's body and echo in the air. He gently traces Reid's features with his fingers before leaning in for a kiss. Reid's mouth is warm; his lips are slightly chapped but cushiony enough for comfort. On second thought, Sebastian realizes as he applies more pressure, Reid's peppermint taste offers much more than a comfortable feeling.

They move together, arms wrapped around each other as if choreographed to sway in a slow dance. After a few beats, Sebastian pulls back and nuzzles his head into Reid's chest. *Inhale.* Reid's scent is even more defined now: he smells of a day's worth of sweat and a hint of citrus, like a freshly planted garden.

Reid strokes Sebastian's hair. Sebastian's eyes widen with the tingle that rises through his body. He swallows hard and gently yet firmly reminds himself (and, once again, his hard-on) to exhale.

The embrace they share feels as solid and warm as the memory of the blankets Sebastian's parents used to cocoon him in at night; as cozy as Arthur's furry, twenty-pound frame spoons against him; as safe as the hugs he exchanges with Chloe. Sebastian's heart pulses at an allegro pace, and a glimmer of dread and dizziness courses through him. But he closes his eyes, commands the fear to subside and, with eyes raised to the sunny sky, offers a smile.

His arms draped over Reid's shoulders, their five o'clock shadows married, Sebastian squeezes tight. He whispers, "I can't tell where all this will lead."

"I know," Reid says. The calluses of his landscaper hands feel sandpaper-rough as he rubs Sebastian's hand. In the sunshine, the sun-bleached hairs on his arms glow a coppery hue.

"But I promise I'll try," Sebastian offers, looking directly into Reid's eyes. "It might be slow, but I'll try to be open to wherever this takes us."

"We've got time," says Reid, interlacing his fingers with Sebastian's.

"There's something else. I finished the number for the recital."

"Excellent!" Reid dances his fingers against Sebastian's palm. "I knew you would."

"Really?" Sebastian says. The pressure of Reid's grip excites him, makes him feel wanted, needed.

"You know, Seb, we're a lot alike."

"What are you talking about?" Reid is certainly no drama queen. Sebastian can't imagine Reid would ever be as neurotic or insecure as himself, nor live in one fantasy world after another.

"I mean it, Seb." Reid strokes Sebastian's hair. "I create and doctor gardens, and you create and doctor dance numbers."

"Oh." Sebastian chortles.

"No, really," Reid says, his brow pinched into what seems like his *serious* face. "Think about it. Dance numbers, landscape projects, all of it. Some take longer than others to realize, but in the end, we're both able to give them just what they need to grow as healthily as possible."

"Thank you," Sebastian says. For being such a know-it-all, he never thought of it that way.

Reid rests his palms on Sebastian's chest. "Thank you for what?"

Sebastian's heart flutters with his breath cycle. He wants to offer gratitude to Reid for still wanting to take a chance but decides those particular words can wait. Instead, he says, "The bamboo and chocolate. Thanks for liking them."

Reid's smile extends to his steel-blue eyes. "What's not to like, Seb?"

"Exactly." Sebastian grips him tighter. "What's not to like?"

Chapter

TWENTY-FIVE

L ife struts by fast when it has a purpose. After three years of work as assistant, then associate choreographer on several projects with his old pal Marcus, Sebastian, much to his utter joy, finds himself promoted to choreographer of the Broadway revival of *No, No, Nanette.* Of course, the production abounds with all-original choreography; every flap, shuffle, ball change, and pirouette nurtures itself inside him first before he ultimately translates it to his chorus boys and girls.

Yet despite all the creative kudos and changes, Sebastian keeps his vow: for as long as he's able to do so, he'll stay with his students at the community center. And in the event he has to say goodbye to his crew, he'll find the exact right captain to keep them anchored, feeling safe and loved. Their meeting time has changed to accommodate his rehearsal schedule, but he still offers a steady date night every Monday.

It's a balmy July day. Sebastian's once-black CREATE shirt has faded to a charcoal gray and it's started to fray at the shoulders. Nevertheless, he'll always remain loyal to the gift Chloe gave him over three years ago. At four months into his forty-third year of life, the drama queen's earned the right to wear whatever the hell he wants.

No papier-mâché vice on his lower extremity, no metal stilts—it's strange now to think Sebastian ever dealt with either impediment. The tan line on his right hand finger, where he and Frank had kept their wedding band, is also long gone, smoothed away after three years' time.

Just last month, Sebastian could've sworn his heart had seized upon the news that the New York State Legislature finally stepped into the twenty-first century and made marriage equality legal. With President Obama helming the country, it's possible the federal government will eventually follow suit, ensuring that civil marriage becomes a freedom available to every US citizen. Sebastian often wonders what Frank would think of it all.

Tonight, however, Sebastian presides over the podium at Film Forum, a movie revival house. He scans the small, yet surprisingly packed house—row upon row of eager faces. His eyes follow the red-carpeted aisles to the back, where two thick pillars claim space on either side of the entrance. Black curtains are draped along every wall. There's no denying it: this place has old-school style, like a movie studio screening room.

He arranged it with the archivist at Film Forum and the community center to book the auditorium for this private viewing. This is their field trip, much like the ones he hosts every month for his students and their families and friends. Tonight's treasure, *Silk Stockings*, particularly close to his heart. Fred Astaire is certainly older (and Ginger-less) in the film, but neither age nor the partner change stunts his luster.

Sebastian adjusts the podium mic and clears the lump from his throat. "So . . . I hope you all enjoy this one as much as I do. As far as I'm concerned, Astaire dances amazingly well with Cyd Charisse, and with as much style and grace as he's ever displayed onscreen or off."

Chloe and Andrew sit in the front row with Taylor, their daughter. With her curly, jet-black hair and narrow face, she looks eerily like a three-year old version of Chloe. But the little gazelle's personality—calm yet linear—is clearly a gift from her yogi father, Andrew.

Mrs. Woo has reversed her look. She swore off her black glasses last year and now wears an orange-rimmed pair whose roundness accentuates her owl face even more. Her iridescent, from-the-bottle orange hair, is now pitch black. A transformed Kathleen is here as well. There's been dramatic weight loss, but she hasn't abandoned the Kewpie doll cuteness, especially seated next to Beau, who still sports his dark hair and trademark grin. Hank and Millie, ever so elegant in his and hers linen suits, complete the row.

Sebastian waves his left hand to the projectionist, blinking as the light bounces off his platinum wedding band. The lights fade, and the syncopated click and sputter of the advancing filmstrip fills the room.

Sebastian gathers images of all his pals in the audience as he finds his way down the dimly lit aisle, and settles next to his husband, Reid.

The movie's soundtrack starts. *Inhale. Exhale. Inhale.* Sebastian closes his eyes. *There's no real goodbye. Anyone I've ever loved will always be a part of me.*

"I am loved," Sebastian says toward the ceiling with a smile.

"What?" Reid whispers in his ear.

Sebastian cups Reid's hand. "Love . . . you."

ACKNOWLEDGMENTS

Thanks to my entire Wise Ink Creative Publishing team. All the interns, you rock! Amy Quale, when I first saw you speak so passionately on a marketing panel at the Writer's Digest annual conference, I was convinced that Wise Ink would be a great home for my debut novel. Your kind words of encouragement have so inspired me. Laura Zats, thanks for your fierce spirit that I've seen on display on social media, and which I'm certain translates as Wise Ink's editorial manager. I can tell you celebrate otherness. Kim Morehead, thanks for the novel's gorgeous interior design—a welcoming home needs just the right décor and attention to detail. Big thanks to you Emily Mahon for your very generous time, effort, and creative vision that produced a stunning cover design. Anitra Budd, your stellar editor's eye combined with an understanding of my story's emotional life helped me strike the right balance in my prose. Roseanne Cheng (fellow theater lover) you really helped me build my skills and confidence in the marketing process, and with so much patience and kindness to boot. Patrick Maloney, I so appreciate your wit, calmness, and guidance as my production manager, as well as your proofreading acumen. And dear Dara Beevas, from the moment I pitched you this novel and my personal story, you believed in me, and gently and lovingly managed me toward its creative birth: I thank you with all my heart. Finally, to all of you at Wise Ink, you set such a fine example for the publishing world; I'm so grateful that you champion diversity.

There are many other fantastic hearts and talents who've been a part of this novel's journey. Thank you Dennis Johnston for my first official author photos; my heart sang during our fabulous time at the shoot reminiscing about George Michael. Helen Schulman, thanks for being my mentor at The New School MFA in creative writing program and helping to guide and shape my earliest drafts; grateful to you since that time for being a wonderful source of author inspiration, support, and friendship. Jordan Rosenfeld: gifted writer, editor, friend, and fierce advocate of social justice, I thank you for your artistic passion and editorial support in helping me find an even deeper understanding of every aspect of this novel.

My heart dances with much gratitude for the brilliantly talented Casey Nicholaw. Thanks, Casey, for trusting my vision and for your enduringly kind spirit. We've come a long way since being in tap class together.

Thank you to these angels of support who, for many years, have offered editorial notes, and unconditionally believed in, and actively supported my efforts: Dr. Aimeé Gerrard-Morris; Karen Ricard; Randi Weidman; Mary Bleier; Pam Wehner.

To my friends, near and far, and extensive, loving family, thanks for all your support. My mother, Geri Naylor; my mother and father-in-law, Tippi & Al Bevan; my siblings Judy, Gwen, Jackie, Kim, Ric, Aimeé, and all my siblings-in-law; my beautiful nieces and nephews; zillions of fantastic aunts, uncles, and cousins on both sides of the family—each of you informs my writing in ways you may not even realize.

Thanks to Gloria Miller and my and my husband's cat, Georgie, both in heaven now, who still live in my heart and have helped me discover the truth about goodbye.

Ruth, a.k.a. the notorious RBG, my lovely and supportive stand-up desk who allows me to transition from sitting to a standing position the whole day long, I thank you for keeping my brain and body in motion.

To my little love, Sebastian, amazing kitty and muse, and namesake for this novel's protagonist, who takes such good care of me, day in and day out, thank you.

And finally, I thank my sweet and patient husband, Scott Bevan. The first reader of all my projects, he offers insight and unbiased advice, and never wavers in his love and support, truly nurtures my ability to write. I'm so lucky sharing my life with you, Scott, for the past twenty-seven years and counting. My love for you certainly finds its way into everything I create and helps make me a better man.